WELLSPRING

ALLAN LEVERONE

For Craig: never stop fighting

PART I

1

May 10, 1856
Southeastern Peru

The three outlaws crouched in the scrub brush, hot and uncomfortable in the midday South American sun. They had discovered shortly after sunrise that trying to stay cool out here in the God-forsaken Peruvian wilderness was damned near impossible.

Jackson Healy wiped the sweat from his forehead with the back of one grimy hand and asked the young native guide, "How much longer?" The words came out a scratchy, low-pitched growl.

The kid—his name was Juan and he claimed to be twelve, although Jackson thought that might be a bit of an exaggeration, not that he cared—stared back uncomprehendingly, then seemed to decipher the gist of the question and smiled brightly. "Soon," he said in his heavily accented English.

"I goddamn well hope so," Jackson grumbled. "It's hotter'n Satan's kitchen out here." The bizarre-looking group of three adults and the child had taken up their position hours ago, disappearing from sight—they hoped—in the folds of a gigantic natural rock formation located less than a hundred feet from what appeared to be a door carved into one smooth, sheer side of a massive boulder.

On their approach, hours earlier, all three Americans had gaped, slack-jawed, at the enormity of the door. Well over twenty feet high and nearly as wide, it featured a smaller alcove carved directly into its center. The alcove itself was perhaps six feet high,

3

roughly the size of a normal door.

Except it wasn't a normal door.

It wasn't a door at all.

It was a door-like shape carved into a solid rock wall disappearing into the side of a jagged, rocky hill in the middle of nowhere in Peru, miles away from civilization, or anything remotely resembling it.

And it was haunted, or so claimed the local legend.

The rock face was known as Puerta de Hayu Marka by the locals, the English translation being "Gate of the Gods," and it had been here for centuries; for as long as anyone could remember. No one could say how it had been carved, or when, or by whom.

But South American legend had it that on rare occasions, the door could be opened, only by shaman priests, and only through an elaborate ritual utilizing a sacred golden disk as key, inserted into the center of the carved door. Once the portal was opened, the legend said that the gods were free to pass through it, crossing between their worlds and ours.

All of this Jackson had learned over the course of many weeks buying drinks – and friends – in a tiny cantina in the dusty Peruvian village of Puno.

Jackson and his two fellow outlaws, Wesley and Amos Krupp, had headed south into Mexico through Brownsville, Texas, following a dispute over accusations of cheating during a poker game. The accusations—all accurate, as if that mattered—had resulted in a gun battle, which had in turn resulted in two dead cattle ranchers and a posse of Texas Rangers hot on their trail.

Mexico had seemed a little too close to Texas for Jackson's taste. He had had run-ins with the Rangers in the past, and felt certain the minor complication of an international border crossing would not deter their pursuers for long, if at all. So he led his fellow outlaws farther south, putting more distance between themselves and the long arm of the Texas law, eventually holing up in Puno, Peru, where the plan had been to drink away a few months, romance a few senoritas, and eventually slip back across the border into the States once the heat died down.

But within a few weeks, after the trio had ingratiated themselves with the locals through a liberal whiskey-sharing policy, Jackson had begun hearing the stories.

The mysterious door carved into the sheer rock wall.

The elaborate rituals.

The golden disk.

The portal to other worlds.

The more Jackson Healy heard of the Puerta de Hayu Marka legends, whispered fearfully in dark corners of the Puno cantina, the more intrigued he became.

The legends themselves were all superstitious South American bullshit, of course. Gate of the Gods, indeed. The notion of a magical doorway carved into a rock wall, accessible only via a golden disk, was beyond believable. But the disk itself wasn't bullshit. This disk, supposedly the key used to open Puerta de Hayu Marka, was said to be large, hefty, and solid gold, through and through.

Getting his greedy hands on a disk constructed of solid gold was the sort of thing no self-respecting outlaw could be expected to pass up. Jackson had no idea how much money such a golden disk might fetch on the open market, but he knew it had to be a lot. And it wasn't like the Healy-Krupp gang was exactly rolling in dough. The cash they had scored from their most recent bank jobs, combined with the money they had taken off the dead ranchers in the ill-fated Texas poker game, amounted to just enough to bankroll this South American vacation.

A solid gold disk could solve a lot of problems.

So, three nights ago, when one of their loose-lipped Peruvian drinking buddies had let slip the secret that one of the rare Gate of the Gods ceremonial rituals was to take place at Puerta de Hayu Marka tonight, a plan had begun forming in Jackson Healy's devious mind.

Finding a guide to lead them to the mystical location deep in the Peruvian wilderness was a simple task. Puno was a poor village, and the three gringos had learned quickly that the U.S. dollar was king in South America. That fact, combined with the natural curiosity of young boys everywhere, easily outweighed any superstitious fears about gods and shamans and imaginary doorways carved into rock formations.

The son of a local goat farmer had enthusiastically agreed to lead the three Americans by burro to the "Valley of the Spirits," as the area containing Puerta de Hayu Marka was known locally.

The strange group—three grown American men sporting scraggly beards and dirty clothes following a tiny brown child with a massive smile creasing his face—had left town before daybreak, Jackson's reasoning being that the team needed to be in-place and invisible well before the shaman priests began preparing for their ritual. Word around the cantina was that preparation would begin sometime in early afternoon.

The trip had taken hours, and while the three Americans started out raucous and lively, joking, swearing and sipping whiskey, as the morning had passed they grew more and more restrained. The heat grew stifling as the sun rose higher and higher into the sky. The terrain was alien and forbidding, flat grassy plains erupting occasionally into massive rock formations resembling animals, strange beings, and alien-looking structures.

Jackson's outlaw partners, Amos and Wesley Krupp, just as devious and bloodthirsty as Jackson if not quite as intelligent, became pale and withdrawn and even began to appear a little afraid as the men journeyed farther and farther from the semi-civilization of Puno.

Jackson would never have admitted it to his partners, but a worm of unease had begun crawling through his belly as well. The farther they rode, the more…*off*…things seemed to become. There was nothing specific he could put his finger on. Rather, it was a vibration, a sensation of encroaching alien-ness. It was as if the South American air was becoming saturated with some weird electrical charge, a pulse unseen but real, altering their perceptions in a slight but noticeable – and frightening – manner.

He shook his head, embarrassed at his schoolgirl fears, thankful Amos and Wesley could not read his mind. As an educated man— he had completed eight years of schooling in Kansas City before moving to the Texas plains with his parents as a child—Jackson Healy was the acknowledged leader of the Healy-Krupp gang and not one to suffer superstitious fears or crises of confidence.

He glanced at their young Peruvian guide and felt even sillier. Juan was clearly unaffected by whatever was causing Jackson's jumpiness. His grin, which seemed permanently glued onto his face, was just as bright now as it had been in the predawn darkness this morning.

After what felt like an endless journey, their guide began gesturing wildly at what looked to Jackson like just another rock formation looming above the flat surface of the plain, far off in the distance. It appeared as alien and forbidding as all the others they had ridden past, but this one, the young boy informed them in broken English, was the one they were looking for.

Puerta de Hayu Marka.

As they approached, even from a distance of at least a quarter-mile, Jackson could see the outline of the gigantic door, the sides of the carving thrust upward toward the sky like long arms.

As they moved closer, the smaller carved alcove appeared, exactly in the middle of the much larger door. Six feet high and sunk into the flat surface, the alcove was bathed in shadows, and the sight of it reignited in Jackson his previous irrational fears, which seemed suddenly not so irrational at all. He glanced at his partners and could see without speaking that they felt the same way.

The tension that had been blanketing the adults in the small group—the boy seemed impervious to anything other than wide-eyed, innocent joy—ratcheted up even higher. The reason for the stress was unspoken between the three outlaws but clear: if the shaman priests who were to conduct tonight's sacred ritual were already on site, a bloodbath was likely about to begin. The consensus among the superstitious locals populating the Puno cantina had been that the priests would not arrive until late afternoon, but none of the men had ever actually attended one of the ceremonies, and they freely admitted all of their information regarding Puerta de Hayu Marka was second or even third-hand.

When the outlaws reached a point several hundred yards away, Jackson called their small caravan to a halt and sent the Peruvian guide ahead to scout the rock formation. The kid was gone less than thirty minutes, and when he returned, smile still plastered onto his face, he announced that the area was deserted. Only then did the group ride the rest of the way.

They examined the curious carving before scouting out a hiding place among the nooks and crannies in the massive formation. The alcove did, indeed, resemble a doorway. It featured a perfectly circular depression at approximately waist height, located precisely in the middle. This depression was close to a foot in circumference, and Jackson thought that if the sacred golden disk he had heard so much about was supposed to fit into that depression, he would be one very rich man before the day was out.

The feeling of unease and paranoia that had been building among the men all morning did not disappear, however, and in fact grew much stronger now that they had arrived at their destination. Jackson had no difficulty understanding why the South American natives feared and revered this place. He didn't give a damn about any of their superstitious mumbo-jumbo, but he had to admit, if only to himself, that something was off-kilter about the place.

After a few minutes' examination of the carving, and sick of listening to the Krupp brothers' endless grumbling about the intensity of the midday heat, Jackson decided it was time to make camp and await the arrival of the shaman priests.

The group moved into the jumble of reddish-brown boulders, climbing steadily upward. Jackson knew that to successfully accomplish their mission tonight, two things were essential: the element of surprise, and occupation of the high ground. It was critical he be able to see everything happening at Puerta de Hayu Marka.

Once hidden safely away from the eyes of the native priests who would be arriving soon, the plan was to rest up, drink plenty of water, and wait.

2

The night was clear and warm, and the air heavy with moisture and the threat of a coming storm. In the distance, a fire burned brightly in a pit that had been constructed roughly fifteen feet directly in front of the Door of the Gods.

Jackson wondered what sort of fuel the Peruvian shamans had used to stoke the blaze, as it burned with greater than any campfire he had ever seen. Flames leapt straight up, as if straining to reach the heavens, roaring to heights greater than that of the men feeding the fire. Wood crackled and the fire seemed to take on a life of its own, emitting a guttural sound like throaty moan of a suffering animal. The rocks forming the edges of the pit glowed a bright red.

The ceremony was in full swing and had been for more than an hour. Drums pounded and men danced, their moves oddly hypnotic, their bones seeming to lose all rigidity, so fluid were their motions. There was no food consumed that Jackson could see, but there was plenty of drink, and pipes with massive bowls were passed among three men at the center of the activity.

Those three men were the shamans, Jackson knew, and he focused most of his attention on them. So far he had yet to observe any sign of the reason for this bizarre journey: the golden disk. He hoped his time had not been wasted, as none of the men performing the ritual in front of Puerta de Hayu Marka seemed to possess a single item worth stealing. They were simple people, dressed in simple native garb, deeply involved in their strange ritual. That was all.

Wesley and Amos had begun mocking the Peruvians almost from the beginning o the ceremony, their voices low, snickering and chuckling, and they turned resentful gazes on Jackson when he shushed them. Their young guide was transfixed. He stared at the activity, taking it all in, watching with all of the reverence the Krupp brothers lacked.

And then Jackson saw it.

The golden disk. The reason they had come out here.

Without warning, a short, squat man materialized out of the pitch-dark Peruvian plains, walking slowly into the ring of flickering light provided by the fire. Even from a distance and in the dim light, it was clear the man was old. He was more than old; he was ancient. Wrinkles lined his face, and skin sagged from his jowls despite – or perhaps because of – the fact that he was thin to the point of emaciation.

The man moved slowly, purposefully, carrying the heavy disk before him at chest height, arms extended and locked in what had to be an extremely uncomfortable position. The man didn't seem to notice. He trudged toward the fire from somewhere out in the wilderness, head up, eyes focused forward.

The drumbeats increased in intensity now, and the strangely fluid dancing of the men around the fire became frenzied. They whirled and jittered, arms moving this way and legs that, seemingly in defiance of the laws of human anatomy. Jackson watched, spellbound, jaw hanging open, one hand resting on the butt of his Colt revolver.

The drums pounded and throbbed and the dancers whirled and the ancient shaman priest moved slowly forward and the pace of the tribal music increased until it seemed something would have to give—

—and then the old man arrived at the fire and stopped moving, and instantly, all activity ceased.

The drumbeats abruptly stopped, although no signal had been given that Jackson could see. The dancers froze in place, their bodies suddenly rigid and unyielding, the men holding themselves in positions that didn't seem humanly possible. They remained as unmoving as statues, the only indication they were even alive being the expansion and contraction of their chests as they panted from the exertion of the dance.

For a long time—Jackson guessed at least five minutes, maybe ten—nothing happened. No one moved. No one spoke. The fire roared and crackled, but otherwise the silence was complete. It was unnerving after the frenzy of activity preceding it. The Krupp brothers had long since abandoned their mockery and stared at the scene below, their skin pale and their eyes nearly as wide as their Peruvian guide's.

Just when it seemed the inactivity might continue forever, stretching into eternity, the ancient shaman priest holding the golden disk began moving. When he had stopped initially, he had done so directly in front of the mammoth door carved into the sheer rock face—Puerta de Hayu Marka—and now he crept forward, the disk still clutched before him like a sacrificial offering.

The old man approached the alcove carved into the center of the door. The other shamans watched but remained motionless. When he arrived at the alcove he stopped again. He stood motionless and Jackson could see his lips moving, like he was reciting some kind of prayer or incantation. When he finished, he reached forward with great solemnity and placed the golden disk into the depression Jackson had seen when they examined the alcove earlier in the day. It fit perfectly, locking into place, glittering dully by the light of the fire.

And then the impossible happened.

The door began to open.

The ground shook and a rumble emanated from deep within the solid rock and then, incredibly, the alcove that was no more than a rendered carving of a door—Jackson knew it to be true, he had examined the cursed thing with his own eyes, had run his own hands over the solid surface—swung slowly outward, and as it did, a brilliant blue light pierced the darkness, appearing from the other side of the door, the side buried deep within the solid stone. The impossibly bright beam burst outward into the South American night.

Still no one moved, either at the site of the ceremony or in the bandits' hiding place above it. The door rumbled open, and when it had formed a perfect ninety-degree angle with the surface of Puerta de Hayu Marka, it ground to a halt. The thick slab of rock stood open, once again solid and immovable, and the strange blue light continued billowing outward from somewhere deep inside the rock, forming a thick rectangular shaft of oddly hypnotic illumination.

And then a figure stepped through the opening.

* * *

The man, if it even was a man, was bigger by far than anyone Jackson Healy had ever seen. He – *it* – glided through the open doorway that had been nothing more than solid rock just moments before. The figure's feet touched the ground but he moved with a smoothness and economy of motion Jackson had never seen out of another human being. His bearing was regal. His skin appeared paper-thin and translucent, and his body pulsed with a pale glow that seemed to emanate from deep within.

In his hands the visitor held a clear tubular container. From a distance the container resembled glass, although Jackson guessed it was not, and it was filled with an amber liquid that sloshed around inside it sluggishly like a thick gel. The rock doorway's brilliant blue light illuminated the visitor from behind, casting his features in deep shadow. His clothing was unlike anything Jackson had ever seen: a billowing robe flowing off massive shoulders, stretched out behind him like the train on a society matron's ball gown.

The visitor moved to a point directly in front of the shaman priest and stopped. He bent and spoke a few words into the priest's ear before handing him the tubular container filled with the gel-like liquid, his movements somehow ceremonial. He straightened abruptly and gazed over the crowd and then up the hill in the direction of the Healy-Krupp gang's hiding place.

For a long moment Jackson froze, certain the visitor's penetrating eyes were locked onto his. Then the otherworldly being turned and glided back through the open Puerta de Hayu Marka, disappearing through the stone door, swallowed up almost immediately by the brilliant blue light.

And then the rumbling began again, seeming to originate from somewhere deep below the surface of the earth. The door swung slowly closed, and less than a minute later was gone, melted back into the surface of the rock, and the alcove appeared exactly as it had before the bizarre ceremony had begun.

And Jackson Healy knew now was the time to act.

3

The bandits herded the ritual's participants into a more or less straight line in front of Puerta de Hayu Marka. The shamans' meager security detail—a couple of tribal warriors armed with spears; it was clear the pagan priests had expected no visitors and certainly no trouble—had been brought under control quickly and easily. Jackson had simply shot the first man to act aggressively in the head, point-blank, and the remainder of the tribal members immediately recognized the wisdom in doing as they were told.

The fire continued to burn brightly in the stone pit behind them, throwing dancing shadows onto the once-again sheer rock face. The Peruvian natives gazed at their captors with stony expressions. They seemed to save the worst of their scorn for the young boy who had served as guide for the Healy-Krupp gang.

For his part, Juan seemed shell-shocked at the sudden turn of events. He had agreed to serve as guide in exchange for more American money than anyone in his family had likely ever seen, but he had clearly not expected violence, believing the three gringos wanted nothing more than to observe the mystical ceremony from a distance. Only in the last few minutes had he learned the truth.

Now he would be put to use as a translator. Although the language being spoken by the shamans was not quite the Spanish Juan was accustomed to, the dialects were similar enough that with a little effort the boy could make the two parties understand each other, more or less.

While the Krupp brothers brandished their revolvers menacingly to keep the natives under control, Jackson examined the alcove. He placed his hand on the rock, sliding it slowly across the smooth surface. It was solid and unyielding, with no sign that any part of it had only minutes ago swiveled as if on a hinge and opened into a door. A vibration, so faint Jackson wondered whether he was imagining it, seemed to emanate from the massive rock formation.

The golden disk, roughly a foot in diameter, remained locked into the depression in the middle of the alcove where it had been inserted to turn the massive rock into a mystical portal. Jackson grazed his fingertips lightly across the disk's surface, and felt the vibration again. It was a little stronger, a humming that was felt rather than heard, and it ran up his fingers and into his hand, dissipating in his forearm.

Jackson shuddered with a sudden and irrational sense of misgiving. He was gripped by the thought that he should abandon this insane project, jump on the back of his burro and get out now, while he still could.

Before it was too late.

Then the feeling was gone, evaporating as quickly as it had arisen.

He shook his head, angry with himself for falling victim to what was clearly no more than superstitious pagan nonsense, and felt around the edge of the disk, probing and prying, looking for a handhold to use to pry the valuable golden relic out of the rock.

Within seconds he found one. On the right side of the circle, near the top, the otherwise uniform depression sank slightly deeper into the stone. It provided just enough room for him to slide his fingers between the disk and the smooth surface. Jackson patiently worked his fingers under the disk, conscious of the skin being rubbed off his knuckles, as well as of the angry stares of the natives from behind him.

At last the disk levered out of the depression. It slid away from Puerta de Hayu Marka slowly, as if doing so only with the most extreme reluctance. It began to fall and Jackson caught it with his left hand. As he did, a mutter of protest arose from the warriors. The sound was brief and ended abruptly, and he knew one of the Krupp brothers had raised his gun to the head of a random tribal member in an unspoken threat.

Jackson examined the back of his hand and observed blood welling through the scraped and shredded skin of his knuckles. He wiped the blood away on his vest, aware that the gesture was futile; more blood was already taking its place. He shrugged. A little scrape on his knuckles was a small price to pay for this solid gold disk, which was big and thick and heavy, and clearly worth a fortune.

He turned and moved away from the alcove. Walked to his burro and slid the priceless treasure into a saddlebag. Walked back to the rest of the gang and stood before Juan. The boy's enormous smile had long since disappeared and he stared at Jackson with a mixture of fear and confusion.

Jackson ignored it. His plan was working to perfection and he wasn't about to alter it because of the feelings of a little boy. He fixed the child with a stare and said, "Ask the priest what that… man…handed him before he disappeared back into the rock."

The boy stared back, and for a moment Jackson thought the kid was going to spit in his face. Then he broke Jackson's gaze and trudged toward the ancient shaman priest, whose skin was lined and weathered and who looked even older up close than he had from a distance.

The boy stopped in front of the old man and began exchanging words. Although Jackson had picked up a fair understanding of the Spanish language from his time in Texas and especially the gang's more recent excursion into South America, the dialect was confusing and the conversation too rapid-fire for him to follow in any meaningful way.

Juan and the old man went back and forth, and then the young guide returned to Jackson. He kept his voice low when he spoke, and Jackson wondered why. What did it matter if anyone heard? "He…he says the liquid is…it is…"

The boy looked away, either embarrassed or afraid to continue, and Jackson waved his hand in an impatient circling motion. "Out with it," he growled.

"He says it is the secret to eternal life," Juan finished. Tears rimmed his bloodshot eyes and he looked miserable.

There was a long silence. No one moved and no one spoke.

Jackson didn't know what he had expected to hear, but he knew that wasn't it. Then one of the Krupp brothers giggled from somewhere behind him and Jackson turned and glared. Both brothers looked away, each appearing equally guilty, and Jackson was glad he would soon be parting ways with the two dullards.

He bent and said to the boy, "I want to make sure there was no misunderstanding. This is important. You go back and ask that old man what happens if someone drinks that liquid in the glass tube he's holding, and then you come back to me and repeat exactly what he says, word for word."

Juan did as he was told, and Jackson watched the exchange with a critical gaze. The old Peruvian shaman lifted his head and shot Jackson a look of hostility that went far beyond anything he had ever seen, even out of the good ol' boys back in Texas just before he put bullets in their heads and made off with their money.

This time the conversation was brief, and when Juan returned, he said simply, "If you drink the liquid, you will live forever." He refused to meet Jackson's eyes and stood shuffling his feet uncomfortably in the dusty South American night.

Jackson Healy smiled. He had come to this desolate spot in the wilds of Peru in search of riches, and would leave with so much more.

* * *

The slaughter was sudden, efficient, and brutal. Jackson instructed Juan to take the tube containing the golden gel-like liquid from the hands of the shaman priest. He accepted it from the boy and walked over to his burro, placing it into the saddlebag already weighted down with the golden disk. Then he strode back to his position in front of the fire, which had begun to wane but was still burning brighter than any campfire he had ever seen.

The Peruvian tribesmen and the American outlaws faced each other, with Juan standing on the side of the gringos only because he had been forced there. The night breezes were humid and carried on them the promise of a coming storm. Off in the distance, thunder rumbled through the heavy air. The hint of a flickering glow appeared over the horizon, winking once, twice, three times, and then disappearing like the end of a nightmare.

Without warning Jackson turned and nodded to the Krupp brothers. The three men raised their Colt revolvers in perfect unison and began firing, and Peruvian tribesmen began falling, and within seconds it was over, the sound of the dying men's moans barely discernible over the screams of the young boy the outlaws had hired as their guide. Juan stood off to the side, rooted to the spot in shock and disbelief, staring with wide, frightened eyes and screaming into the muggy night.

And then Jackson turned his pistol on Juan and fired.

And the screaming stopped.

* * *

The smell of gunpowder hung in the air as the three outlaws prepared to flee. Jackson Healy surveyed the devastation, the fallen bodies littering the flat plain in front of Puerta de Hayu Marka like a child's dolls after a tantrum. Wesley Krupp asked, "How long d'ya suppose it'll be before someone finds this mess?"

Jackson shrugged. "Couple of days. The kid's ma and pa will wait for him to come home tomorrow, and when he don't, they'll get a search party together and head out here at first light the next day."

"So we'll have about a day-and-a-half head start on the locals. That ain't much. We'll have to ride non-stop for the next few days."

"One of us will," Jackson agreed, and then he drew his Colt again and gut-shot Wesley Krupp, then turned and fired on Amos almost before Wesley had hit the ground. Amos was so stunned he never even reached for his gun.

"Sorry about that," Jackson said agreeably, aiming his voice in the direction of his fallen partners. "It's nothin' personal, but you fellas have outlived your usefulness. Know what I mean?"

He waited for an answer, but none was forthcoming. Pained gasps, punctuated by the occasional shocked curse, seemed to be the limit of the Krupp brothers' current vocabulary.

Jackson shrugged, unsurprised. He gathered the reins of the four burros into one hand and began walking away from the carnage in what he hoped was the direction of Puno. He had no intention of entering the village—to do so would be the height of stupidity, given what he had just done to the twelve year old former resident of the place—but intended to skirt it to the west, then head north toward the good old U.S. of A.

Three of the burros he would release into the wild shortly, and the fourth—the one carrying the saddlebag containing a fortune in pure gold, not to mention the fountain of youth—would transport Jackson Healy until he could steal a horse to use to escape South America and move on to his suddenly limitless future.

As he departed, leaving in his wake bodies and blood and devastation, he could hear the muttered curses and vain threats of his now-dying former partners. He ignored them and walked on into the night.

4

Lucas Crosby had just finished wiping down the bar at the Paskagankee Tavern when the horse-drawn carriage arrived. The evening's last drinker had departed over an hour ago, and Luke would normally have been asleep in bed by now, but not on delivery night. Delivery night was different.

The clop-clop-clop of horse hooves on hard-packed dirt became stronger as the wagon approached from the south, then faded away again as it drove straight past the tavern's front entrance. Luke knew the routine. It was always the same. The driver would turn his horse into the small delivery area hacked into the dense forest just past the building, then guide the wagon along the side of the tavern until reaching the rear service entrance.

Luke waited a couple of minutes for the driver to navigate the narrow, rutted pathway, then walked through the kitchen and out the back door to begin unloading supplies.

Receiving deliveries in the middle of the night was unusual, Luke knew that. And in fact the strange nocturnal schedule had raised a few influential eyebrows five years ago, when Luke had purchased the Paskagankee Tavern with his wife, Sarah. But he explained to the Town Council that arranging for supply deliveries to a location as far out in the wilderness as Paskagankee was no easy task, and when the distributor—located all the way down in Portland—offered Luke a discount if he would agree to the unorthodox schedule, he had jumped at the offer.

"It's all in the name of giving the people of Pakagankee a place to wet their whistles," Luke had explained, and while the town fathers were none too happy about the deal, they didn't interfere, either, especially when Luke told them it was either that or he would not be able to open the tavern.

He walked out the back door into the uncertain light provided by two flickering gas lamps mounted on the exterior wall, one on either side of the door. Delivery man Matt Fulton grunted a greeting, his heavily muscled arms straining under the weight of three cases of liquor as he stumbled by, moving in the opposite direction. "Hotter'n the hinges of hell, ain't it?" Matt mumbled after placing the cases just inside the door and returning to the wagon for more.

Luke nodded and said nothing. All of his concentration was focused on unlatching a small iron hook fastened unobtrusively onto the rear of the wagon. He struggled with the latch—it was intentionally difficult to loosen for their protection, a fact Luke could appreciate but which was, nonetheless, extremely frustrating at two o'clock in the morning. Finally the offending latch popped free with a heavy *clank,* and Luke pulled the wagon's false bottom straight backward, as if opening a gigantic dresser drawer.

The contraption rolled straight out about four feet, then swiveled on an iron bar mounted under the wagon as a hinge. Luke lowered the free end of the false bottom to the ground and a man tumbled out. It was a black man. The man was sweating profusely, having been trapped inside the tiny space for virtually the entire ten-hour trip north from Portland.

The hidden traveler rolled onto the dusty ground and pushed himself onto all fours. He struggled to his feet with difficulty, his limbs clearly stiff and sore. It was painful to watch. Luke extended a hand to help the man but was ignored. The man was old. Wizened, with receding gray hair and rheumy brown eyes.

Most slaves willing to risk everything for a shot at freedom were younger, often with families; men and women with more of their lives ahead of them than behind them. This man seemed to be the opposite. He walked with a slight bend to his frame, as if unable to fully straighten his spine. He was short and frail looking, and it looked as though a strong wind might reduce him to smoke and blow him away.

Luke was stunned that the frail-looking old man standing unsteadily before him had made the long, dangerous trip. He tried to guess the man's age and settled on seventy-five, maybe eighty. That would make him easily a quarter-century older than any other slave that had ever used the Paskagankee Tavern waypoint.

Luke had purchased the tavern with the intention of making it the final stop along the Underground Railroad's Portland route almost five years ago. After making some special modifications to the building's basement, he did exactly that. The Canadian border was located just a few short miles to the north, close enough for escaping slaves to make the final freedom-seeking dash on foot, after resting up at the tavern for anywhere from a few hours to a few days.

For the last five years Luke had been helping make slaves' dreams of freedom come true. There had been hundreds of deliveries just like this one, and in all that time, he had never seen anyone of this advanced age and frail physical condition tumble out of the wagon's false bottom. The space was so small and cramped that one decent-sized adult was forced to lie either on his back or his front, with barely enough hip-room to turn over. Luke couldn't imagine how this man had managed ten hours.

Luke waited patiently while the elderly slave brushed himself off. His clothes were threadbare and dirty and his brushing motion accomplished nothing besides smearing the dirt around. Finally he gave up and shook out his arms and hands vigorously in an attempt to restore some of blood flow.

The man glanced around disinterestedly, as if falling out of invisible compartments and into deserted, out-of-the-way courtyards in the middle of the night was nothing noteworthy. Probably it wasn't, having ridden the Underground Railroad hundreds, if not thousands, of miles over many days and weeks.

Luke smiled gently, again extending his hand. "Welcome," he said quietly. "You'll be safe here tonight, if not quite comfortable. My name is Lucas."

"Jedediah," the stranger answered, finally breaking down and shaking Luke's hand. His eyes, though, never met Luke's. He continued to scan for potential danger, his head swiveling in all directions.

Luke's smile widened. "You needn't worry," he insisted. "Nobody lives within shouting distance of this place, and everyone in town 'cept for me and Matt has long since gone to bed."

"Not everyone," the old black man muttered. "Someone's coming."

Luke withdrew his hand and stared into the dark night, listening hard. If someone was indeed approaching the Paskagankee Tavern during a nighttime delivery, it would be a first. The tiny village was a workingman's town. Folks liked to drink hard, but they also worked hard, and getting a good night's sleep was important.

"I'm sure you're wrong," he said. "I don't hear a thing. But just to be on the safe side, let's get you inside and bunked down for the night." Luke bent down and retrieved a tiny valise that had slid off the wagon's false bottom at the same time the slave did. The bag was dusty and torn, and it depressed Luke to think it contained every last item the old man owned.

"Too late," Jedediah said, and at that moment a man rounded the corner at the side of the inn, emerging out of the darkness into the half-light of the flickering torches. The man approached along the path the wagon had taken just minutes before, confidently following the ruts worn into the grass from hundreds of deliveries on hundreds of nights just like this one.

Luke knew everyone in the small town, at least by sight. The moment the man stepped into the torchlight, Luke understood immediately he was not a Paskagankee resident. The stranger was on foot—if he had ridden into town he had tied his horse to a tree some distance away in order to ensure a stealthy approach—and Luke's first thought was to wonder how in the Lord's name the elderly slave had heard the man coming when *he* hadn't heard a thing.

Then he forgot all about the slave, all about how the old black man had ridden ten long hours crushed into the false bottom of the delivery wagon. He forgot about everything. Because being dragged along behind the stranger, the man's left ham fist wrapped securely around the collar of her nightdress, was Luke's wife.

Sarah.

Her eyes were wide and terrified and a heavy layer of dust caked the bottom of her dress, and after a moment's shocked hesitation, Luke took two steps toward her. He would attack the man if necessary to rescue his wife, he would die to save her if he must, he would do whatever it took, and—

—and the man calmly lifted a big Colt revolver and placed the barrel against Sarah's temple. "Stop right there," he said, and Luke stopped right there.

"Well, well, well," the stranger said thoughtfully, glancing from Luke to the slave and back. "Whatta we have here?" He caressed the side of Sarah's beautiful head with his gun and Luke prayed he wouldn't pull the trigger. Luke could see Sarah trembling, but she stood quietly and said nothing.

The slave was positioned behind Luke. He didn't move or speak. Luke could feel his presence although he could not see him. It was obvious the old man was waiting to see what would happen next, something Luke was more than a little curious about, himself. He calculated how long Fulton had been gone and what he might be doing. The deliveryman should long since have returned from inside the tavern for another armload of flour or case of beer or sack of clean linen.

"What's your business here, friend?" Luke asked.

"We all friends now, are we?" the man countered without any trace of a smile.

"Well, we ain't enemies. Least not yet. I certainly mean you no harm, although it'd sure be easier to *stay* friends if you release my wife. What brings you to Paskagankee at this time of night?"

The stranger chuckled. He was relatively young, maybe thirty-five, and relatively handsome, if you discounted the small pair of scars running in thin parallel lines along his right cheek. His face was flushed and his hair mussed and his manner abrupt. "So, this little filly wasn't lying, after all. She told me I could find you here. Ya see, I need a place to hole up for a bit. They's some people chasin' me and they ain't exactly what you'd call the highest of high society fellas."

"What does that have to do with me, and what does it have to do with my wife?" Luke longed to lunge at the stranger; the urge was almost overwhelming. He wanted to punch the man into submission, six-shooter or no six-shooter, then sweep Sarah into his arms and hold her until she stopped trembling, to convince her everything would be all right.

But Luke was very afraid everything was not going to be all right.

"What's it got to do with you? Nuthin' really, 'cept you happen to own the house I busted into a few minutes ago lookin' for shelter. Once I showed her my gun, your very kind—and might I add, very beautiful—wife volunteered that they wasn't much of anyplace to hide in that house, and if it was the first shelter *I* considered it would probably be the first one the folks chasin' me would consider, too." He spit on the ground. "Smart lady."

Matt Fulton poked his head around the corner of the building. The stranger couldn't see him, but Luke had a clear view of the deliveryman. Matt had apparently heard the commotion back here and exited through the front door of the tavern, circling around to approach the stranger from behind.

Luke knew Matt was always armed—it would have been suicide driving a wagon full of liquor and bar supplies all over northern Maine without some way to protect himself, and a weapon was even more critical given the illegal human cargo Matt carried— but he knew also that the deliveryman had left his gun on the seat of the wagon in order to lug the supplies into the building. He knew because that was how Matt always did it.

The stranger continued speaking, unaware of Fulton's presence behind him. "Your beautiful wife told me you was down here takin' a delivery at the waterin' hole and that this would be a much better place than your house to lie low. Turns out it was a slightly different kind of delivery than I woulda expected, though, wasn't it? It was the kind of delivery that tells me you must truly have some good places for me to hide out for a while."

The man grinned, and even in the uneven light of the flickering torches Luke could see his teeth were yellowed and stained; some of them were missing entirely. "So whaddaya say," he said, smiling wickedly. "Is there any room at the inn?"

As the stranger talked Fulton approached stealthily from behind, taking his time, moving with care. Sarah stood resolutely, trembling and clearly afraid but trusting in Luke to handle the situation. Fulton had nearly reached the stranger when Luke realized he had just made a critical mistake. He had been so caught up in tracking the deliveryman's progress and trying not to give anything away that he had fallen silent for much too long. He had completely lost track of the stranger's words.

The gunman's eyes widened and he threw Sarah to the ground as he spun left and ducked. Fulton launched a roundhouse right at the stranger's jaw, a dangerous punch from a dangerous man which, had it been thrown one second earlier, would have ended the fight before it began.

But by the time the punch reached the stranger's jaw he was no longer there. Fulton's roundhouse whistled harmlessly through the air, leaving Matt off-balance and vulnerable to a counterattack. The stranger's foot shot out and connected solidly with Fulton's knee. Luke rushed forward as the sound of Matt's kneecap shattering filled the air. It was loud and unmistakable and horrifying.

Fulton gasped in shock and pain and the stranger lifted his six-shooter, pointing it directly at Luke's face. "That's far enough," he said coldly.

Luke stopped short. "No," he said. "No, no!"

The gun barrel looked enormous and deadly. From somewhere in his panicked brain Luke could hear Sarah sobbing quietly. The stranger swiveled his arm, holding the big pistol one-handed, aiming it at Matt Fulton's head.

And then the stranger fired, and instantly Matt Fulton's head caved in, pulverized by the .38 slug. Blood and bone and brain tissue exploded into the night air and the elderly slave—in his panic Luke had forgotten all about the old black man standing behind him—screamed and Sarah screamed and Luke realized he was screaming, too.

Matt wasn't screaming, though, he was too busy dying, and his body slumped to the ground, his head a pulpy mush, bludgeoned by the mass of the bullet fired almost point-blank into his skull.

The stranger was panting and jittery and his eyes were wild. He turned the gun on Sarah next, and Luke sank to his knees in the dirt and the weedy grass. "Please stop," he said. "Please. We'll do whatever you want. We can hide you. We can hide you for as long as you want to be hidden. Just, please, stop."

For a long moment nothing happened, and then the stranger lowered his gun. "Show me where I can hide or everyone dies," he said.

5

The Paskagankee Tavern had been constructed on a foundation of rough-hewn, sound-deadening granite blocks, each several feet thick. From the moment Lucas Crosby had first set eyes on the basement, he had known exactly how he was going to modify the structure to allow Underground Railroad travelers to remain safe and secure during the final stopover in their long journey to freedom.

The day he finalized the purchase, Luke had begun modifications on the property. He did most of the backbreaking work alone, contracting out what few jobs he could not handle himself to Railroad sympathizers who rode up from Connecticut and Rhode Island. They completed their tasks, one or two at a time to avoid raising suspicion among Paskagankee's residents, and then disappeared, returning to their hometowns and states.

Within a few months the illicit basement modifications had been completed, along with improvements to the rest of the building, allowing Lucas Crosby to open the Paskagankee Tavern. The community knew nothing of the structure's dual purpose.

In the dank basement, Luke had chipped away a small handhold in one of the seams between the massive granite blocks. The handhold was virtually invisible, indecipherable to anyone unaware of its existence, and until memorizing its location even Luke occasionally had to search for it by running his fingers along the block.

Inside the handhold, a spring-loaded latch had been inserted.

A heavy pull on the latch would allow one entire block of granite to swing ponderously outward on a thick iron hinge, revealing a tunnel dug into the earth. The primitive six-foot wide corridor sloped gradually downward and appeared to terminate at an earthen wall fifteen feet away.

That wall, however, was just an illusion. What appeared to be a tree-root thrusting several inches out of the wall was in reality another spring-loaded latch. A tug on the "root" would result in a second door, this one smaller and constructed of dark-brown wood almost perfectly matching the wall, opening on its own hinge to reveal a small room hacked even farther into the earth.

The room had been outfitted with three pairs of bunk beds, a rudimentary table, and six chairs. Shelving lined the walls from floor to ceiling, stocked with food and water and various other supplies an Underground Railroad traveler might need to stay alive—and safe—for weeks, if necessary. Luke had even provided a makeshift lavatory, erecting a wooden wall across one small corner of the room and outfitting the space behind it with a chamber pot.

Luke's purpose in tunneling into the earth had been to provide for temperature moderation. Thus, even on the coldest of the northern New England village's bitter winter nights, the secret room stayed at a reasonable temperature. It wasn't warm, exactly, but with the proper clothing and plenty of blankets, would prevent a traveler from freezing to death.

Providing ventilation had presented the biggest challenge, and Lucas had been forced to bring an engineer all the way from Boston to solve the problem. Eventually, they constructed a series of small tunnels running from the ceiling to ground level, terminating at different locations around the tavern's property. Each of the ventilation tunnels was integrated into the landscape and was as indecipherable to the unknowing observer as the door built into the basement's granite blocks.

The product of Lucas Crosby's backbreaking labor was a hidden room of the highest quality; one that allowed Luke to serve the needs of freedom-seeking slaves without putting his safety or the safety of his beloved Sarah at unnecessary risk. As many as a half-dozen Underground Railroad riders at once could remain safely concealed inside the room for as long as necessary if suspicious strangers – or even locals – seemed to be asking the wrong kinds of questions around the Paskagankee Tavern.

The thick granite blocks, long tunneled entrance and deep-in-the-earth construction deadened all sound, so once sealed inside the hidden room, escaping slaves were free to talk as loudly as they wished without fear of being discovered.

Luke had placed several crates of supplies inside the access tunnel behind the granite blocks in the event his basement doorway were ever discovered, planning to explain away the tunnel as simply an extra, if unusual, storage area. In five years, though, the secret construction had not come close to being discovered. Even Sarah had never actually seen the room.

She was about to see it now, though.

Luke led the way down the rickety stairs leading from the tavern's small first-floor storage room into the basement. Following silently behind him was the slave. Sarah and the stranger brought up the rear, the stranger's assumption seeming to be that Luke would not dare try anything stupid with a gun barrel caressing the side of his wife's head.

The stranger's assumption was right.

Luke had no idea what, or who, this man might be running from, but at the moment he didn't care. Seeing Matt Fulton's head blown almost completely off his shoulders was enough to convince Luke to do as he was told. He knew he could not live with himself were he to be responsible for the same fate befalling his beloved bride.

The sound of the footfalls on the wooden stairs seemed to drop into the basement and disappear. It was as if the building simply swallowed up the noise, leaving behind an eerie and somehow alien silence. Luke stepped off the final tread and felt his way in the darkness to the side wall, lighting a series of candles mounted on sconces, and waited in the resulting insubstantial illumination for the rest of the strange little party to join him.

When everyone had gathered in the basement, the stranger looked around critically and said, "This is it? This is your wonderful hiding place? I ain't gonna be safe here. The sons of bitches looking for me will sniff me out in seconds!"

The stranger cocked the big .38 and Luke panicked. He had

a vision of Sarah lying facedown on the dirt floor, blood leaking out of her body as her life ebbed away. "No, no, this isn't it! Settle down, please, and I'll show you the real hiding place."

The man's eyes narrowed. Quietly, he said, "You do understand what's going to happen here if I don't see some results, and soon, correct?"

Luke nodded, breathing heavily, and walked quickly to the rear of the basement. He reached into an unassuming-looking gap between two of the huge granite blocks and the stranger instantly lifted his Colt to eye level, suspicious, training it on Luke. Luke winced—the gun looked massive with the business end pointed between his eyes—but continued. He tugged sharply and the stranger's eyes widened as the block swiveled outward. A smile crossed the man's face. "Now, this is more like it," he said approvingly.

Luke gestured everyone forward and the stranger walked to the entryway, clutching Sarah tightly by the arm, his gun again aimed at her head. He waved Luke away and then peered inside the tunnel, his vision limited to the first few feet by the flickering candlelight. "Looks like a storage area," he said.

"That's what it's meant to look like," Luke said. "But there's a hidden doorway at the other end and an actual room behind it. Might not be as comfy as a four-star hotel in Boston, but you'll be safe and warm for as long as you'd like to stay hidden."

Luke walked past the stranger, careful not to make any sudden movements that could be interpreted as threatening. "Follow me," he said. "I'll show you inside."

"Stop right there," the stranger snarled. He spit on the floor. "Just how goddamned stupid do you think I am?"

"What do you mean?"

"There's a corpse lying in your back yard, remember? Shot with this here gun, remember? I gotta get that body out of there before the guys chasin' me stumble over it. If they see the dead man, they'll know I'm here. And I'm runnin' out of time. So you're going to help me." He pointed the gun at Luke, and Luke felt a surge of hope. He would help the stranger dispose of poor Matt Fulton's body, and while the gunman was occupied, Sarah could make her escape. She would alert the authorities, and Luke might or might not survive the ensuing confrontation, but at least Sarah would be safe.

Luke's tiny flame of hope was extinguished immediately, however, when the man said, "This pretty little thing is going to come with us, just to be sure you don't get the bright idea to try something you'll regret later.

"And as for you," he continued, turning the gun on the old black slave. "Seems you ain't no use to me at all. No reason for you to come with us, and if I leave you here, I figure you'll just go runnin' straight to the law, won't cha?"

The old man stared at the stranger, saying nothing, exhibiting no fear, betraying no emotion at all. The stranger cocked his .38 and the black man seemed to stand a little taller, straightening his bent spine and glaring at the killer with baleful eyes. It was almost as if he was daring the stranger to shoot.

Luke's blood chilled. "No!" he interrupted. "There's no need to kill this man. He can't go to the authorities, because if he does, he'll get shipped right back to . . . to . . . where are you from?" he asked the slave desperately.

"Plantation just outside N'Awlins." The old slave's words were the first and only ones he had spoken since giving Luke his name just after tumbling out of Matt Fulton's delivery wagon. He seemed to part with his words reluctantly, like a Vanderbilt paying his taxes.

"New Orleans," Luke said, nodding. "See? He can't go to the law any more than you can, because if he does, he'll find himself on his way back to New Orleans before the day is out."

"I can't take that chance," the stranger said coldly. "How do I know he don't want to go back?" His grip tensed and his eyes narrowed and Luke knew there was about to be a second murder if he didn't take action right now. But what could he do?

The slave looked the stranger in the eyes and spit on the floor, hawking up a gob of saliva that floated gracefully through the air and landed with an audible splat at the stranger's feet.

He was going to die.

"Wait!" Luke practically shouted. "We can keep him out of the way and I can guarantee he won't be able to go anywhere."

The basement fell deathly silent and nobody moved. Finally the stranger said, "How?"

Luke realized he had been holding his breath and blew it out forcefully. Maybe he could save the old guy's life. The slave didn't seem to care one way or the other; he continued glaring at the stranger.

"The hidden room at the end of this hallway was built specifically to hide escaping slaves. There's only one way out of it, and the door has no handle on the inside. We simply stash Jedediah here," he gestured at the old man, "inside the room – he would be spending the night in it anyway – and everyone will be happy."

"Show me," the stranger said, so Luke did.

6

Luke's stomach was doing flip-flops as he grabbed Matt Fulton by the ankles. He tried not to look at the deliveryman's ruined head. The two hadn't exactly been friends, but they had maintained a business relationship for over five years, a relationship involving tavern supplies and freedom-seeking slaves, and the sense of regret he felt at being responsible for the man's death was like a physical weight hanging from his neck.

He breathed a sigh of relief that the homicidal stranger had agreed to spare the slave's life—at least for now—after being shown the secret room and accepting that there was no way out once locked inside. They had ushered Jedediah into the room together and then retreated down the tunnel, with Luke pushing the earthen door closed behind him.

The slave had not said another word after his brief, and nearly deadly, confrontation with the stranger. Luke sensed a rage smoldering inside the old man that was so strong it was almost as terrifying as the .38 the stranger waved around so carelessly. He felt certain that were it not for the revolver, the ancient slave would have been able to whip the outlaw in a fistfight, the difference in their ages notwithstanding.

Luke shuddered as he pictured the horrible fate facing the old black man if the stranger were to shoot him and Sarah after they disposed of Matt Fulton's body. No one else in the world knew of the secret room's location, and no one else in the world knew the slave had traveled here to Paskagankee, Maine. The man would slowly starve to death, but only after several long weeks spent alone, desperately trying to make his food and water last.

Luke guessed the stranger would not kill him yet, and risk not finding the entrance to the secret room again, but he had no illusions about the man allowing him and Sarah to live once he no longer needed them. He had to survive the next few hours, and stay alert while protecting Sarah. Perhaps an opportunity to overpower the stranger would present itself.

He grunted as he lifted Matt's body, thankful the stranger had elected to carry the corpse by the armpits, where his grotesquely misshapen head lolled lifelessly just inches away from the stranger's trousers.

Matt's blood looked as black as tar—even blacker than the old slave—by the dim light of the torches. It had splattered onto the ground where he fell, draining from his head wound as he lay dying in the dirt, and Luke prayed death had been instantaneous, that the deliveryman had not suffered. He realized he had never had a single conversation of a personal nature with Matt Fulton; didn't know whether the man had a family, or if he enjoyed a hobby. Knew nothing about him at all, when he came right down to it.

A sense of hopelessness overwhelmed Luke without warning and he shook his head violently. He would not allow himself to give up. He had to remain focused. Sarah was counting on him. Luke had dared hope he might grab Matt Fulton's gun from the wagon and turn it on the stranger, but of course the man had been a step ahead of him. He plucked it off the well-worn seat and slid it inside the waistband of his trousers as they walked past carrying Matt's body, smiling wickedly at Luke as if reading his mind.

"Put him in the back," the stranger muttered through clenched teeth. Together, the two men swung the body of the dead deliveryman into the wagon, dropping him onto the floor among the supplies. The stranger withdrew a pocket watch from his vest and examined it carefully, turning it this way and that to catch the light from the torches.

"We gotta hurry," he said. "They'll be here soon." Luke said nothing and the man continued. "I'm guessing I had maybe two hours on 'em, and we've already wasted far too much of that time."

"Why are they chasing you?" Luke asked.

The man glanced at Luke, eyes narrowed to slits, and said, "Shut up and get in the wagon."

* * *

The forest felt alive and malevolent as Luke forced the horse off the road and into a narrow gap between the trees. They had traveled no more than a quarter-mile from the tavern when the stranger said, "This is far enough. We'll hide the wagon here and dump the body in the woods. With a little luck neither of 'em will be found until I'm long gone."

"The sheriff's going to know Matt made his delivery the minute the wagon's discovered. Supplies are missing. The first thing he'll do is come to the Paskagankee Tavern; it's the only place for thirty miles in any direction Matt delivers to."

"I don't give a damn about the tin-star lawman in this two-bit village," the stranger said. "All I need is one night. The men looking for me will assume I kept traveling when they can't find me in your hayseed town. They'll move on toward Canada and when they do, I'll head south. What happens around here after that ain't my concern."

The wagon lurched to a halt. The forest was ancient, primeval, filled with millions of massive fir trees broken up by the occasional hardwood, and underbrush so thick it was nearly impossible to walk, much less drive into with a delivery wagon. Once they had replaced the branches and brush matted down by the horse and the big wooden wagon wheels, Luke felt a sense of defeat wash over him. He was convinced the abandoned wagon would be invisible to passersby, and would not be discovered until a concerted search had been launched.

"Now," the stranger said with a look on his face that was half grimace and half leer, "let's us three take a little stroll with a corpse, shall we?"

"Please," Luke said, knowing he was wasting his breath but trying anyway, "allow Sarah to wait here. She doesn't need to be exposed to the nighttime disposal of a murdered man."

The stranger shook his head and turned a glare Luke's way. "I swear," he said, "you can't possibly be so stupid as to think we're going to carry a dead man into the woods and leave your little woman all alone back here, so she can hike into town and raise the alarm. Please tell me you ain't that stupid."

Sarah placed a hand on Luke's arm and shook her head, a tiny smile on her face. *Don't make this volatile man any more unstable than he already is,* she was trying to tell him. *I'll survive.*

Luke hoped she was right. He wasn't so sure.

The three clambered off the front of the wagon in the suffocating darkness, one anxiously, two reluctantly. Luke stepped to the ground and then helped Sarah down with one hand, steadying himself against the wagon with the other. The thick brush instantly closed in around them, surrounding them from all sides, filling Luke with a sense of claustrophobia. The moon, two-thirds full tonight, had disappeared almost immediately after they left the road, lost somewhere high above the canopy formed by the ancient forest.

The silence seemed preternatural, the only sounds being their heavy breathing and the scratching of branches and brush against clothing. They fought their way to the rear of the delivery wagon, and the stranger said, "We're gonna carry the stiff along the side of the wagon, then deeper into the forest, as deep as we can manage without wasting too much time. I'm almost out of time."

Luke wondered about the men chasing this homicidal stranger. The thought occurred to him that maybe he could intentionally delay the disposal progress long enough for the murderer's pursuers to catch up with him, but he discarded the idea almost immediately. If this man—with his cold eyes and amoral personality and the ability to murder an innocent man as easily as if he were lighting a cigar—was as worried about his pursuers as he appeared to be, it didn't seem likely he would be the only one to suffer the consequences were he to be caught. Luke guessed he and Sarah would as well.

The two men struggled under the dead weight of Matt Fulton's body, climbing over downed trees, around boulders and through scrub brush. After maybe ten minutes, during which time they made little progress, the stranger grunted, "Far enough," and dropped Fulton's upper body to the forest floor. It landed with a thud.

Luke eased the distributor's ankles to the ground and stood hunched over, hands on his knees, breathing heavily. He knew Matt was beyond caring what happened to him, but still Luke hated the desecration of the man's corpse. He hoped it would be found soon so he could receive a proper burial, in front of family and friends.

The stranger had bent over to catch his breath at the same time Luke did, and now he straightened and said, "Let's go," still breathing heavily. "We've got a bit of a walk ahead of us, and it won't be long before the boys hunting me stumble on to your place. If you want to live – and more importantly, if you want your wife to live – you'll make damned sure I'm tucked away inside that secret room with your new black friend before that happens."

Luke nodded and they began retracing their steps. They reached the wagon much more quickly now that they were not burdened by the weight of the body, and almost without breaking stride Luke took Sarah by the hand and continued toward the road. He believed without question the man's threat to kill he and Sarah if they were intercepted, and there was no way of knowing how close the stranger's pursuers were. For all he knew, they might be in town already.

Minutes later the strange trio reached the road and turned left, walking quickly toward the tavern. They encountered no other travelers, an unsurprising development given the location and time of night.

For the first time since this horrifying saga had begun more than two hours ago, Luke found himself with a few minutes to think, and something occurred to him that was so obvious he couldn't believe he hadn't thought of it until now: all they had to do was make it back to the Paskagankee Tavern undetected and seal the stranger in the secret room! The man would then be trapped and Luke could alert Sheriff Cowles to the situation. Cowles could round up as many men as he thought necessary – the more, the better as far as Luke was concerned – then come out to the tavern, open the room, and subdue the stranger.

This plan, of course, if successful, would result in the

discovery of the secret room. Such a discovery would shut down the Paskagankee stop along the Underground Railroad forever, and quite possibly result in jail time for Luke. But under the circumstances, incarceration was the least of his worries.

He glanced over at Sarah, her face blurred and indistinct in the inky northern Maine nighttime blackness. He flashed her what he hoped was a reassuring smile and kept walking.

* * *

Several hundred yards south of the Paskagankee Tavern, the stranger growled, "Stop right here." He flicked his wrist, indicating they should enter the forest on the side of the trail, and after a moment's hesitation, Luke plunged off the road and into the underbrush. Sarah followed right behind him. The stranger brought up the rear.

A sense of disquiet, not quite panic but damned close, gripped Luke's heart. What was happening? Why would the stranger herd them into the forest when they were now so close to the hiding place he claimed to need so badly?

In his head Luke knew the man was not going to kill them; not both of them, anyway. Not yet. He still needed at least one of them, because although the stranger now knew the secret room's location and how to enter it—assuming he had been paying attention—no one else in the world would know he was in there. He would be trapped forever if he killed both of them.

Of course, it was entirely possible he intended to put a bullet in *Luke's* head. He needed one of them, but he didn't need both, and from the stranger's point of view, it would make sense to eliminate the one who could cause him the most trouble.

Luke thought desperately, trying to decide what to do if the stranger leveled his Colt at him. There weren't many good options. He supposed he would lunge at the man and try to wrestle the gun away from him. Of course, as the stranger was walking behind him, he might never see the kill shot coming.

All of this went through Luke's head in a matter of seconds, and then, no more than ten feet into the woods he struggled through the underbrush and nearly ran right into a horse. The animal was secured to a tree, standing motionless, staring through the near-complete darkness at Luke with accusing eyes.

The stranger brushed past Sarah and then Luke. He reached into a saddlebag and rummaged through it quickly before pulling out a large disk, roughly the size of a chef's serving platter, only much thicker, and apparently, much heavier. The stranger hefted it with his left hand and reached back into the saddlebag. He pulled out a second item, this one smaller and lighter. It was a long, clear tube, filled with what looked in the darkness like a thick liquid.

The gunman spoke quietly, his voice hard and gravelly. "These things stay with me. Now, let's get to that secret room so I can snuggle up with an old black man." He gestured again with his gun, indicating that Sarah and Luke should return to the road. They began working their way back through the brush, Luke wondering what in the hell was going on.

7

Luke had been getting increasingly nervous the closer they came to the Paskagankee Tavern. Push was coming to shove, and he began to wonder whether he had been fooling himself to think the homicidal stranger would really allow himself to be locked in the slave's hiding place, leaving himself completely at Luke's mercy.

The man was vicious and brutal, that much had become obvious the moment he pulled the trigger on the defenseless Matt Fulton, but for all that, he didn't strike Luke as dumb. Just the opposite, in fact. He seemed intelligent and, even worse, cunning and clever.

Luke decided he would find out soon, because the hulking structure of the Paskagankee Tavern suddenly materialized out of the predawn darkness as if by magic and now loomed before the exhausted trio like some haunted house straight out of a two-penny serial novel. They trudged through the front entrance, trooped past the bar and into the kitchen, then descended the stairs to the basement.

No one spoke. Luke felt as though the supper he had eaten nearly ten hours ago might come back up at any moment. It was now or never. Would the stranger suddenly recognize the flaw in his hastily devised plan and simply shoot Luke and Sarah before high-tailing it out of Paskagankee on his hidden horse, hoping to outrun his pursuers? Or would he slip inside the secret room, leaving himself at the mercy of Luke and Paskagankee's only lawman, Sheriff Stanley Cowles?

Luke strode to the wall and felt around for the latch hidden in the seam between the granite blocks. With one tug, the massive block rolled outward on its hinge and stopped. Luke breathed deeply and said a silent prayer, then turned and lifted his hand to the opening and waited to see what would happen.

The stranger eyed him critically and walked into the hidden entryway. Luke's plan was going to work! Another step or two and the man would be inside the passageway to the secret room and Luke could pull the lever, effectively trapping him inside, ending this nightmare.

Then the man turned, his body half in and half out of the entryway. He fixed Luke with a baleful stare and then, ever so slowly, a smile crept across his face. The smile was hard and devoid of any good humor, and it told Luke the man knew exactly what he had been thinking. He had known all along.

"Well?" the stranger said.

"Well, what?" Luke said.

"Please. You can't believe I'm stupid enough to allow you to lock me in here with only a hundred year old slave for company. Why, the minute the door closed, you'd be running as fast as your little legs would carry you to the local sheriff's house. Hell, you'd probably steal my horse just because you could."

"I...no, I...of course not." Denials were pointless, yet Luke couldn't stop himself from issuing them.

"It don't matter," the stranger said, waving his revolver like he was shooing away a pesky mosquito. "I've got the perfect solution to our little problem."

Luke felt all hope slipping away. He closed his eyes, wishing this whole cursed night was just a bad dream, wishing he would wake up and be in his bed and it would be seven-thirty in the morning, but when he opened his eyes the stranger was still standing there, waiting. "What?" he finally whispered.

"Your beautiful bride will join me inside this impressive little hidey-hole. Consider it my personal insurance policy, because if anyone besides you, and you alone, is standing there tomorrow morning when you open that door, pretty little Sarah here will be the first to die. She'll catch a bullet in the head before she knows what hit her. But you'll know, though." He gave a sly, hideous wink, "because I'll make sure you're watching when I pull the trigger."

Luke stared in open-mouthed horror. Sarah? Trapped in that underground room with a cold-blooded killer? This was worse than anything he had imagined since seeing Matt Fulton gunned down. How could he be expected to function over the next few hours, knowing Sarah was trapped in there with this…this… amoral madman? Wondering what he was doing to her, how he was hurting her, what liberties he might be taking with her?

Again the stranger grinned. It was as if he could see straight into Luke's head. "Who knows?" he said. "Maybe we'll have us a little party, you know, just to pass the time."

The urge to rush the man was almost overwhelming. Luke wanted to hit him, strangle him, to send him to hell where he belonged. Luke was willing to risk taking a bullet to the brain just to bring an end to this madness. He even took a step forward, his hands clenched into fists.

But then the stranger lifted his Colt and pointed it, not at Luke but at Sarah.

The gunman's cold eyes locked onto Luke's and he said, "Not one more step, friend, or your last memory of your wife will be of seeing her brains splattered all over the walls of this basement."

Luke froze, his hands still balled at his sides.

"That's better," the stranger said. "Now, you listen to me. Don't say or do nothin' out of line, and both you and your little woman will walk out of this place tomorrow with nothin' worse than a few unpleasant memories. But if you go to the sheriff, if you tell my old friends where I'm hiding, or if you say anything to anyone about that dead body you helped dump in the woods, the next time you see pretty little Sarah, you ain't gonna be pleased with the changes in her appearance. Got it?"

Luke nodded, swallowing hard. A black despair unlike anything he had ever experienced washed over him.

"But there is a bright side. I was just funnin' ya about getting close to your wife. She ain't my type. Hell, I'll bet she ain't ever even had more'n one man at a time."

"What? I never!" Sarah said angrily, her face flushed.

The stranger smiled, cruel and hard. "See?" he said. "Not my type, so as long as you do exactly as you're told and don't step outta line, you got nothin' to worry about on that front. Take too long, though, and that could change," he added with a sly grin. "My type or not, a man's got needs, and like the sailors say, 'any port in a storm,' ain't that right?"

The man's mocking, teasing tone disappeared in an instant, and his voice turned icy. "So, do we understand each other, friend?"

Luke nodded, unable to find the strength to form words.

"Good. Now, come with me, little lady." The stranger half-turned and indicated the earthen passageway with a flourish.

Sarah looked stricken. She stared at Luke with horror in her eyes. Then she trudged forward, head down, like a condemned prisoner walking to the gallows. As she passed, Luke reached out and gave her forearm a quick squeeze. She eased past the stranger without meeting the man's eyes and then disappeared down the gloomy passageway.

The stranger winked at Luke and then said, "All you have to do now is close this here magic door, and you'll be on your way to saving your little woman."

Luke moved slowly forward. He was confused. There was no need for him to pull the lever to close the granite slab. The whole point of the design was to eliminate the need for a second person to be in the basement if a slave was forced to hide quickly. There was plenty of time for the stranger to pull on the lever and then get out of the way of the slow-moving granite block as it swung closed.

He reached the basement wall and stopped directly in front of the stranger, sliding his hand into the seam between the massive chunks of granite to locate the lever. As he did, the stranger said, "I ain't convinced you won't run to the law the minute this here door closes, even if I do have your beautiful bride with me."

Luke shook his head. "I...what are you talking about?"

"How the hell do I know this ain't exactly the break you're looking for? Maybe you've grown tired of life with the ol' ball and chain, and you see this here scenario as the perfect opportunity to kill two birds with one stone. So to speak."

"No," Luke protested weakly. "I love my wife; I'd never do anything to put her in danger."

"You mean like letting her enter a sealed room with a man who just murdered a friend of yours? Like that?"

Luke's face flushed red and he balled his hands into fists. He cocked his arm and froze as the stranger lifted his Colt and placed the barrel between Luke's eyes.

"That'll be enough of that," the man whispered. "Anyway, like I said: I *think* you won't do anything stupid, but I need to *know* you won't do anything stupid."

"How can I prove it to you?" Luke asked beseechingly.

The stranger smiled. "Luckily for you, you don't have to." He pulled the gun away from Luke's face, drawing his arm out to the side. Then he pivoted his wrist and whipped his hand forward, clubbing the butt of the .38 against Luke's head, just behind his ear.

Luke heard a sound like a thunderclap and a bright light exploded behind his eyeballs. Then everything went dark.

8

Jackson Healy was an expert at inflicting deadly violence. Killing the deliveryman who had been foolish enough to try sneaking up on him outside the Paskagankee Tavern was only the latest in a long line of murders he had committed, a string that had begun when he was just twelve years old on the Texas prairie.

But inflicting *non*-lethal violence was a different story. It turned out that injuring someone without putting him six feet under was complicated. He had succeeded in hitting the tavern owner hard enough to knock him out, as evidenced by the man dropping to the floor like an empty whiskey bottle.

The question was, had he killed him? Jackson hoped not, because he needed the guy alive and at least functioning well enough to open the hidden basement door after the Krupp brothers had given up looking for him and moved on.

From the darkness of the corridor behind him, he heard a gasp of shock from the man's wife as her husband hit the floor. She rushed forward to tend to his injuries, and Jackson pivoted and thrust his weapon in the woman's direction, not planning to shoot her, but assuming the sight of the Colt would be enough to frighten her into reconsidering her actions.

It was. The woman skidded to a stop. "Please," she said, "please let me make sure he's alright."

"I'll just handle that for you," he said politely. "I'd hate to be considered ungentlemanly, especially considering how kindly I've been treated by the two of you." Before he turned, he added, "And don't even consider trying anything stupid, or the first person I shoot will be your husband. He ain't conscious, so I'm not likely to miss."

The woman moaned, the sound high-pitched and squeaky, like what might come out of a dying mouse. "You understand me?" Jackson said, and she nodded weakly.

He turned and knelt next to the unmoving man. The side of the tavern owner's head had begun swelling and blood oozed out of an ugly gash. It flowed out from under his hairline and dripped in roughly equal proportion under the collar of his shirt and onto the floor.

Jackson didn't care about blood or where it was falling. His only concern was that he hadn't accidentally killed the man. He took a quick look into the passageway to make sure the little woman wasn't considering doing something foolhardy—she wasn't, luckily for her—and then he eased his head down onto the unconscious man's chest and listened for a heartbeat.

It was strong and steady.

Then he felt for a pulse.

Strong as well.

The man would be fine. His brains had been scrambled a bit, but he would awaken in a little while, and when he did, he would find he was suffering from one hell of a massive headache.

But he'd live.

Jackson smiled up at the man's terrified wife. "Your husband's got one high-quality skull," he said. "I'll bet he barely even felt it when I hit him."

The woman shook her head and Jackson thought he could see tears rolling down her cheeks in the semi-darkness. He knew he should feel guilty for what he was putting these two innocent people through, but he didn't. Didn't feel anything at all, in fact. His only emotion was worry, because if the Krupp brothers got their hands on him after what he had done to them two years ago in Peru, he knew he would suffer in ways he could not even begin to imagine.

Why he hadn't taken a few extra seconds to make sure Amos and Wesley were actually dead before starting off across the plains, he didn't know. He had asked himself the question a thousand times. The answer, of course, was simple: he had assumed they would simply crawl off somewhere and die. They were miles from any civilization and suffering serious gunshot wounds. What other option had they had?

But he had underestimated their will to live, or perhaps their desire for revenge. The brothers had somehow escaped Puerta de Hayu Marka, seemingly rising from the dead and dragging their worthless carcasses out of the wilderness, and then finding some sympathetic South American doctor to stitch them up and send them on their way.

Jackson had been utterly, blissfully unaware of their continued existence for nearly eight months after sneaking back across the United States/Mexican border and making his way north. The pair had caught up to him in a boarding house just outside Wichita, bursting into his room one night with whiskey in their bellies and vengeance in their wild eyes.

And they should have gotten him, too. Jackson had erased his two former partners almost completely from his memory by then. He figured—when he thought of the Krupps at all, which was rarely—that their long-dead corpses were by now moldering in a couple of unmarked shallow graves in the plains of Peru. And that was assuming their bodies hadn't been picked clean down to the bone by scavenging wild animals.

He had gotten lucky in Wichita, plain and simple. There was no other way to describe it. Jackson Healy had survived that night only because he wasn't asleep in his bed at three a.m. as he should have been. He had bedded the wife of a local rancher when the man departed on what was supposed to be a three-day trip to evaluate and purchase cattle. The man had cut his trip short after losing most of his capital in a poker game and nearly caught Jackson with his pants down, both figuratively and literally, when he returned home early.

Jackson had barely had time to throw his clothes on and scramble out a bedroom window before skulking back to his room, angry and humiliated.

And horny.

He had hunkered down at the small writing desk in his room, whiskey bottle in one hand and glass in the other, prepared to drink his anger away, when down the street staggered the Krupp brothers, both drunker than skunks and brandishing their revolvers.

How they had located him Jackson had no idea, but Wesley and Amos burst into the rooming house and marched directly to Jackson's room. They smashed the door in and proceeded to empty their guns into his bed, too drunk to notice it was empty.

By this time Jackson was gone. For the second time in less than two hours he departed a residence via a back window, and as shaken as he was to discover the Krupp brothers alive and well – and gunning for him – he decided he was getting damned tired of running away from people.

But run he did, with the Krupp brothers hot on his trail. They were relentless, single-mindedly chasing him around the United States. Memphis, Chicago, Detroit. Atlanta, Boston, Louisville. No matter where Jackson went, the Krupp brothers were never far behind. It was exhausting.

Now, though, Jackson thought he might have gotten his first bit of good luck since appropriating the golden disk and tube of life-juice from those crazy shamans two years ago in Peru. His plan up until a few hours ago had been to keep running, to cross the border into Canada—just a pistol-shot from here in Nowhereville, USA—and then head to Vancouver, hopefully shaking the damned Krupps along the way once and for all.

But finding the secret room in the basement of this dumpy small-town tavern had changed everything. He would never be discovered in here, not even by the Krupps, with their hound-dog noses, and once his former partners reached the only conclusion they could – that Jackson had continued north into Canada – he would bolt from his hiding place and reverse course. Backtrack. Maybe head to California's Gold Coast. That was where he belonged, anyway, he figured.

But everything depended on the Krupps not finding him. Holding the tavern owner's wife captive in the secret room was a good plan for keeping the man from talking; immobilizing the tavern owner so there was *no way* he could give up Jackson to the Krupps or the local law was an even better plan.

And he was executing his plan perfectly. The tavern owner was injured but would live. He would awaken in a little while and let

Jackson and his precious wife out after Amos and Wesley Krupp had come and gone, and with a little luck, Jackson could finally get on with his life. He had yet to find a buyer for the massive golden disk that would make him rich beyond his wildest dreams; he had been too busy trying to stay alive with the goddamned Krupp brothers on his tail for the past year-plus.

The Gold Coast was the answer. He would find a buyer for the disk there, Jackson was sure of it, and now that he stood a reasonable chance of putting some distance between himself and the vengeful bastards chasing him, he might actually be able to begin living the lifestyle he had earned.

A greasy smile slid across Jackson Healy's face as he stood and brushed dust from the basement's hard-packed dirt floor off his trousers. He froze, though, and the smile vanished, as one floor above, he heard an insistent banging on the tavern's front door, followed by a loud *crash* as the door was smashed back against the wall. A moment later, the sound of boots clomped across the barroom floor and a pair of booming voices echoed through the empty building, shouting curses and threats.

The Krupp brothers had arrived.

Jackson backed into the entrance leading to the secret room. He fumbled around in the hidden gap between the stones, finally locating the lever that would close the big slab of granite and seal him in. The door closed smoothly and quietly, and in seconds, a blackness unlike anything Jackson had ever experienced enveloped him and the tavern owner's wife.

All he could now was wait.

9

Wesley Krupp stalked into the Paskagankee Tavern two steps ahead of his brother, gun drawn and ready to rain lead on anything that remotely resembled that devil, Jackson Healy. The place appeared deserted but Wesley knew otherwise. The Healy stink was all over the place.

Since being gut shot two years ago by the lying, cheating sack of horse manure who had then opened fire on Amos, Wesley had devoted his every waking moment to the extraction of revenge. The quest for vengeance was the one thing that had kept him and his brother going over the long days and weeks spent recuperating under circumstances he could now barely believe, despite having lived through them.

The quest for vengeance had kept them going through fever and infection, through choices made that were more difficult than any others they would ever face, no matter how long they lived.

The quest for vengeance was everything. It defined their lives and gave them a focus and single-mindedness of purpose greater than that exhibited by the greatest outlaws – or the greatest lawmen – who had ever lived. It had kept them going through their painful rehabilitation, followed by months trekking north back into the states and picking up Healy's trail.

It had kept them going through disappointment after disappointment, the frustration peaking in Wichita, where they nearly caught the traitor, only to have the trail go cold again for three long weeks.

But Wesley Krupp never wavered. He never doubted they would eventually run Healy down like the cowardly dog he was. And when they finally found the yellow bastard, he would die slowly. Painfully. Wesley would make sure of that. Every moment of the brothers' agony over the past two years would be repaid with interest, of that Wesely Krupp was certain.

And now they had found him.

The lame-brained coward—he had never been quite as clever as he gave himself credit for—had hidden his horse in the forest less than a quarter-mile south of here, fifteen feet off the rutted path that served as a road in this piece of shit little village. The saddlebags were still slung over the horse's ass, and although a quick check of the contents didn't turn up anything specific that would identify the beast as belonging to Jackson Healy, Wesley nevertheless had known it was his.

Who else would it belong to? No resident of this out-of-the-way hamlet—trust Jackson Healy to find the most obscure village in North America to hide out in—would have hidden his horse there, what would be the point? And besides, Wesley could just tell. The animal reeked of Healy.

Therefore, Healy was here. It was technically possible he had dumped his horse, then stolen another and continued on, but Wesley knew that wasn't the case. The Krupps had been gaining ground on their prey for weeks, until by now they were no more than a few hours behind him. Wesley guessed they would be able to run him down before his arrival at the next decent-sized city, Quebec, and he figured if *he* assumed that, Healy would as well.

The yellow-bellied traitor had to be desperate. He knew he couldn't run any farther, so he hid his horse and hunkered down somewhere, hoping the Krupps would assume he had continued into Canada. But Wesley assumed nothing of the kind. Healy was here—and by *here* he meant inside this God-forsaken bar—and he was going to find him. Tonight was the night his insatiable thirst for vengeance would be quenched.

He clambered across the dirty tavern floor, Amos right behind him, past tables with chairs stacked on top of them as if the proprietor had been preparing to sweep when he had been interrupted. "Healy!" he bellowed. "You can't run no more, Healy! Get your sorry ass out here and take what's comin' to ya!"

He stopped and waited.

No response. The bastard was going to be a coward right to the end. He was hiding in a closet or something, and they would have to haul him out by the hair. Wesley hoped Healy hadn't had time to set up some kind of booby-trap before going into hiding; he had been gut-shot once and had no desire ever to repeat the experience.

"Healy!" he yelled again, and again received no answer. He wondered where the tavern owner had gone. Had Healy killed him and dumped the body somewhere? It wouldn't have surprised him.

"Come on," Wesley mumbled to Amos, and the two men resumed their search, marching behind the bar and through a set of swinging wooden doors into the combination kitchen/storage area. Supplies had been stacked haphazardly across the floor, again suggesting at least one man had been working when he was inter-rupted. Why that man would have been working in the middle of the night, Wesley couldn't imagine and didn't care.

The brothers searched the tavern methodically, starting at one end and working their way to the other. They opened every closed door, even those on storage cabinets clearly not big enough to conceal a full-grown piece of shit like Jackson Healy.

Nothing.

They checked behind furniture, in the washrooms, under tables and behind the bar, and within minutes concluded the tavern was empty.

And that left one possibility. The basement.

Wesley nodded toward the stairs and the pair started down, guns drawn, moving slowly, alert for an ambush. Wesley was in the lead, and he swiveled his weapon smoothly back and forth in an attempt to cover the entire basement.

It became immediately clear Jackson Healy wasn't here, but he had been. The flickering light of a half-dozen candles revealed the unmoving body of a man crumpled in one corner of the basement, next to the building's granite-block foundation. The man had been suckered just like the Krupps had been suckered two years ago; Wesley would recognize Healy's handiwork anywhere.

But Healy was nowhere to be found.

Somehow he had escaped again, vanishing into thin air at the last possible moment.

And Wesley Krupp exploded. The rage that had been eating away at him for the last two years, smoldering like last night's campfire at sunrise, suddenly and without warning burst into flame. This was too much to take. Tracking Healy, forcing him to run nearly non-stop for the past two years, finally trapping him—again—only to see him disappear like a ghost or that strange being they had seen walk out of solid rock at Puerta de Hayu Marka, it was all just too much.

He raised his gun into the air and let loose a wild shot into the basement ceiling, screaming something unintelligible, even to himself. Amos put one hand on his arm in a calming gesture and Wesley shook it off angrily. "I've had it!" he shouted into his brother's face. Amos jerked away as spittle flew.

"I've had it," he repeated, and reached into a pocket, removing a box of matches. "Follow me," he said, clomping up the stairs. "This place is gonna burn. Healy's here somewheres and we're gonna smoke him out."

"Wes, we searched every inch of the damned building. He ain't here."

"He's here, I can smell him. Wherever he's holed up, he'll come runnin' out once the flames start nippin' at his sorry ass."

"What about the guy in the basement?"

"What about him?"

"We're just gonna kill him?"

"He's probably already dead anyway if Healy's had at him, and besides, he don't matter. Nothing matters 'cept finding Jackson Healy, and if putting match to wood on this piece of shit tavern accomplishes that, we're gonna do it right now."

Wesley knew Amos wouldn't stand up to him and he was right. His little brother simply shook his head, lips compressed into a thin line on his wide dumb face, and said nothing. That was how it had always been in the Krupp pecking order, Wesley taking charge and Amos following behind, and that was how it would always be.

Wesley strode to the bar and grabbed a nearly full bottle of whiskey. He tossed it to Amos and said, "Start splashin' this around on the walls." Then he grabbed a second bottle for himself. He smashed the neck on the edge of the bar. Amber-colored whiskey flew everywhere and Wesley inhaled the heavenly aroma. Then he moved to the far end of the building and got to work.

Within minutes, the tavern was ready. It had already smelled of stale beer and alcohol when the brothers entered, and now the stench was almost overwhelming, even to a veteran whiskey drinker like Wesley Krupp. Wesley struck a match and handed it to his brother. "Start at that end," he said, nodding at the far side of the room. Amos took the match and wandered away and Wesley lit another for himself.

He bent down and touched the match to a corner of the room, at the point where the interior wall intersected with the wide pine floorboards. Instantly the match flared bright yellow, and flames danced away, shooting across the floor along a track of spilled whiskey, and climbing the wall along another.

Smoke began to billow, a lot of smoke. It gathered just below the ceiling like a rapidly building storm cloud. Wesley dropped the match into a puddle of whiskey and stepped back quickly as the puddle burst into flame. He fumbled for another match, lit it and tossed it into the center of the room before shouting to Amos, "That's enough. Let's get the hell out of here while we still can!"

The brothers rushed across the barroom and through the front entrance, bursting into the refreshing night air, both men gagging and coughing, Amos with wide, frightened eyes and Wesley with a smile on his face the like he had not displayed since before being betrayed by Healy in South America.

The men leaned over, hands on their knees, catching their breath. After a moment, Wesley chuckled. "That'll get Healy's ass out here, and when it does, we'll be waiting to give him the welcome he deserves."

"What about the back entrance?" Amos asked.

"You go cover that. I'll stay here and watch the front."

Amos glanced around nervously, the light from the blaze flickering in his eyes. "We can't be here when this fire's discovered, Wes, we'll go to jail for sure."

"Look around you. This place is so far off the beaten path it'll burn for hours before anyone even notices something's wrong.

We'll be long gone before that happens. Now just get back there and wait for Healy to come stumbling out; it should happen any minute now."

In front of them, nearly the entire building was ablaze. Flames licked around the eves and reached for the nighttime sky. Wesley watched as his brother headed for the back entrance, stumbling around the corner, giving the intense heat of the still-building fire a wide berth.

When Amos disappeared, Wesley focused his attention determinedly on the front door. His feet were planted solidly on the dusty ground, his weapon ready. He was certain Healy would show his double-crossing face any second now.

The fire continued to grow, burning out of control as flames devoured the tavern with shocking speed.

And Jackson Healy never showed.

PART II

1

Modern day
Paskagankee, Maine

A steady rain fell from slate-gray skies as temperatures hovered just above the freezing mark for the third consecutive day. The conditions were more appropriate to mid-December than mid-May, and the sound of the raindrops pelting the roof of the Caterpillar earthmover was almost hypnotic.

Dan Melton yawned and stretched inside the cramped cab of the Cat. It had been another late night last night—almost all of his nights were late ones now that Mary had split, sick and tired after three years of putting up with his drinking and his constant unfulfilled promises to quit—and he wanted nothing more than to call it a day and go home. Maybe pull the top off a brew and watch the Sox on TV; they were scheduled for a rare weekday afternoon game at Fenway, assuming they weren't rained out.

But watching TV and drinking beer didn't pay the bills, and until he could figure out a way to *make* them do so, Dan knew he needed to finish this job. Completion would be the only way to force that asshole Bo Pellerin to pay the demolition fee, and Dan had a feeling he'd be needing cash, and lots of it, once Mary got tired of crying on her mother's shoulder and decided to contact a divorce lawyer. Hell, for all he knew, maybe she had already taken that step.

Dan sighed. He should have known better than to get hitched a second time after his first marriage had been such a fucking nightmare, but Mary had always told him he was one of those people who needed to learn every lesson the hard way, and apparently her insight had been right on target, if a little late to do Dan any good.

As usual.

This job had started out as an easy one. He would spend half an afternoon clearing the sod over the failed septic system behind the run-down Ridge Runner roadhouse, so that the concrete baffles of the system could be removed and disposed of. Then he would come back tomorrow or the next day and fill in the whole shebang once the new baffles had been delivered.

Simple. Easy money.

But then it had started raining, and he had explained to Pellerin that he didn't dare operate his Cat behind the Runner with the ground saturated the way it was, because he was afraid the damned thing would get stuck in the mud and he wouldn't be able to remove it until July.

Pellerin had pissed and moaned and made like he was going to call another contractor, but better men than Pellerin had tried to bullshit Dan and hadn't succeeded yet. Dan Melton was the only contractor north of Portland with the equipment necessary to complete this job, and there was no way Bo Pellerin was going to pay what Dumas Construction down in Portland would charge if they had to haul an earthmover all the way up here.

So after hemming and hawing, cajoling and threatening, Pellerin had finally agreed to wait. He was in a hurry because the state health department wouldn't allow him to operate his business without working restrooms, and the failure of his septic system had put the Men's and Lady's out of commission until a new system could be installed.

"Christ," Pellerin had groused, "none of my male regulars would have a problem stepping out back and pissin' behind a tree. And we don't get any women in here, 'cept for old Blanche Raskiewicz, and she don't count 'cause she's tougher than the rest of my customers put together. I'll bet she pees standing up, anyway."

But that was three days ago, and the drizzle had fallen steadily ever since, broken up only by the occasional heavy downpour. Each day had seen Dan field two or three calls from Bo, and each day had seen him explain the issue with the Cat getting stuck in the mud again and again.

But each day had also seen Pellerin's calls become a little more aggressive than the last. The bar owner was losing a fair amount of money from the forced closure. Hell, Dan guessed by now half the male population of Paskagankee was probably suffering from the DT's, thanks solely to the Ridge Runner's shutdown.

This morning everything had come to a head. Pellerin's voice had been rough and insistent. "Listen here, Melton," he said the minute Dan picked up the phone, not even giving him the chance to say hello. "The weather guessers say we're going to have *at least* another day of this shit and I just can't afford to be out of commission that long. You get your goddamn equipment over here and finish the job, or our deal's off, and you can forget about getting paid."

Dan sighed heavily and agreed. His concern about the Cat was still just as valid as it had been three days ago, but that goddamn Pellerin had just worn him down, plain and simple. Dan Melton didn't like arguing—although he supposed Mary might dispute that claim—and besides, Pellerin did have a point. A business owner could only keep his doors closed for so long just because of the weather.

So now, the Cat slipped and slogged through the mud, rain falling on and around the enclosed cab, while Dan tried not to fall asleep. So far the earthmover seemed to be maintaining traction, and maybe with a little luck he would be able to drive the thing out of here when he was finished, which he very nearly was.

The leach field was laid out in a rectangular grid pattern; each corner marked with a red stake. Dan had scraped the top couple of feet of earth off the baffles, and then carefully removed each one with a chain connected to the Cat's big bucket. He had piled all of the baffles neatly together and was now in the process of digging the pit a little deeper in order to satisfy zoning requirements that had changed in the decades that had passed since the old system was constructed.

And he was almost finished. He had dug in a pattern, starting with the land farthest away from the back of the Ridge Runner, and working his way in toward the building. Now, though, he was running into a problem. He sighed. It figured. That guy Murphy had really had his shit together when he invented his Law.

The teeth of the Cat's iron bucket had snagged on something just under the surface of the earth. Dan swore softly under his breath and manipulated the bucket, maneuvering it back and forth like a driver trying to free his car from a snowbank in the winter.

Finally the bucket lurched free and Dan extended it a little farther before trying again. This time it plowed through the obstruction, the Cat's big diesel engine straining for just a moment.

Dan stared through the windshield. It looked as though someone had buried a massive beam in the ground at some point in the distant past. It had to have been a long time ago, because the beam was splintered and eaten through by rot. Had it been solid, Dan knew there was no way the Cat's bucket would have been able to split it like it had.

He stared for a moment and then shrugged. It was strange, but no stranger than a lot of other shit he had seen or heard about in this weird-ass town. He muttered, "Ain't that the damnedest thing you ever seen," aware that he was alone but not caring.

He clambered out of the cab and into the pit, hooking the chain around the biggest section of rotted wood. Then he climbed back up, lifted the beam, and deftly swiveled the bucket, dropping his discovery onto the ground next to the big hole. He would bring it to Bo Pellerin's attention tomorrow, or whenever the hell it stopped raining. He sure wasn't about to stand around in this shitty weather and talk about a rotting piece of wood.

Dan turned his attention back to the big hole in the ground and smoothly ran the bucket along the edge nearest the building, filling it with mud and preparing to dump the load on top of the massive mountain of dirt he had already manufactured. When the bucket was halfway to the pile, something now visible at the bottom of the hole caught his attention.

The bucket filled with saturated earth hung suspended in the air, forgotten, as Dan gaped in slack-jawed surprise at the unlikely sight visible through the Cat's rain-drenched windshield: there was a hole *under* his freshly-dug hole.

A second hole.

It was big, and deep, and had the vague appearance of a rudimentary room. It looked as though it had been there – a man-made rabbit hole – for a very long time.

And that wasn't all. There were bones lying at the bottom of the hole. From his position up in the cab of the Cat, Dan thought they looked like human bones. Two sets.

Dan Melton was no expert on human skeletal structure, but both sets of bones appeared intact and complete. They also both appeared at one time to have been clothed, as little bits and pieces of tattered fabric remained, the rest having long-since rotted away.

Dan swallowed hard.

He was suddenly very cold.

Because as bizarre as it was to find bones lying at the bottom of the newly dug, suddenly-much-deeper-than-it-should-have-been septic system pit, they weren't the strangest thing down there. Lying next to the two sets of apparently complete human skeletal remains was a third body.

An actual body.

Its clothing, too, had rotted mostly away, but the body itself looked whole, alive even. It was a man, complete with flesh-colored skin and a full head of hair. The body was unmoving, lying in repose with its eyes closed, but from Dan's perspective looked an awful lot like a nearly naked guy taking a nap.

At the bottom of a hole.

A hole that, until moments ago, no one knew existed.

A hole that, until moments ago, had been buried under tons of Paskagankee earth.

Dan Melton shut down the Caterpillar. The earthmover's diesel engine fussed and complained and eventually gave up the ghost. Dan gaped out the windshield a moment longer, the chill in his bones deepening, and wished very much he was not alone right now. He was suddenly sure the man lying at the bottom of the whole would pivot at the waist and rise. He would rise and open his eyes and fix them on Dan's face, and the eyes would be alive but also dead, devoid of any humanity, any compassion, and then the man would climb out of the muddy hole and come for Dan, and when he did, Dan knew the result would be worse than bad. The result would be horrifying.

Dan took a deep breath to steady himself. It came out shuddery and paper-thin, like an old man's. He knew he was being ridiculous but couldn't help himself. He glanced back down at the bottom of the hole, half-convinced the body would be halfway to the Cat, but it wasn't. It was still unmoving, lying in the septic system pit like a nearly naked guy taking a nap.

He reached for his cell phone and wondered when he would be able to finish this job. It appeared suddenly quite obvious it would not be any time soon.

2

Sharon Dupont shut down her cruiser and shrugged into her rain gear. She gazed glumly across the Ridge Runner parking lot to where the back half of a gigantic yellow earthmoving vehicle was visible beyond the building. Its corrugated iron tracks had sunk into the mud halfway up their hubs, and she wondered briefly how in the world Dan Melton was going to get his equipment out of there.

Then she sighed and stepped out of the vehicle. Sharon was intimately familiar with the Ridge Runner, both from her days spent holding down a bar stool inside the place before getting her shit—and her life—together, and from the investigation last year into the strange case of former drinking buddy Earl Manning's disappearance.

But her familiarity with the place didn't translate into any overwhelming desire to be here. The Ridge Runner represented a time in her life Sharon would just as soon forget. Just driving past the place never failed to bring her back to her lost days before meeting Mike McMahon, when she was rudderless and adrift, alone and doing her best to drink herself into an early grave, exactly as her father had done.

Meeting Mike had changed all that, and while it wouldn't be entirely accurate to say she had never again thought about drinking, avoiding her old demons was a much easier proposition now that she found herself in a stable relationship with the older ex-cop.

Sharon crunched across the gravel lot past two pickup trucks parked nose-in to the closed bar, like horses outside an old-West tavern. One of them she recognized as Dan Melton's vehicle, the other she assumed belonged to Bo Pellerin, owner of the Ridge Runner. The men stood waiting for her at the corner of the building, Pellerin currently involved in an animated, mostly one-sided conversation with Melton that included hand waving, angry gestures, and the occasional finger stabbed into Melton's chest for emphasis.

She wondered how much more verbal abuse Melton would put up with before hauling off and slugging Pellerin. From the look on his face, she guessed the answer was not much. The last thing she wanted was to have to break up a fight between two men who each outweighed her by eighty or more pounds, and she picked up her pace.

"Gentlemen," she said sharply, skidding to a stop in the wet scrub grass. Pellerin flinched in surprise; he had been so involved in haranguing Melton that he hadn't even noticed her drive into the lot. "Someone reported the discovery of a body?"

"That'd be me," Melton said, raising his hand in a little half-wave as if maybe Sharon might need help determining who had spoken. "And it's not just one body, exactly. It's more like...well..."

Sharon scratched her head. "Well, what? How many bodies did you find? Aren't you sure?"

"Maybe you should just take a look and see for yourself," Melton said.

Sharon looked at him quizzically. "Okay," she said. "Lead the way."

They began walking along the side of the building in the direction of the earthmover. "I still don't know why you couldn't have called me first," Pellerin said, apparently resuming the conversation that Sharon's arrival had interrupted. "Thanks to you, I'm going to be out of business even longer now."

Melton stopped on a dime and turned. Sharon was surprised such a big guy could move so nimbly. Pellerin had been directly behind him and nearly ran into him. "There's dead people lying in a hole in the ground right behind your bar," Melton said, his voice rising in volume as he spoke. "What would you have wanted me to do, just cover them back up and pretend I never found them?"

Sharon had known Bo Pellerin a long time and knew without a shadow of a doubt that was exactly what he would have preferred Melton do. "Of course not," Bo said after a long pause. "I just think that since this…incident…occurred on my property, I should have been notified first."

Melton shook his head, exasperated, and said, "Just give it a rest, Bo, and let me show Officer Dupont the hole so we can all get the hell out of the rain."

All except me, Sharon thought.

They rounded the corner and Melton waved a hand in the general direction of the portion of the hole closest the back wall of the Ridge Runner. "You can see it for yourself," he said uneasily, refusing to look into the pit.

Before turning her attention to the hole, Sharon let her gaze linger on Dan Melton's face, scrutinizing him. His skin was pale, his lips a grayish-white, and it occurred to her with stunning clarity that he was afraid. *This is more than just being shaken up by the discovery of a dead body. Melton's actually terrified.* She knew the contractor would never open up with Bo Pellerin standing right next to him, though, and made a mental note to talk to him later, alone.

She turned her attention away from the heavy equipment operator and at last looked into the pit he had dug. It was nearly finished, measuring roughly ten feet long by eight feet wide, maybe four feet deep.

Except for the area in question. That portion of the hole was much deeper, extending perhaps another six feet *below* the four feet Melton had already excavated. It opened up into what at one time had clearly been a small room. Melton had dug right through the ceiling and exposed the hidden room by stripping away the layer of earth covering it.

She squatted down on her haunches in the wet grass and looked more closely and saw what Melton had called the station to report: the bones of two skeletons, sprawled on the hard-packed dirt floor of the room. The falling rain and drizzle had turned the floor into a gooey, muddy mess, but the off-white bones were still easily recognizable from above.

The flesh surrounding the bones had long-since disappeared,

meaning either the bodies had been down there a very long time, or the victims had died somewhere else and been transported to their present location only after decomposition was complete. Sharon guessed it was the former, as small bits of muddy, mostly-decomposed fabric—presumably the clothing the victims had been wearing when they died—still clung to the bones and lay scattered in the immediate vicinity.

She furrowed her brow and looked up at Melton. He had turned his back on them and was staring resolutely in the direction of the parking lot. "Dan," she said softly.

He turned and cast a questioning look in her direction. Sharon noticed he still did not look into the pit. "Two bodies," she said. "Why didn't you just tell me there were two?"

"Two?" he answered. "What about the other guy?"

"Other guy? What other guy?" Sharon dropped to her knees now and examined as much of the room as she could. The steel-grey light provided by the glowering skies made it nearly impossible to see much of anything besides the bones through the relatively small gash in the room's ceiling.

She produced a Maglite flashlight and shined it down through the hole, examining as much as she could of the room's interior. It looked exactly like some kind of ancient underground bunker. As far as she could see, no other bodies were present. "There are two sets of bones here," she said. "Probably human, although we'll have to wait for lab analysis to be sure. But that's it. There's no other guy."

"What are you talking about?" Melton said. He trudged forward reluctantly, the saturated ground sucking at his work boots, producing an audible *slurp* with each step. "How can you not see it? Lying right next to the bones is another guy, and this one looks alive, his skin color is—"

He stopped short and stared in horror down at the secret room under the hole he had dug less than an hour ago. "Oh, my God," he whispered, his already pale face turning chalk-white. His eyes widened in panic and he stumbled backward and almost fell, wind-milling his arms in a desperate attempt to maintain his balance. For a moment Sharon though he might drop right into the pit, but then Bo grabbed him by one arm and steadied him.

"What is it?" Sharon said, and for once, Bo had nothing to add, he simply stared mutely at Dan Melton like a moviegoer waiting for the killer to be revealed in the final scene.

Melton swallowed hard and made an obvious effort to get his emotions under control. "The guy...the guy is gone."

* * *

"I'm telling you," Melton said, "there was another body at the bottom of that hole, and it wasn't just a loose collection of bones, either. The skin color was normal and the dude appeared as alive as you or me. He looked exactly like some guy sleeping one off, except he had no clothes on."

Sharon had prevailed upon Bo to fire up the Ridge Runner's coffeemaker, and the three of them sipped coffee and stood at the bar, trying to pretend they weren't all soaking wet and freezing cold. And in Melton's case, terrified beyond all reason.

"Well," she said. "Not to dwell on the obvious, but if there was another body down there, where would he have gone?"

"Beats the hell out of me. But I know what I saw."

Sharon turned to Pellerin. "Did you see another body down there, Bo?"

He shrugged. "I didn't see anything until just now. I got here no more than two minutes before you drove up. I never even went behind the building until we all went together." Sharon glanced at Melton for confirmation and he nodded.

"Maybe you saw something else and only *thought* it was another body," she suggested. "Uncovering those bones would startle anyone, and—"

Melton shook his head resolutely and raised his hand, cutting her off. "There was another body in there. It was a man, maybe mid-to-late thirties, and although his eyes were closed and he wasn't moving, I would bet a hundred bucks he was alive. I know what I saw," he repeated.

Sharon looked between the two men and then drained her coffee. "I have to get back outside. I've got work to do."

3

Bronson Choate urged his seven-year-old Jeep Cherokee up the rutted dirt trail leading to his cabin. Twenty miles per was about the best speed he was ever able to achieve on the mile-long weed-strewn cow path serving as his "driveway," and even then he was grateful for his safety harness. It was about the only thing preventing him from being bounced right out the driver's side window.

A merchant marine engineer based out of Portland, Bronson typically spent six weeks at sea, followed by four weeks at home. He considered the relatively long drive from Portland to his cabin in Paskagankee well worth the time, given his love of solitude. Hunting, fishing and hiking were the perfect methods of relaxing after the grueling work schedule he was forced to endure—four hours on, eight hours off, over and over, for weeks at a time—while at sea.

Plus, with the low cost of living up here at the far end of the known universe, Bronson was able to bank most of his salary, and had been doing so since signing on right out of high school fifteen years ago. His plan was to work his ass off for another ten years and then retire. He figured by the age of forty-three he would have enough cash salted away to live quite comfortably off the beaten path for the rest of his life.

And that was good enough for Bronson Choate.

The Cherokee ground on through the dense forest. The drizzle had been falling steadily during the drive north, and although it was still only early afternoon, between the low clouds and the thick canopy of centuries-old fir trees it felt to Bronson more like dusk. He had flipped his headlights on over an hour ago, but here in the dense forest the beams seemed to wither and die a few feet from the car, gobbled up by the looming darkness.

At last the little cabin materialized in the mist, the unrelenting mass of Paskagankee forest encroaching on it from all sides. Hauling construction materials way out here ten years ago while building his home had been no picnic, but Bronson had never doubted his struggles would be worthwhile in the end, and he had been right.

He pulled to the side of the narrow pathway and shut down the Jeep. Parking was tricky, but if done properly, left him just enough room to turn the vehicle around between two trees when it was time to drive away, rather than being forced to back out through a mile of wilderness.

Bronson yanked on a watch cap and slid into his jacket. He hefted his canvas duffle off the passenger seat and worked the nylon strap over his head, allowing him to carry the bag while keeping both hands free. Then he opened the Jeep's door and stepped into the falling rain.

Standing water filled the potholes in his forest driveway, some of them upwards of eight inches deep, and Bronson reminded himself to tread carefully. Breaking an ankle this far from help would be a problem, especially given the historically spotty cell coverage in the Paskagankee area. Even after the recent construction of their very own cell tower, residents of the remote town could never count on receiving a steady signal from one location to the next, or even from one *moment* to the next.

The steady, days-long precipitation had saturated the ground, even here under the thick forest canopy, and Bronson slipped and slid to his front door. He was fumbling around in his pocket for the house key—he hadn't used the damned thing in nearly two months, where the hell was it?—when furtive movement, sensed rather than seen out of the corner of his eye, caught his attention.

He froze, hand in his pocket, and glanced to the right. The movement had seemed to come from somewhere beyond the corner of the cabin, back among the trees. Bronson Choate was not what anyone would consider to be a jumpy person, not given to flights of fancy or unfounded fears, but now he was reminded exactly how isolated he was out here.

He pictured his Ruger 9mm semiauto pistol, currently less than ten feet away but stashed securely in a gun safe and out of reach behind his closed and locked front door. Carrying the gun aboard ship was strictly prohibited, so Bronson's policy was to unload it and lock it up before leaving for a stint at sea.

He wished he had it now.

Squinting, Bronson willed the heavy rain to ease up for a moment so he could just freaking *see*. The rain paid no attention.

He stared for a few more seconds in the direction he thought/felt he had seen movement.

Nothing.

A light breeze ruffled the evergreens and Bronson heard the soothing sigh that accompanied the wind in the middle of the forest, but there was no sign of anything unusual.

False alarm.

Maybe you're becoming just another pussy in your old age. He smiled at the thought. Rough, tough Bronson Choate, veteran seaman, globe-trotting merchant marine, survivor of bar fights the world over, from the Philippines to the Hawaiian Islands to Portland's roughest Old Port taverns, quaking like a little girl on the front steps of his own house, frightened by nothing scarier than the wind in the trees.

He shook his head at his foolishness and pulled the house-key from his pocket. He slid it into the door lock and turned it.

And again sensed movement, this time from his *other* side. A figure rushed at him from out of the gloom on his left, and Bronson knew immediately he had been suckered. Whoever—*what*ever—had raised his hackles a moment ago on the right side of the cabin had crossed behind it while he was staring like a dumbass into the forest.

He spun to the left and raised his hands to defend himself against the unknown attacker, but the bulky duffel bag slung over his shoulder had thrown his balance off. He slipped and lurched sideways.

Nearly fell.

Recovered.

But by now it was too late. The attacker raised one arm and slashed at his face. Bronson reacted instinctively, ducking and turning his head, but he was too slow and whatever the attacker was holding slammed into the side of Bronson's skull.

A white-hot explosion of pain bounced around inside his skull and he tried to counter with a roundhouse right as he was falling, but his motor skills had vanished, he felt numb and tingly, and the punch missed its target badly. He crumpled to the ground, dropping onto his duffel bag like he was falling onto a mattress. *Small favors,* he thought.

He felt consciousness slipping away and forced himself to focus on his attacker, determined to identify the son of a bitch so that on the off chance the guy didn't kill him right here and now, he could hunt the fucker down later. Even as the circuits in his brain were shutting down, shock flooded his system at what he saw.

His attacker was a man; no surprise there.

But the man was buck naked.

4

The man went down in a jumble of rubbery arms and legs and Jackson Healy wondered for just a second whether he had killed him. He didn't *care*, but he did wonder.

He would have preferred to shoot the guy, rather than rushing him without a stitch of clothing covering his bare ass, but his Colt .38 was somehow rusted and corroded all to hell and when he had pulled the trigger experimentally a few minutes ago, not a goddamned thing had happened.

So he had improvised. It was a talent Jackson had always been blessed with.

He stepped over the unconscious man and tried the cabin door. A key hung from a strange-looking lock built into the knob, and it had apparently already been turned, because the door swung open noiselessly.

Jackson stepped inside, then turned around and dragged his victim in behind him. It seemed unlikely anyone would come along and see the man way out here in the middle of nowhere, but there was no point in taking unnecessary chances, especially considering he had no idea what in the hell was going on.

He needed to find clothing. That was the first order of business and the only thing Jackson was really sure of at this point. Things had been moving so fast since he had opened his eyes, awakening out of a deep sleep and finding himself at the bottom of a muddy hole, naked and being pelted with freezing-cold rain, that he hadn't had much of an opportunity to think about anything else.

The cabin owner coughed weakly and moaned on the floor, and Jackson decided he'd probably live. He guessed the guy would regain enough of his faculties to become a problem again fairly quickly, and decided he had better hurry up and neutralize the man.

He padded down a short hallway into the tiny home's only bedroom and began pulling open dresser drawers at random. Before long he had found underclothes and stockings, as well as a pair of denim trousers. He found a button-down flannel shirt hanging in a small closet.

The owner of the clothes looked to be relatively close to Jackson's own height and weight, and in any event he didn't have any other options, so he stepped quickly into them. They fit well enough and were certainly better than running around naked as the day he was born.

Jackson spied a pair of work boots tossed haphazardly under the dresser and fished them out. He laced them up and returned to the cabin's sitting room and found the man he had attacked still lying on the floor. His eyes were fluttering, though, and it seemed clear he would be recovering soon.

Jackson knew he should leave now, cut his losses, get out while the cabin's owner was still incapacitated. Thanks to the man's unwitting generosity, Jackson now at least had clothing and boots to wear, and undoubtedly there was a nice, warm coat hanging in the closet next to the front door. He should grab that coat and go.

But there was a problem with that plan.

Jackson Healey had no idea where *to* go.

Hell, he didn't really even know where he was. His mind was foggy, his memories vague and unclear. He had an almost dream-like recollection of hitting somebody in the head, hitting them in the head because…because…someone was chasing him….they were chasing him and had almost caught up to him…

And then it all came back to him.

Everything.

Shooting the Krupp brothers in South America and stealing the Peruvian golden disk and the strange immortality juice from the man who had stepped right through the solid rock formation.

Fleeing north into the United States thinking he was home free.

Finding out the Krupps had survived and were hunting him.

Running again, month after month spent with the Krupps dogging his every move, finally arriving in the tiny northern Maine village with the Krupps right on his tail, killing the liquor distributor and then knocking the tavern owner out to keep him from blabbing about the secret slave hideaway to Amos and Wesley.

But then what had happened? His plan had been a good one, and the innkeeper was out cold, as he remembered. He had felt his way along the pitch-dark subterranean passageway and into the secret room, practically dragging the barkeep's little woman behind him. The granite-block door had barely closed ahead of the Krupps' arrival, so he knew they had searched the tavern.

The last thing he remembered was hearing the muffled, faraway sounds of destruction: walls crashing down, timbers and beams falling, the tavern being destroyed. Wesley and Amos must have known he had outsmarted them—again—and one of them had snapped. Probably Amos, he thought, the man had never had an ounce of patience in his entire big ugly body.

One or both of the Krupps had done something rash. Given the level of destruction that seemed to have been occurring beyond those thick foundation blocks, the damned fools had probably set fire to the tavern, burning it down with the innkeeper—the only man with the knowledge that three human beings were trapped inside a secret underground room with no way out—lying unconscious on the basement floor.

That meant the innkeeper had either burned to death or been killed by falling rubble, and that had been the beginning of the end for Jackson Healy, the innkeeper's lovely wife, and one very pissed off old black slave. The three people paced back and forth inside the tiny room, mostly trying to stay out of each other's way, all attempting, with varying degrees of success, to quell their rising panic.

When two hours had elapsed and the innkeeper had not yet returned to release them from their subterranean prison, Jackson knew he wasn't going to return.

Ever.

The innkeeper had been so stricken about his wife being held hostage that Jackson knew he would not have let one extra second elapse after the Krupp brothers departed before would rush to the basement and release her.

Thus, he was dead or dying and they were never getting out.

They had gone through their supplies slowly, rationing them more or less on an equal basis, although it became much easier to accomplish when Sarah mostly stopped eating. Once she realized her husband must have been killed and there was no hope of rescue, it seemed to Jackson that she was anxious to get on with the business of dying in order to join the innkeeper in whatever came after this life.

And she did it, too. She was the first to die.

Jackson had lost track of the number of days they had been trapped underground when the young woman slipped away, but it seemed as though her death had happened much more quickly than it should have, given her apparent good health. But what did he know? He was no doctor, and her fate didn't concern him, anyway.

What *did* concern him was the prospect of sharing their earthen prison cell with a decomposing corpse, that concerned him a lot, but by this time there were much more serious issues to worry about. Their food was running low, and the old black slave's health was deteriorating rapidly, and Jackson knew the man would also die soon. Then he would be down here alone, trapped with two corpses, and would likely go mad before following his fellow prisoners into death.

But Jackson had a secret, something he had carried with him for two years, afraid to use but unwilling to discard. Day after day—or perhaps night after night; Jackson had long since lost track of hours and days down here, and what difference did it make, anyway?—when the old man drifted off to a troubled sleep, Jackson would pull the long, clear tube out of the breast pocket of his overcoat and examine its gel-like contents, recalling the words the young Peruvian guide had spoken just minutes before Jackson had shot the kid: *If you drink the liquid, you will live forever.*

What had the boy meant by that? The words seemed clear enough, but were they really?

The words had been a translation, uttered for his benefit by a child with a child's unquestioning belief in their truth. The boy had spoken them with such conviction, Jackson had almost believed them himself, and why wouldn't he? He had just seen with his own eyes a solid, seamless boulder transform – impossibly – into a door, using nothing more than a solid gold doorknob. He'd seen a massive humanoid figure appear out of nowhere, dressed in foreign, almost alien-looking clothing. He'd seen with his own eyes a mystical ceremony probably not observed by any other living white man.

He'd seen things he would never understand.

After all of that, and in the dead of night, under the starry South American sky, what the hell else *could* he believe?

He had put enough stock in the child's words to be sure he took possession of the bizarre gel-like liquid sealed inside the clear tube before stealing the gold disk and murdering everyone—or at least, thinking he had murdered everyone—and then fleeing the continent.

But that was where it had ended. Jackson Healy never quite developed enough faith in the story enough to actually drink the stuff.

Now, though, with the body of the innkeeper's wife moldering in a corner of the room not eight feet away, with the stench of death and decomposition filling his lungs with every wretched breath he took, with the ancient black slave already weak and getting weaker, soon to follow the dead woman into the great beyond, he supposed he had no choice. It was either drink the liquid and take his chances, or suffer for a few more days or weeks and then die like his two fellow prisoners, alone and miserable.

So he had drunk the liquid and taken his chances.

5

Mike McMahon was pacing. He paced a lot these days, having resigned his former position as chief of the Paskagankee Police Department over concerns raised by the Town Council about a potential conflict of interest, given the fact he was living with one of his subordinates on the force.

At the time of his resignation, no one had as yet approached him about his living arrangements, but it would only have been a matter of time, so he had saved them the trouble. He submitted his letter of resignation the very day he proposed to Sharon.

He had known for months that the day was coming when he would be forced to choose between the two things he loved – his job and his girl – and the results of a bizarre plot hatched by a power-hungry maniac last year involving a sacred Navajo stone and the kidnapping of a world-renowned software developer had served to simplify the decision in a way nothing else could have.

Sharon had nearly died.

Her quick thinking and unerring cop instincts had allowed her to narrowly escape a horrific death at the hands of Earl Manning, a local drunkard and former lover of Sharon's who had been turned into the unwitting – and unwilling – pawn of cult leader Max Acton. Mike's inability to save Sharon and the knowledge that he had nearly lost her forever had made the choice an easy one: he could always find another job, but the idea of living without the petite, fiery Sharon Dupont was unacceptable.

And he had never regretted his decision, not once. But finding work with strictly a law-enforcement background in a town as remote as Paskagankee, Maine, a stone's throw from the Canadian border, was easier said than done, and he had spent most of the time since his resignation cooling his heels.

He would have a temporary but lucrative gig in a couple of months. Hollywood was coming to Paskagankee in the form of a film crew and a bunch of actors Mike had mostly never heard of to do location shooting for the upcoming motion picture based on Portland *Journal* reporter Melissa Mannheim's book, NIGHTS OF TERROR.

Mannheim had written the book two years ago, based on the string of brutal murders that gripped Paskagankee almost immediately upon Mike's arrival in the little town. The book became an instant bestseller, earning Mannheim lots of money—nobody knew how much and Mannheim wasn't saying—and, of course, the obligatory movie deal.

As the hero who single-handedly stopped the violence, Mike had been approached by the film's production company, which had insisted on hiring him as a credited "special consultant."

The problem was Mike McMahon had no desire to be listed as a consultant on a horror movie. He had lived through the experience first-hand and felt no desire to revisit those awful days, with Sharon Dupont missing and feared dead. That, combined with Mike's certainty that no movie could do justice to the story, led him to turn the offer down flat, despite the fact it came with a fat paycheck and few actual duties.

Unused to being rebuffed, NorthStar Productions management refused to take no for an answer, and after weeks of email negotiations, they reached a compromise. Mike would not be listed anywhere in the film's credits, but would agree to sign on as temporary head of security for the short time the crew was in town. He would make himself available to answer questions from the film's director and stars on an unofficial consulting basis, and in return would receive a fat check.

Mike still wasn't convinced he had done the right thing in signing the contract, but money was money, and at least the gig would give him something to do for a while. Unfortunately, the film crew wasn't due in town for eight weeks, leading to Mike's current situation: wearing a pathway in the carpet of Sharon Dupont's living room.

He traipsed through the kitchen, pausing to take a sip of coffee from a cup strategically placed on the stovetop, then resumed his restless wandering: through the kitchen, across the living room in front of the couch, sharp left turn just before crashing into the rarely-used TV, through the dining room, and then back into the kitchen for more coffee and to start the circuit again.

For the thousandth time over the last three days, Mike wished the rain would stop falling so he could walk outside, but a glance out the window confirmed what he already knew: his wishes weren't being well-received by the weather gods. The rain sluiced down in dark gray sheets.

Mike shook his head in disgust and had just begun another trip around his personal walking circuit, when the telephone rang, making him jump. He squinted at the Caller ID screen, surprised to be hearing from Sharon. He had seen her briefly at lunchtime and didn't expect to hear from her again until she returned home at the end of her patrol shift.

The number glowed on the screen and he realized it wasn't Sharon after all. The caller was new Paskagankee Police Chief Pete Kendall, the man who had succeeded Mike in the chief's job – despite not yet being thirty years old – following Mike's glowing recommendation. Pete rarely phoned, and when he did, it was almost always after hours. This clearly wasn't a social call.

"Huh," he mumbled to himself, and pressed the *Talk* button. "Hello?"

"Hey, Mike, this is Pete Kendall. How's the life of a semi-retired gentleman treating you?"

"It's not all it's cracked up to be," Mike answered with a smile. "Although at least I don't have to deal with dumbass cops every day anymore."

Pete laughed. "I can see you've given the issue a lot of thought, but remember, it takes one to know one. Anyway, I'm sorry to pull you away from your deep philosophical musings, but we've got a situation, and I was hoping you might be available to provide a little input on it."

"Of course. What kind of situation?"

"I don't know if you're aware, but the septic system failed at the Ridge Runner, and Bo Pellerin was forced to replace the whole thing."

"Listen, I know I agreed to serve as occasional consultant to the Paskagankee PD, but I'm not sure I'm qualified to take on the job of digging a septic system. Or that I want to, for that matter."

Pete laughed again, the sound warm and friendly. It reminded Mike how much he missed his old life. "No, I'm not asking you to play in the mud and…you know, the other stuff. Bo's already hired Dan Melton to do that. But here's the thing: Dan was digging the pit for the new septic system this morning and he uncovered what appears to be human remains in some kind of hidden underground bunker next to the Ridge Runner."

"A body buried next to the Ridge Runner?"

"More than one."

"How many more?"

Kendall paused, and Mike wondered why. The question seemed pretty straightforward. Then the young police chief cleared his throat and said, "It depends who you believe. There are two sets of what I'm certain are human skeletal remains positioned almost right next to each other at the bottom of the hole, but…"

"But what?"

"But Dan swears there were *three* bodies down there when he made the discovery."

Mike ran a hand through his hair. "What? How long was the hole left unattended?"

"Melton says he called us on his cell from the cab of the earthmover the minute he discovered the bodies, and that he waited for the arrival of the cruiser—Sharon responded, by the way—in front of the bar."

"How long did it take her to get there?"

"She happened to be in the area on patrol at the time, so she was very close. Mike, she radioed in on arrival at the Ridge Runner not five minutes after Gordie took Melton's call."

"Let me get this straight. Someone stole a dead body that no one even knew existed until this morning, within five minutes of its discovery, with Dan Melton right around the corner? And Dan didn't see a thing? That's impossible, Pete."

"I know that. Even if someone had been watching Melton dig the hole and had snuck down there the minute his back was turned, it just would not have been possible to bring the body up from the bottom of the hole and spirit it away without being observed."

"So what happened? The corpse got up and walked away by itself?"

"Melton says that's exactly what happened."

6

Mike was inside his car and on the way to the Ridge Runner five minutes later. He had been a Paskagankee resident long enough by now that navigating the winding, remote roads, often roads badly in need of repair, was second nature and required little conscious thought. As he drove through the fuzzy afternoon drizzle, he considered Dan Melton's odd claim that three bodies had been at the bottom of the hole when he called the police, and only two were there upon Sharon's arrival just minutes later.

The obvious conclusion was that Melton was mistaken, that he had been so shaken up by his gruesome discovery that he had counted wrong in his shock and his haste to notify the authorities. It was the only thing that made sense.

But Pete Kendall was not a stupid man; he wouldn't have needed Mike's input to figure that one out. If Pete had gone to the trouble of calling Mike, then he obviously felt there was more to the story. Something else was going on, or at least Pete thought so.

Mike pulled into the gravel lot and parked as close to the front of the Ridge Runner as possible. Scowling out through the bar's front plate-glass window was Bo Pellerin, clearly unhappy with this latest development. The owner of the Ridge Runner wasn't the easiest man to get along with under any circumstances, and three-plus days of lost revenue—with who knew how many more to be tacked on to that total now—had undoubtedly pushed his patience right to the breaking point.

Pete, Sharon and Dan Melton were gathered in a tight cluster in front of the door, apparently preferring the cold, wet weather outside the bar to having to listen to Bo complain inside. Mike offered a smile and nodded to each of them as he stepped out of the car. Sharon looked exhausted, but she returned his smile brightly, and for maybe the ten thousandth time in the last two years he thanked God for her and wondered how he had ever gotten so lucky to wind up engaged to the beautiful young patrol officer.

"So," he said, shaking hands with the two men and kissing Sharon lightly on the cheek. It felt awkward, but he had given up his position as police chief to avoid the appearance of impropriety that came from sleeping with a subordinate, and he felt he had earned the right to a little PDA. Sharon didn't seem to mind. "We started out with three bodies and now we have two?"

"That's right," Melton replied defensively, like he was tired of being second-guessed. Probably he was. Mike looked him in the eye and winked, trying to put the man at ease. The last thing they needed was a witness who had grown tired of cooperating.

"I'm sure you guys have had enough for one day," he said, speaking mostly to Melton, "but would you mind slogging out to where the bodies were discovered one more time?" No one objected, at least not out loud, and the group began walking along the front of the bar.

As soon as they turned the corner Mike could see the massive yellow Caterpillar earthmover parked in the open field behind the Ridge Runner. It sat just beyond the edge of a rectangular-shaped pit, with a big mound of muddy earth piled up beside the hole and a stack of concrete baffles next to the dirt. The Cat seemed to be settling into the mud on its tracks, as if in anticipation of a long stay. Two halves of a thick beam, partially rotted away, lay on the far side of the mound.

At the edge of the pit, Mike looked down and saw what did, indeed, appear to be a room dug out of the earth adjacent to and a few feet away from the granite-block foundation of the Ridge Runner. With his earthmover, Melton had neatly stripped part of the reinforced ceiling of the room away while digging the new septic system leach field.

Two sets of bones lay in the mud, positioned in close proximity to each other, and the ruined remains of what might at one time have been rudimentary furniture—perhaps a table, a few chairs, and some shelving, now collapsed and almost entirely rotted away—littered the space. Tree-roots had grown through the ceiling and thrust downward into the room in a tangled mess, suggesting to Mike that this was no recent construction, but had been buried next to the Ridge Runner, undetected, for years, maybe decades. The obvious question was had the bones been down there the entire time, or were they a more recent addition?

Mike straightened and turned to Pete Kendall. "Has anything been disturbed?"

Kendall shook his head. "Nope, not a thing. Soon as we're done here, I'll transport the remains to Dr. Affeldt, but I didn't want to move anything until you had had the opportunity to examine it on site."

Mike nodded thoughtfully and then turned to Dan Melton. "And you saw a third set of remains, which have now gone missing, before you called for help?"

"Well, yes and no. They weren't remains. It wasn't a set of bones like these." Melton gestured in the general direction of the construction site. "It was an actual body, Mike. A man, and he was naked, sort of draped across that table-thing down there, like he had fallen asleep without getting dressed first."

Mike was watching Melton closely as the man spoke. Dan saw Mike's look and said, "I know what you're thinking, but you asked me what I saw. That's what I saw. You can believe me or not; I don't really care. But that's what I saw."

Mike raised his hands in a calming gesture. "I'm not question- ing what you saw, Dan, I'm just trying to figure out what possible explanation there could *be* for what you saw, especially given the fact that this naked man is now missing. You didn't see anyone come or go in the time between your call to the station and Officer Dupont's arrival?"

Melton shook his head. "I already had this conversation with Officer Dupont, and then again with Chief Kendall. *Nobody* came and *nobody* went, at least not from the front of the Ridge Runner. I can't speak for what was happening behind the building, because I wasn't back there."

Mike knelt down on his haunches and examined the sidewalls of the subterranean room, as well as the much newer pit Dan Melton had been digging before making his gruesome discovery. If someone had stolen human remains out of the bottom of that hole, they would have had to climb in and out somehow, and the distance from ground level to the hard-packed dirt floor of the newly unearthed secret room had to be close to ten feet.

The grade of the sidewall was steep, nearly ninety degrees, but thanks to the roots that had forced their way through the ceiling and walls, there were plenty of hand-and-foot holds available. It would not have been impossible for a determined climber to work his way down there and back out again. *Why* he would do so was anyone's guess, but it would definitely have been possible.

Any evidence of such a climb, though, had disappeared hours ago. The steady-falling drizzle had turned the entire pit into a morass of sticky mud, eliminating potential boot or shoe tracks any intruder might have left behind and rendering the hole practically inaccessible. Mike didn't envy Pete Kendall the job of retrieving the remains, but was glad the new chief hadn't assigned the job to tiny Sharon Dupont.

He rose to his feet and wiped his hands on his jeans, smearing mud on the now-rain-saturated denim. He glanced at the three people gathered in a rough semicircle around him and smiled. "You guys look like drowned rats."

"Speak for yourself," Sharon said, smiling at him.

"So what do you think?" Pete said.

"I wish I could give you some insight, but I'm as baffled as you are. Maybe when the autopsies are complete on these remains, we'll get some idea how long ago they were killed and how long they've been down there. I assume you're going to light a fire under our esteemed ME?"

Kendall nodded. "I'll ask him to put a rush on the lab work, but you know Dr. Affeldt. He's about as cooperative as a hibernating bear most of the time."

Mike thought back to some of the run-ins he had had with the County Medical Examiner while he was running the department. Pete Kendall's description of the man was as accurate as any he could have come up with. "Okay," he said. "If you'd like my assistance, keep me apprised of any developments and I'll help in any way I can. For now, though, I'm afraid I'm useless to you."

The small group trudged through the wet field to the front of the Ridge Runner and parted company. The last thing Mike saw as he backed out of the lot was Bo Pellerin, still gazing out the bar's plate-glass window. He looked as though he had just bitten into a lemon.

7

Bronson Choate swam up to consciousness like a diver breaking the surface of a lake. The first few moments consisted of a dark void, followed by utter confusion as he began processing information again. His brain's first order of business was to advise him he was suffering from one whopper of a headache and would likely continue to do so for the foreseeable future. Its second was to instruct him to open his eyes.

The world swam and blurred and his head throbbed, but his vision slowly cleared. He blinked and glanced around slowly to minimize the pain. He was inside his cabin. Tied to a chair, hands lashed behind his back.

He craned his neck and turned his body as much as possible, which was not much, but enough to see that a length of electrical cord had been ripped out of a floor lamp and used to tie him up. The cord was stiff and not terribly pliable, and Bronson thought that with a little effort he might be able to loosen it enough to free his hands. He wondered why anyone would have used it in the first place. He began working at the wire, feeling with his fingers, picking at the knot.

From down the short hallway he heard the heavy clomping of footsteps, and then a man emerged from his bedroom, dressed in a pair of his jeans and work shirts. And his boots. Bronson assumed this was the same man who had attacked him outside his front door, but everything out there had happened so fast he couldn't be sure.

The intruder saw that he was conscious and stopped in his tracks, eyeing him suspiciously. "What's that buggy out there?" he said, nodding in the direction of the front yard.

"Buggy?" Bronson repeated, confused.

"That's right, the buggy you were riding in when you arrived here. What is it?"

"Are you talking about my Jeep?"

"Jeep," the stranger said hesitantly, trying the word out, repeating it like a man might mimic something in a language he had never heard before.

"Yeah, that's right," Bronson said, "and if you want it, you can have it. It's all yours, just take it and go."

"Take it? How? Where's the horse?" the man asked, as if he hadn't heard a word Bronson said.

Bronson shook his head slowly, wondering if his injuries might be more severe than he realized. His attacker wasn't making any goddamn sense. "Horse? What horse?"

"Don't play stupid," the man said menacingly. For the first time, Bronson noticed he was clutching an ancient pistol in his hand, a revolver. The gun was rusted badly, corroded to the point where it had to be unusable. "The horse that pulls your carriage. Where is it?"

"There's no horse. It's just a car. You know, you drive it. A car. With an engine."

"Car," the man said, and the word seemed as foreign to him as "Jeep" had. Bronson wondered if he might be mentally challenged. He examined the man's face and noticed two thin scars running in parallel lines across his right cheek. The lines disappeared under the collar of the shirt the man had taken out of Bronson's closet.

He wondered what the man was planning to do to him.

He wondered whether he would to survive the day.

He continued to work at the electrical cord, knowing the bulk of his body was shielding his efforts from view of his captor. For now.

* * *

Jackson was hungry. He was also upset and confused and a little afraid of the man he had trussed up in the chair, who seemed to be talking gibberish: a buggy with no horse? But more than anything else, he was hungry.

When he had opened his eyes and seen daylight streaming through the ceiling of his underground death trap, Jackson had been momentarily disoriented. His clothing had somehow disappeared – where it had gone was anyone's guess – and the steady rain soaking his naked body had chilled him to the point where he felt colder than he ever had in his life. The skies were slate-grey and threatening, but to Jackson Healy it was the most welcome sight he had ever witnessed.

He had examined his surroundings cautiously despite the freezing cold because he was unsure of what in God's name was happening. Then he had seen a man. The man's back was turned to Jackson and he was walking away from a massive yellow iron machine, which was sitting on the ground next to the ceiling of the underground room.

And Jackson had panicked. He leapt to his feet, nearly crying out in fear but somehow forcing himself to stay quiet. He maintained the presence of mind to pick his Colt revolver out of the mud, and then he rushed to the closest wall of the suddenly liberated prison cell. He scrabbled up the muddy side, using exposed tree roots as handholds, and when he reached the top he flung himself out of the hole, flopping face-first onto the ground. Wet grass had never felt so good.

The man Jackson had seen upon waking was still looking in the other direction. He was leaning against a building located exactly where the Paskagankee Tavern had been, although the structure looked nothing like what he remembered. The man was hunched over against the driving rain, holding his hand to his ear and talking quietly.

The man was alone. He was clearly crazy.

Jackson bolted. He sprang to his feet and sprinted around the hole, past the strange-looking yellow machine, and ran full-speed into the comforting cover of the forest. He continued on as fast as he could, no destination in mind, just moving, too confused and frightened to think. He skirted boulders and climbed over fallen trees, trying to remember where he had left his horse, but nothing looked familiar. He kept moving.

Eventually he had burst through a small clearing and seen a cabin. By this time, Jackson had regained enough composure to realize he needed to find clothing immediately. It was his top priority, even above figuring out what the hell was happening. He was now shivering uncontrollably and his teeth chattered like someone was shaking a bag full of dice.

And he was hungry. Unbelievably, stomach-crampingly hungry.

He had glanced once again toward the small cabin in the middle of the clearing and shrank back behind the cover of trees just as the strange-looking carriage rolled up. A moment later a man, presumably the shack's owner, had climbed out. Jackson thought for one brief moment about calling out to the man for help, but he abandoned the idea immediately as sheer folly. He was completely unclothed and holding a pistol he only now realized was corroded to the point of uselessness.

Appealing for help would be foolish, so Jackson had taken the man by surprise, attacking and immobilizing him, and gaining access to his cabin.

And now the man had finally regained consciousness, which was wonderful, because Jackson was famished. He realized now that he had made a mistake while addressing the cabin-owner. He had been asking about the odd-looking buggy in front of the cabin, when that was not the critical question, at least not at the moment. He had more pressing concerns.

"I need food," he said as his victim blinked rapidly in an obvious effort to reorient himself following the blow to the head.

The man squinted at him. "Take whatever you want. I've been gone for a while, so you won't find much in the fridge, but I've got some canned stuff in the pantry. You're welcome to it. Pile it all in the Jeep and take it with you."

Jackson narrowed his eyes at the man. He was talking gibberish again. "Fridge?"

"Yeah, you know, the fridge. The refrigerator. In the kitchen." The man nodded in the direction of the only room in the tiny cabin Jackson hadn't yet had a chance to explore. "Like I said, there's not much in it, but go check it out. Take whatever you want."

Jackson followed the man's eyes and decided he had nothing to lose. If this "fridge" was where the food was, then the "fridge" was where he needed to be. He could not believe how hungry he was, the sensation was building and building, rapidly approaching the point where he could think of nothing else. He shot one last suspicious glance in his prisoner's direction, then turned and trudged into the kitchen.

* * *

The minute his captor turned his back and began walking toward the kitchen, Bronson was up and out of his chair and moving across the room. He had unfastened the stiff electrical wire binding his wrists with little effort and now moved as quietly but as quickly as possible. It was critical he take advantage of the surprise factor to regain control of his home, because Bronson was growing more and more certain the man now dressed in his clothing was suffering from severe schizophrenia.

That his captor had attacked him while naked was strange enough, but their brief conversation, just concluded, was even more bizarre. Ranting and raving about extreme hunger while not seeming to understand what a refrigerator was? And what were all those weird questions about his Jeep?

This was bad. At the rate things were going, Bronson Choate felt there was every reason to believe the man might simply kill him and continue living for the foreseeable future in Bronson's isolated cabin.

And there was a more pressing concern. His girlfriend was on her way here.

They hadn't seen each other for six weeks, the entire time Bronson had spent at sea, and Jodie Miller had refused to accept the notion of waiting one minute longer than absolutely necessary for their reunion. She in her car right now and was due to arrive from her home in Bangor at any moment.

Bronson had to take advantage of the window of opportunity his attacker had opened by tying his hands in such a shoddy manner, or the situation would soon go from bad to much, much worse.

He crept to the kitchen entryway and flattened his body against the wall. Took a deep breath. Eased his head slowly around the doorframe.

The man's back was to him. He stood unmoving, staring at the refrigerator. He reminded Bronson of a cow watching a car drive past. For a guy who was supposedly "famished," he didn't seem in any hurry to examine the contents of the fridge.

Finally the strange intruder eased a hand forward and grabbed the handle. He pulled the refrigerator door open and recoiled, seemingly surprised by the yellow light spilling out of the appliance's interior.

Again, Bronson was struck by a feeling of unreality. Something was not right about this guy, but he didn't have time to mull over what that something might be. He took a step into the kitchen, grateful for the cabin's solid construction. He had built most of it himself and knew his location wouldn't be given away by a creaky floorboard.

He eased slowly forward. The man seemed utterly captivated by the interior of the fridge. He bent at the waist with his head stuck halfway into the open door. Another three feet and Bronson would be able to take him down. The fucking home invader would never know what hit him.

Bronson raised his arms above his head. His plan was to lower the boom on the son of a bitch, to clasp his hands together and bring them down on the back of the guy's neck. Whether he could actually break the man's neck using that technique Bronson had no idea, but he had no doubt the blow would incapacitate him, and the fight would be over before it started. The son of a bitch had some serious payback coming.

A foot and a half. The guy's back was still turned, and there was almost no way he could avoid taking a beating now, unless—

--Outside, a car horn honked, a series of excited staccato bursts that indicated Jodie had arrived, and just like that, everything went to shit.

Bronson froze, hands in the air, caught completely off-guard. He watched in shocked disbelief as the stranger whirled, moving much more quickly than Bronson would have expected. The man burst out of his crouch and hammered a fist into Bronson's gut. The air *whooshed* from his lungs and he dropped to the floor with a teeth-rattling crash.

The stranger advanced. Bronson kicked at his knee, aiming to shatter a kneecap, but his rushed blow went high. Instead of connecting with bone, he drove his foot into the meat of the man's thigh.

The home invader cursed and staggered backward, and Bronson struggled to his feet, retching and wheezing. Instead of advancing on his attacker, he staggered through the living room, thinking only of Jodie, knowing he had to warn her away. If she entered the cabin she would die, Bronson was certain of it.

He weaved into the living room and stumbled into an end table. A glass table lamp wobbled and then fell to the floor, where it shattered with what sounded like a mini-explosion. He ignored it and crunched on the glass shards to the door, yanking it open, the sound of pounding footfalls telling him the attacker was right behind him.

On the front landing stood Jodie Miller, blonde hair tied back in a ponytail, her face radiant. She opened her mouth in a joyful greeting, and then her excited smile faltered and turned to confusion. "What's the matter, what…"

"Get out," Bronson managed, still struggling to breathe. The words came out barely louder than a whisper. "Get out of here and bring the police."

Jodie's eyes darted up and over his right shoulder. Her confused expression turned to alarm, and Bronson knew she had caught sight of the stranger. She took one hesitant step backward on the landing and then Bronson felt a crushing blow to the back of his skull, and as consciousness faded, Bronson Choate prayed to a God he had not thought about in years that Jodie had understood his warning and was even now escaping before she too fell victim to the murderous stranger.

8

Mike took one look at Sharon as the meeting broke up at the Ridge Runner and decided to drive back to the station and meet her there. Her shift had officially ended long before they left the crime scene – or whatever the hell it was – and she looked so exhausted he didn't want her driving home by herself. He would pick her up in his own vehicle and they could share a ride to her home on the outskirts of Paskagankee.

Rainwater dripped steadily off Mike's soaked clothing onto the lobby floor as he waited for Sharon. He was daydreaming about a hot shower and change of clothes when a distraught young woman burst through the double glass front doors, sobbing and wild-eyed. Paskagankee was a small town and over the course of his two-year stint as chief of police, Mike had gotten to know every resident, at least by sight. He had never seen this girl before.

She advanced across the big, open lobby, not quite running, and pulled up sharply when she caught sight of Mike. "Help me," she said. "I need someone to help me!"

Mike reached for her elbow and led her to a metal bench, where she sat reluctantly. He could see dispatcher Gordie Rheaume peering curiously through the big plate-glass window separating the lobby from the offices within. "What's your name, Miss?" he asked quietly.

"Jodie Miller," she said between sobs. Her eyes were bloodshot and red-rimmed.

"Hi, Jodie, I'm Mike McMahon, former police chief here in

Paskagankee. What seems to be the problem?"

"My boyfriend…it's my boyfriend."

"What happened to your boyfriend?"

"He was attacked inside his house. He…I think he's hurt bad," she said, dissolving into a fit of tears. By now Sharon had entered the lobby from the interior of the station and she watched the exchange curiously, saying nothing. Mike noticed with a hint of jealousy she had changed into dry jeans and a University of Maine Black Bears sweatshirt.

"Who attacked your boyfriend, Jodie?"

"I don't know who he was! I walked up to the house and before I could use my key, Bronson opened the front door."

"Bronson is your boyfriend?"

She nodded distractedly. "He was all out of breath, like he had just run the Boston Marathon or something, and his clothes were torn and his hair a mess. He told me to get out and bring back the police, and then…and then…"

The young woman broke down crying again, and Mike said softly to Sharon, "Go get Pete." She nodded and used her ID to buzz through the locked doors, disappearing the way she had just come. Gordie continued watching from the dispatcher's office, his eyes wide and curious.

Mike turned his attention back to the distraught woman. "So, you got to Bronson's front door and he was disheveled when he opened it. What happened then?"

"And then some guy came up behind him, from inside the cabin, and smashed a gun down on the back of Bronson's head! He moaned and his eyes rolled up into his skull and he dropped straight down. He fell half in and half out of the house. Oh, God, I'm afraid he's hurt bad, please, you have to get help!"

"We're getting help right now, I promise," Mike said gently. "An officer is already notifying Chief Kendall. A unit will be on the way to Bronson's house in a matter of seconds. What's the address?"

"He lives way up in the woods off Route 28."

Mike furrowed his brow. "Route 28? Does he live anywhere near the Ridge Runner?"

The woman nodded. "Yes, the trail leading to his cabin is maybe a half mile north of the Ridge Runner on 28. It's called Long Pond Road. But to get to his cabin, you have to drive a long way on the trail. His house is probably three-quarters of a mile into the woods, more or less directly behind the Ridge Runner."

Alarm bells started going off in Mike's head. What were the chances this attack – if it was an attack – was unrelated to the disappearance of a body from the strange underground room discovered earlier today at the Ridge Runner? Mike had spent a lifetime in law enforcement and knew the answer to that question: virtually none.

The interior station doors opened again and Sharon stepped through, followed by Pete Kendall. They moved quickly next to Mike and the young woman. He nodded to them and then turned his attention back to Jodie Miller. "So," he said. "Bronson told you to get out and you saw the attacker strike him on the head. Then what happened?"

"I sort of froze for a second, then I took off running. I jumped back in my car and headed straight here."

"Did you try calling 911?" Mike asked, already knowing what the answer would be.

"Of course," she said. "But the signal kept fading in and out. I couldn't get my cell to work at all."

He nodded. It was a common problem in Paskagankee.

"I was scared to death," she continued, reliving the moment, "because Bronson's driveway is tiny and very narrow. So is Long Pond Road, for that matter. I had to turn my car around before I could get out. The guy who attacked Bronson had plenty of time to get to me and stop me from leaving if he had wanted to."

"What happened?" Mike asked. He had worked more than one home invasion while a member of the Revere Police Department, and he knew the typical suspect in that time of crime would go to great lengths to avoid allowing a witness to escape.

"I'm not sure," she said, a sense of wonder creeping into her voice. "He didn't come after me. He stepped over Bronson and followed me down the stairs at first – he was right behind me! – but the minute he saw me heading to my car, he backpedaled like nobody's business. I took one last look at him after I had gotten my car turned around, and it was like he was...I don't know...

cowering in fear or something. It was almost like he had never seen a freaking car before. Like he was afraid of it."

The alarm bells clanged louder in Mike's head. Something was very wrong here, far beyond a home invasion in the sticks, an occurrence that was rare but not unheard of around Paskagankee. The region was vast and remote, making it ideal for the construction of meth labs, and sometimes disputes among cookers escalated into deadly violence. This was more than such an incident, Mike was certain, and he could see by the look on Sharon's face she felt it as well.

Pete cleared his throat and said, "I'm sorry to interrupt, but I'm Chief Kendall, Ms...."

"Miller," the young woman answered automatically.

"Ms. Miller," he said. "Our dispatcher copied the address while you were talking to Mr. McMahon. An officer is on his way to your boyfriend's cabin now. Why don't you come inside with me and have a seat until he reports back. I'll get you a cup of coffee."

Pete led the young woman inside the station and moments later returned alone. He said, "Harley's on his way now and we should have this mess straightened out soon." He fixed Mike with an intense stare. "My first thought was drugs, but it seems awfully coincidental that this guy would be attacked in a home invasion not a mile away from where a body disappeared earlier today, don't you think?"

Mike smiled tiredly. "I knew there was a reason I recommended you for this job."

"You mean above and beyond my pretty face?"

Now he laughed. "Yeah, above and beyond that." To Sharon he said, "I don't think there's any more we can do for Ms Miller, and you look exhausted. Let's get out of here."

9

Mike sat at the kitchen table eating apple pie and sipping hot coffee as Sharon rinsed the dinner dishes and loaded them into the dishwasher. He had briefly considered a glass of something stronger, but decided to follow his general rule of thumb: support Sharon, a recovering alcoholic, by passing on the alcohol.

He had half-heartedly offered to help her clean up, knowing she would refuse since he had cooked dinner. When she did, he smiled in satisfaction. He much preferred watching her petite but shapely form glide around the kitchen to scrubbing and rinsing a meat loaf pan.

A hot shower had rejuvenated his spirits after the long afternoon spent in the cold northern Maine rain. He avoided discussing the Ridge Runner case over dinner to give Sharon a break – he had been away from the job for months and over that time his old love for law enforcement had returned with a vengeance, but he knew being a cop was still a day-to-day grind for her – but now that the roast was gone and cleanup mode was in full swing, he decided it was time to approach the subject.

He cleared his throat and she turned away from the sink, wiping her hands on a dishtowel. "The disappearing body," she said with a knowing smile before he had said a word.

"You know me so well."

Sharon laughed. "Dude, you're not that hard to figure out."

"My ex-wife never seemed to manage it."

"Her loss," Sharon said.

"Well, you're right on target about the topic for discussion, wise ass, but what am I thinking now?"

"Let's see," she said, biting her lower lip and furrowing her brow as she feigned intense concentration. She looked beautiful. "You're torn between wanting to get me into bed right now and the desire to discuss a potential connection between the disappearing body and the attack at Jodie Miller's boyfriend's cabin."

Mike shook his head with a grin. It was spooky how this young woman could almost see right into his head. "I give," he said, raising his hands in surrender. "You're amazing. So, what do you think? It seems to me there's no way those two events could be unconnected. You must have an opinion on the subject. I want to hear it."

She opened her mouth but before she could answer, the phone rang.

*   *   *

Pete Kendall's voice was grim. "I'm sorry to bother you after a long day," he said, "but Jodie Miller wasn't exaggerating about an altercation at Bronson Choate's cabin. If anything, she might have understated the seriousness of the situation."

Mike waggled his fingers at Sharon, calling her over. "Pete, I'm putting you on speaker so Sharon can hear." He pressed a button and said, "Okay, go. How bad is it?"

"Choate is dead. His body is crumpled right in his front door. The positioning is consistent with the way Ms. Miller described the attack. And his skull was caved in from the back. Blunt trauma. Multiple blows, from the looks of it, although obviously we'll need Dr. Affeldt's confirmation of that."

"The doer is long gone, obviously."

"Yep, but the crime scene is…strange…to say the least. I know it's late, and I hate to ask, but I'm in way over my head here, Mike. Would you mind coming out and giving the scene a once-over with me?"

"No problem, Pete." Sharon pointed at Mike and then at herself, and he added, "Sharon says I'm not allowed to leave without her. I'll have company, is that okay with you?"

"Hell, the more the merrier, although that's probably not the best phrase to be using right now."

"We'll be there in thirty minutes."

* * *

An overcast layer blocked out the dazzling spray of stars normally visible in the northern Maine sky as the Explorer bounced and jolted along the rough trail officially known as Long Pond Road. Evergreens crowded the vehicle from all sides, combining with the weather conditions to form an inky blackness as nearly complete as Mike had ever experienced. The truck's headlights stabbed through the night and were quickly gobbled up by the encroaching darkness.

"Jeez," Sharon remarked after they had crept along the rough trail for nearly ten minutes. "This guy really valued his privacy, didn't he?"

"For all the good it did him," Mike answered as they turned a corner and the trail widened slightly. The headlights washed over an SUV with Paskagankee Police markings that had been parked in front of a tiny but solid-looking cabin constructed in the middle of a small clearing. The SUV sat dark and silent. Chief Pete Kendall was nowhere to be seen.

"Pete must be inside," Sharon said.

"Yeah, I guess," Mike answered, noting the cabin's open front door and an indistinct lump of shadow, presumably Bronson Choate's body, positioned half in and half out of the home. Mike eased to a stop behind the police vehicle, which had been squeezed into a small space next to a Jeep Mike didn't recognize. He shut down the engine and sat for a moment, staring at the scene through the windshield.

"You seem uneasy," Sharon said. "What's bothering you?"

"Something's not right. Pete calls us asking for help and then doesn't come to the door when we show up?"

Sharon shrugged. "Maybe he doesn't know we're here."

"It's as dark as the bottom of a coal mine out here. Our headlights lit up the front of that cabin like the noontime sun. Pete should have known we were coming long before we arrived."

Sharon stared at him, saying nothing. Finally Mike said, "Well, this isn't accomplishing anything. Let's go find Pete and get this show on the road."

They picked up their flashlights and stepped out of the truck, then walked side by side across the small front yard. "I'm liking this less and less," he mumbled.

"What is it?" Sharon said.

Mike held out an arm to stop their progress. "Listen," he said. "What do you hear?"

Sharon paused for a moment, concentrating, and said, "There's a small engine running behind the cabin. Probably a generator, which makes sense, right? There are no power lines running this far out in the boonies, so Choate must have used the generator to power his lights and such. Pete must have started it up when the light began to fail."

"Exactly," Mike said. "So how come the cabin is pitch-dark? Pete starts the generator and then doesn't bother to turn on any lights?"

"Oh-oh," Sharon whispered.

"Exactly." Mike eased his gun out of its shoulder holster and Sharon did the same. He lowered his voice. "We're not going inside until we've cleared the exterior. You circle around the house that way," he gestured to the left, "and I'll go this way," he nodded to the right. "We'll meet up at the generator and *then* enter the cabin."

Sharon nodded and began moving slowly away.

"*Hey!*" Mike whispered.

She stopped and turned.

"Until we know what's going on, don't walk directly in front of any windows, you'll just make yourself a target if anyone's inside."

She nodded a second time, shielding her flashlight with a palm, and then flitted along the front of the home like a wraith.

Mike watched until she disappeared around the corner of the cabin, then he eased the other way, alert for trouble, skirting a row of small ornamental shrubs that seemed incongruous to the setting. Who the hell would ever see them way out here besides the guy who had planted them?

Rounding the corner, he scanned the tree line to his right, the edge of the massive forest barely visible in the all-encompassing darkness. It was no more than a slightly darker smudge looming high above in the blackness; a presence felt more than seen.

It seemed somehow malevolent.

Mike's unease intensified. Something was very wrong.

He took a step.

Another.

A third, and he was almost but not quite surprised when he tripped over…something. Whatever it was had been piled on the flat ground directly in his path. Mike had been so intent on scanning the tree line he had walked right into it. He wind-milled his arms and took a half-step to the right to keep from falling, and then he uncovered his flashlight and swung the beam to the ground.

And discovered Pete Kendall lying in a heap, unmoving, his glazed eyes staring sightlessly into the black Paskagankee night.

10

Blood had pooled on the ground around Pete's head. It was beginning to congeal at the edges, but much of the puddle remained wet and gruesome-looking in the weak beam of Mike's flashlight.

He knelt and felt for a pulse.

Nothing.

Pete Kendall was gone.

Mike shone the light on the face of his watch. Nine forty-five. It was less than forty minutes ago that they had received the call from an obviously alive Pete Kendall. He had been upset at finding Bronson Choate's body but nothing in the tone of his voice had indicated he felt he was in any personal danger. Whatever happened to him after the phone call had occurred within a very small window of opportunity, and the now-dead cop had never seen it coming.

"Goddammit," Mike muttered.

From behind the house a quiet disembodied voice asked, "What's taking you so long?"

Sharon Dupont rounded the corner, her form mostly indistinct in the dark, and then she gasped as she rushed to Mike's side. "What happened to Pete? Is he okay?"

Mike looked up bleakly and shook his head. "He's dead," he said. "It looks like his skull was smashed in, exactly the injury he told me on the phone that Bronson Choate suffered. He never even drew his weapon, which meant he was caught completely by surprise."

"Or he knew his assailant."

Mike shook his head. "I don't think so. Even in the dark, you can see that his skull was split open from behind. He was ambushed."

Sharon stared at Mike, her eyes wide and spooked. "What do we do now?"

"We call for backup and then clear the house. Whoever did this *should* be long gone, but he stuck around after killing Choate; there's no guarantee he isn't still here…somewhere…right now. After that, we need to get the bodies transported to the morgue to be examined by Dr. Affeldt. Then we need to notify the Town Council. We're down one Chief of Police."

* * *

Vehicles lined the trail leading to Bronson Choate's isolated cabin, choking the narrow path like weeds in an untended garden. Police cruisers, ambulances, unmarked civilian cars. All had been hastily parked anywhere their drivers were able to find – or make – room. Flashing red, blue and yellow emergency beacons splashed around the clearing in headache-inducing repetition.

After radioing for backup, an impatient Mike and Sharon had cleared the cabin, refusing to take the time to wait for Harley Tanguay – the only Paskagankee cop on the night watch still alive – to drag his ass out to the middle of the forest. They moved steadily from room to room, flipping lights on as they went, discovering quickly that the brutal executioner of at least two people was nowhere inside.

Mike still had his doubts about whether the killer was really gone, though. He could be within fifty feet of the cabin right now, watching the cops' every move from the darkness and safety of the forest, secure in the knowledge he was virtually invisible in the impenetrable blackness.

A pair of gurneys trundled Bronson Choate and Pete Kendall side-by-side to waiting ambulances, their bodies sealed inside the zipped and sealed black body bags. Hours had now passed since their discovery of Pete's body, Mike quietly seething while the corpse of his friend and successor cooled on the ground as the crime scene was examined and photographed from all conceivable angles.

It was now past one a.m., and the darkness of the primeval forest seemed to have thickened further. Mike wouldn't have thought it possible and wondered if it was his imagination. He stifled a yawn as a lone vehicle approached the cabin, headlights bouncing and yawing, the car's operator struggling to avoid driving off Long Pond Road and into a tree. It was the first car to arrive in over an hour.

The headlights flicked off and the engine died as the driver took his place at the end of the long line of vehicles. A moment later a hefty, jowly man of around sixty heaved himself out of the car and clambered along the trail to where Mike and Sharon stood side-by-side near the front of the cabin.

Mike offered his hand and the man shook it perfunctorily. Paskagankee Town Council Chairman Van Beebe was a blue-blood Yankee descended directly from riders on the Mayflower – or so he claimed – and projected a dour, cheerless demeanor even in the best of times, which this clearly was not. Adding to Beebe's natural gloominess, Mike assumed, was the fact that Mike's resignation as police chief had been spurred largely by the council's displeasure at learning he was sharing a bed with a subordinate. Mike doubted Beebe had ever planned on dealing with him again and was surprised the councilman had even consented to the brief handshake.

"A terrible business," Beebe growled, ignoring Sharon and avoiding eye contact with Mike. "Did Chief Kendall suffer?"

"I don't think so," Mike said. "He was hit from behind. I doubt he ever saw his killer coming. Obviously, you'll have to wait for Dr. Affeldt's report, but my guess is he never knew what hit him. He was probably dead before he hit the ground."

"Yes, well, that's something, I suppose."

"Councilman Beebe," Mike said, "I'm sure you're aware of why we called you out here at this time of night. Losing Chief Kendall puts the Paskagankee Police Department in a terrible position. Given the fact Pete was the only management representative in the department, Officer Dupont and I thought the Town Council would appreciate as much planning time as possible to determine where you go from here. Presumably you'll want to call in outside help to investigate these two murders, and get your search started as soon as possible for a replacement for Chief Kendall. He was —"

Beebe cleared his throat and held up one beefy hand in interruption. His discomfort with the situation was palpable, but he pressed on. "Mr. McMahon, you and I have not always seen eye to eye. The situation with Officer Dupont," his gaze slid briefly to Sharon before returning to Mike, with whom he resumed reluctant eye contact, "showed poor judgment on your part. However, your law enforcement credentials are impressive and your performance running the department was sterling, especially given the two horrific scenarios you were forced to deal with in the two years of your stewardship. I've already spoken to the other council members – that was what took me so long to get here – and we are in unanimous agreement. We would like you to consider coming out of retirement, on a temporary basis only, to guide the department through this ugly situation. We know you'll provide steady leadership, and the town will benefit from being able to perform a thorough search for a replacement, rather than having to make a hasty decision, one we might later regret."

Mike said nothing for a moment. It occurred to him that he must be more tired than he realized, because he should have seen this coming. In the chaos of the events over the last few hours, he hadn't even given a thought to the possibility of being recruited back into the job he had so recently been forced out of.

The town council chairman yawned and looked at his watch pointedly. Mike said, "Councilman, you understand nothing has changed with my living arrangements. Officer Dupont and I are still sharing a home and are, in fact, now engaged to be married. We haven't set a wedding date yet, but my personal life today is exactly the same as it was when I announced my retirement. I loved my job as chief here in Paskagankee, but I love my fiancé more."

"We understand, Chief McMahon, and our position on the matter of you and Officer Dupont's relationship remains unchanged. However, given the current circumstances, we believe it to be in the town's best interest to disregard your situation

– temporarily and unofficially, of course – as we move forward. We are prepared to offer you a six-month contract, at your former salary, with your former benefits package intact as well. We believe it's a generous offer. I'm sorry to rush you, but we really do need an answer immediately."

Mike thought Beebe didn't sound sorry, he thought he sounded stuffy and self-important, but said, "As long as we understand each other, I accept your offer. I assume I'm to start immediately?"

"Of course."

Mike thought for a moment and frowned. He lowered his voice, not sure why he was doing so but doing it anyway. Saying what he had to say next at any volume above a respectful whisper would have seemed profane and somehow blasphemous. "Do you know if anyone's been to see Pete's wife yet?"

Beebe shook his head. "I'm told your dispatcher, Gordie…"

"Rheaume," Mike said, suddenly remembering why he disliked the town manager so much. Paskagankee was tiny, not much more than a village, and there was no reason for Van Beebe not to know Rheaume's name, other than a callous disregard for his employees.

"Yes, Rheaume," he continued. "All Mr. Rheaume told Mrs. Kendall was that there has been some trouble, and the chief has been delayed indefinitely."

Mike sighed and glanced at his watch. He wouldn't be getting any sleep tonight. "I guess I know what I'll be doing first thing in the morning."

11

Jackson Healy watched the flurry of activity around the cabin from the safety of the forest with a sense of disbelief and the growing conviction that the world as he knew it had somehow vanished. He had felt that way since awakening in the secret underground room next to the Paskagankee Tavern, and the events of the last few hours had only reinforced the notion. It came as no surprise the killing of the cabin-owner would be investigated – the law had very little patience when it came to murder – but the speed with which the lawmen had been able to marshal a response had caught him completely off guard.

When the victim's lady friend had scrambled down the steps of the front landing and begun running in the direction of her strange horseless carriage, Jackson had initially been right on her tail. Another second or two and he probably could have caught her.

But then she leaped into the belly of the bizarre-looking beast, and moments later it began to growl obscenely, and Jackson had been struck with a fear unlike anything he had ever experienced. He immediately veered off from his pursuit and began backing toward the house, afraid to take his eyes off the machine. Then he froze in his tracks in utter disbelief as the young lady somehow piloted the buggy down a barely visible overgrown trail and out of sight.

After the roar of the horseless buggy faded away, Jackson had taken a moment to collect himself and then retreated to the cabin. He stopped to check on the man lying half in and half out of the front door – dead, exactly as he had expected – and then hurried into the kitchen. His hunger had been overpowering.

He returned to the odd humming icebox – the "fridge," the cabin owner had called it – and after rummaging around inside it had come up with some meat and cheese that was, if not exactly fresh, at least edible. He had stuffed the food down his throat and then finally taken a moment to sit down and really give some thought to his situation.

The young woman would go straight to the law, that much was certain, but Jackson didn't feel there was any real cause for concern. From what he had seen riding into this backwoods village, houses were spread widely apart and it would likely be hours before the law could muster any kind of response to her claim of an attacker at this out-of-the-way cabin. Hell, it might not even happen until tomorrow.

He had concluded fairly quickly that there was no reason to abandon the dwelling he had fought so hard to acquire, at least not immediately. Besides, where else did he have to go? He was in an unfamiliar town with no supplies besides the clothes on his back, and even those didn't belong to him.

As he considered his situation, Jackson felt an extreme drowsiness begin to overtake him. He was no longer hungry, but he *was* exhausted. The couch he was sitting on was small but extremely comfortable and before he realized what was happening, he had fallen asleep. He was awakened some time later – how much later, he had no idea, as his pocket watch had chosen the worst possible time to give up the ghost – by the sound of a thick metallic clunking noise somewhere outside the house and then a man's voice cursing, "Holy shit!"

Jackson had scrambled off the couch with just enough time to hide in a closet before a man dressed in blue, apparently the color of the sheriff's department here in Paskagankee, examined the cabin's owner – he was dead, as Jackson well knew – and then hurried off and began talking excitedly into some strange device he picked up from inside his own horseless carriage, this one painted blue and white with the words "Paskagankee Police" on the side.

Jackson waited until the sheriff's back was turned and then eased as quietly as he could out the front door. Once down the steps he bolted around the side of the house and straight into forest. He expected at any moment to hear a shout of surprise from the lawman, followed by the pistol shot that would knock him off his feet, but it never came. Whatever the lawman was doing, he was so wrapped up in it he didn't see a thing.

The sheriff's deputy had hung around for a time, wrapping yellow ribbon around everything in sight, and then had climbed back into his strange horseless carriage and disappeared in what Jackson thought must be the least effective murder investigation ever. By the time the deputy had departed, Jackson's hunger was nearly overwhelming again and he decided a return trip inside the cabin was a risk worth taking.

He had just started across the clearing when *another* sheriff's deputy showed up, catching Jackson by surprise and confirming what he had already begun to suspect: that there was no way to anticipate what the crazy lawmen in this town might do next. Jackson once again managed to retreat to the safety of the forest without being seen, and then watched while this new lawman repeated most of the actions of the first one, checking the body – still dead – and then actually searching the cabin.

When the lawman strode to his carriage and began talking into his own strange device, Jackson had erroneously assumed this sheriff's deputy would further repeat the actions of the first one and pilot his buggy away. He was by this time so ravenously hungry he had begun to care less and less about the presence of the law and had started across the small clearing behind the cabin, hoping to get inside it and back to the "fridge" the minute the deputy departed.

But the lawman surprised him. He didn't go anywhere; instead he began a search of the exterior grounds of the cabin.

The man had nearly walked right into Jackson, who by now was so flustered – and hungry, *goddamn* was he hungry! – that he had not been able to stop himself from attacking the deputy. He crouched behind the only cover available – a big piece of roaring machinery in the middle of the clearing – and then took the lawman from behind, killing him in much the same manner as he had taken down the cabin owner. Jackson was discovering a Colt .38 revolver could be quite a useful tool even *without* bullets.

Shortly after that, two more people, a man and a woman, both dressed like civilians, had shown up. If Jackson hadn't known better, he'd have thought the dead cabin owner was running the world's smallest rooming house, there was so much goddamned activity. The man discovered the body of the dead lawman in short order and then all hell had broken loose. Within minutes, hordes of people were swarming all over the cabin after rumbling up the trail inside more of those frightening horseless carriages, some of which seemed nearly the size of a small barn.

Jackson had watched it all, thanking his lucky stars for the soothing anonymity provided by the darkness and the thick underbrush of the forest. How so many people had managed to mobilize so quickly he could not imagine.

There was much he did not understand about what was happening here, and it was frightening. He knew he would now be a hunted man after killing two people, one of them a lawman.

It got worse. He didn't know a single soul in this town. He had no horse. And, he realized with a sudden sinking feeling, no money either. He had completely forgotten about the solid gold Peruvian disk until just now. It must still be somewhere in that damned secret underground room.

All of which was bad enough, but it wasn't the worst development. The worst development was that he was getting hungry *again*. The hunger was building rapidly, *again*. Soon it would rule his existence. It would be all he could think about.

He had killed because of the hunger last time, and it was coming again.

And he had no idea what to do.

12

Mike glanced tiredly at his watch as he drove the deserted back roads toward the cement-and-brick Paskagankee Police Department building. Breaking the news of Pete Kendall's murder to his wife was not the way he would have chosen to begin his second stint guiding the department, but there was no putting it off. It wouldn't get any easier by delaying, and more importantly, the young woman had a right to learn her husband's fate.

He had stayed with the distraught widow for over an hour, sipping strong coffee at the kitchen table listening to Jane Kendall talk, sometimes about her husband, sometimes about things entirely unrelated to his loss, until a neighbor had arrived to drive her to her parents' home outside Bangor.

Now he felt washed-out and jittery, no surprise given the fact it was nearly nine a.m. and he had not slept in more than twenty-four hours. Mike rubbed his eyes and tried to formulate a plan with which to approach the rest of the day. The first priority would obviously be the investigation into last night's two murders. But there was also the issue of the body that had disappeared out of the excavation pit behind the Ridge Runner to consider.

Mike mulled over how the two events might be related as he drove, becoming increasingly frustrated with his inability to focus thanks to his building exhaustion. He slowed the car and turned into the police station parking lot, surprised to discover he had been so deep in thought he could not recall more than the most basic details of the cross-town trip he had just made. *Guess I should add "get some sleep" to my to-do list.*

He shut down the engine and glanced at a vehicle he didn't recognize. It was a coal-black Chevrolet Suburban with blacked-out windows and U.S. Government plates, angled carelessly into a spot a few spaces away. Mike wondered what the vehicle's presence might signify and decided it was probably nothing good. He stepped out of the car and walked to the station, entering as a cop for the first time since his forced resignation.

Dispatcher Gordie Rheaume smiled grimly and waved through the heavy plate glass window separating the public lobby from the interior of the station. Gordie stood and weaved his way through the bullpen, realizing Mike would not have received an access card yet. He unlocked the reinforced door and offered his hand. "Welcome back, Chief," he said warmly. "I'm sorry about the circumstances of your return, but it's good to have you back."

"Thanks, Gordie, it's good to see you, too. It seems we have a lot of work to do."

The older man nodded. "You got that right. And the first order of business is waiting for you in Chief Kendall's – I mean, in *your* – office."

"Waiting in my office? What are you talking about? Is it the Maneater?" Mike's first thought was *how the hell did Melissa Mannheim get word of the double murders already?* He had known he would have to deal with the *Portland Journal* reporter and the rest of the press at some point today, but couldn't imagine how the Melissa "The Maneater" Mannheim had managed to get on the story so soon.

He pictured her slinking into the chief's office before poor Pete Kendall's body was even cold, all flame-red hair and provocative clothing, spouting off about freedom of the press and expecting an exclusive on the search for Kendall's killer. Suddenly he felt even more exhausted than he had a few minutes ago driving into the parking lot.

"No, it's not Mannheim," Gordie answered. "Although I'm sure you'll be seeing her soon. You're lucky she's distracted by all the hoopla with the Hollywood film crew coming in a couple of weeks, otherwise she'd be up your ass already."

Mike scratched his head. "If it's not Melissa waiting to speak to me, who is it?"

"FBI," Gordie said.

Mike flashed back to the government car in the lot and realized he should have made the connection immediately. He would have, too, if he hadn't been so damned tired. "What does the FBI want?" he asked.

"Beats me. They refused to speak to anyone but the chief. I told them it's been kind of hectic around here and that you've only been chief for a few hours. Even told them I didn't know when you'd be in. They just said 'no problem,' and that they'd be happy to wait. They've been drinking coffee and sitting in your office like a couple of ugly statues ever since."

Mike glanced at the big clock on the wall. "What time did they get here?"

"Little after six."

"Okay, thanks, Gordie." He sighed and trudged to the small coffee mess set up in the rear of the bullpen, then poured into a paper cup a thick black sludge that looked as though it had been festering in the pot since his resignation. He examined it with distaste, choked a little down, and walked into his new/old office to meet with the Feds.

When he opened the door he stopped short and blinked in surprise. The two agents sat silent and ramrod-straight in chairs placed side-by-side in front of the chief's desk. They looked almost like they could be twins, dressed in nearly identical dark blue suits, plain white dress shirts, and maroon ties. At the sound of the door opening both men glanced at Mike in a move that appeared slickly choreographed.

"Gentlemen," Mike said, extending a hand first to the man nearest him and then to the other. Their grips were firm and cool. "I'm Mike McMahon, Paskagankee Police Chief as of about three o'clock this morning."

The man nearest Mike shook his hand and said, "Nice to meet you, Chief. I'm Special Agent Alton Ferriss, and this is my partner, Special Agent Ward Cooper. We operate out of the bureau's Portland Field Office." The man sitting next to Ferriss nodded once, all business, and shook Mike's hand briefly before letting it drop and returning his attention to the empty surface of Mike's new desk.

Ferriss's tone was frosty and belied his pleasant greeting. Facing a long day with no sleep under his belt, Mike decided that making nice with two stone-faced feds would require more effort that he was willing to expend, and elected to get right down to business.

He moved to the wheeled leather chair behind the desk and sat heavily. "You've probably heard about the two murders last night, one of the victims being my immediate predecessor, so I'm sure you realize we're pretty busy here. I don't have a lot of free time. Keeping that in mind, what can I do for you gentlemen?"

This time Cooper piped up. He glanced at Mike with a look that suggested he would rather be drinking acid than sitting here. "We received a report of the bodies discovered at the site of the excavation out on Route 28 yesterday. We believe the discovery may be related to a missing-persons case we worked several months ago. We wanted to take a look at the site, but thought it would be appropriate to check in with you first."

Mike nodded slowly. "What sort of missing persons case?" he asked. Even though he had been out of law enforcement for months, he knew any case that would pull two FBI guys way up here to the middle of nowhere, a stone's throw from the Canadian border, on such short notice would have been an extremely high profile one. He couldn't recall hearing of any.

Cooper gazed at him, simmering with barely concealed hostility as Ferriss hesitated for a moment and then said, "We're not at liberty to discuss the case at this time, Chief."

"Really," Mike answered. He felt his patience beginning to slip away. "Who notified you about this discovery out on Route 28?"

The two agents glanced at each other uneasily before Ferriss said, "I believe it would have been your former chief."

"You believe," Mike said.

The two agents stared straight ahead. He wondered when Pete Kendall would have had time to call the FBI about the bodies with all that was going on yesterday, and why he wouldn't have mentioned it to Mike. "What time was this notification made?"

"I really don't recall," Ferriss said immediately, staring at Mike flatly as if issuing a challenge. Mike returned the look, wondering just what in the hell was happening here. Something wasn't right, but he couldn't imagine what it might be.

"Let me get this straight," Mike answered. "You got a call from Chief Kendall about the discovery of human remains in a pit out by the Ridge Runner. You don't remember what time the call came in, but you immediately linked this discovery to a long-dormant missing-persons case you were working out of the Portland Field Office."

"That's about the size of it."

"Right. If I check the call logs here at the station, I'm not going to find any record of this notification, am I?"

A trace of a smile crossed Ferriss's face and then disappeared. No such trace made it anywhere near Cooper's face. "I think the dead chief...what was his name again?"

"Kendall," Mike replied shortly.

"Kendall, yeah. I think Chief Kendall made the call on his personal cell."

"Is that right?"

"Yep. Anyway, this visit is just a courtesy call. We wanted to drop by and let you know we'll be poking around your crime scene later today. Didn't want anyone to see us out there and panic, do something stupid. We wouldn't want anyone to get hurt, would we, Agent Cooper?"

Cooper sat silently until Ferriss leveled a gaze at him, and then mumbled, "Nah," spitting out the single syllable like it was causing him pain.

Mike flashed back to his last experience dealing with the FBI, during the Chief Court fiasco nearly two years ago, and grimaced inwardly. The two agents he had dealt with back then had been assholes, but at least they operated with a modicum of professionalism. This pair handled themselves like a couple of hoodlums. "Well, we agree on that," he finally offered. "I don't want anyone else getting hurt; we've had enough of that around here already to last several lifetimes."

The two agents pushed their chairs back and stood in unison. Ferriss offered Mike a tight-lipped smile while Cooper scowled like he had just found out Mike was sleeping with his wife. Neither man offered his hand again. "Be seeing ya around," Ferriss said. "We'll let you know if we need anything else."

"You do that," Mike answered as the men exited his office. He watched them wind their way through the bullpen and out the front door. This was going to be a long day.

13

The hunger was now so bad that Jackson Healy thought he might be going insane. Cramps wracked not just his stomach but his entire frame, and eating was all he could think about. Despite the fact he had chowed down less than twelve hours ago, he felt as though he had been wandering in the wilderness for months since his last meal.

Since awakening from his strange slumber down in that secret underground room he had felt mostly confused, like something momentous had happened to him but he couldn't figure out what it was. But now, the awful hunger pains thundering through his system had the effect of focusing him in a way that nothing else could. He crashed through the thick underbrush of the forest, lost, no idea of where he was going or what he would do when he got there, clutching his ruined Colt revolver like a talisman.

From somewhere far off his right, Jackson began to make out an occasional low humming noise. It was barely noticeable at first, like a pesky mosquito buzzing around his head as he tried to sleep. Then the noise would rise slightly in volume, and shortly afterward fade away. Varying intervals of time would pass, and the mosquito-buzz sensation would begin again.

The sound was unlike anything he had ever heard, but Jackson was pretty sure it wasn't coming from an animal, which meant it must have a human origin. Where there were humans there would be food, and Jackson needed food.

Badly.

So he stopped walking, forcing himself to stand and listen despite the powerful hunger ravaging his belly, and when he next heard the strange noise, he began moving, changing course slightly, navigating – he hoped – in the direction of the humming sound. He moved as fast as he could, driven by the overwhelming need to eat, a sensation now joined by a powerful thirst.

The forest was thick, thicker than any he had ever encountered, but he moved at a steady clip, enduring scrapes on his face and arms from the underbrush, and bruises on his shins from collisions with low-lying logs and boulders. He skirted massive fir trees, walked up gentle rises and down steep drops, continued moving doggedly forward.

His throat felt parched.

He was so damned hungry.

Just when he began to doubt he would ever exit the forest, when he began to fear he would walk in circles under the thick canopy of trees until he simply dropped dead from exhaustion or hunger, just when he thought it might be *better* to die than to put up with the unwavering hunger and intense thirst, he stepped through a thick screen of wild prickly undergrowth into a field of tall grass gently waving in the light breeze.

And on the far side of the field was a house.

Beyond the house, off in the distance, Jackson could see another of those terrifying buggies, somehow moving without the assistance of a horse, propelling itself along a trail that looked flatter and smoother than any he had ever seen. The low humming noise he had been using for guidance accompanied the carriage's movement, fading away and eventually disappearing as the buggy turned a corner and disappeared. Jackson stopped and watched, spellbound by the sight even in the face of his nearly overwhelming hunger.

Once silence returned, Jackson resumed his examination of the house in the distance. Behind it, in direct line between himself and a screened back door, a length of rope had been strung in a zigzag pattern back and forth between two poles shaped like a T. A lady stood in the sunshine hanging laundry out to dry. The lady was probably a hundred feet away, but even from here Jackson could see she had a thick mop of snow-white hair, leading him to believe she was probably in her sixties, or maybe even older.

Her age didn't matter, though, because Jackson was approaching the limits of his endurance. Cramps rifled through him almost continuously and his throat felt as though someone had sandpapered it when he wasn't paying attention. He needed food and he needed water, and he was going to get them both here, come hell or high water. No woman, young *or* old, was going to stop him.

He broke into a trot, crossing the field with long, loping strides, and for a few moments the woman didn't even notice him. She was engrossed in her chore, working with machine-like efficiency. Finally, though, she spotted him out of the corner of her eye, stiffening noticeably and turning to face him head-on.

He slowed to a half-trot, not wanting to spook the old woman until he could get close enough to handle the problem if she drew a gun on him. She watched him approach, her forehead crinkled with concern at this unexpected development, but said nothing. Just when Jackson thought maybe she was mute, she raised a hand and pointed a finger in his direction.

"This is private property," she said with the clipped tone and confident certainty of the righteous. "I don't know what you think you're doing here, but you can just turn your ass around and drag it right back the way you came…"

Jackson kept moving, picking up his pace at the woman's words rather than stopping or slowing. The closer he came to her, the less authoritative her voice sounded, until her words simply faded away and she stared with her mouth half-open, a look of shocked distaste frozen on her wrinkled face.

Jackson had seen that look plenty in his life, mostly from women but occasionally from men. He had even seen it a few times from his ma before he left home. He wasn't surprised. He realized he must appear intimidating, with ill-fitting stolen clothes covering his unwashed body, blood stains splashed liberally over everything.

"Food," Jackson croaked, stopping in front of the woman and swaying like he had drunk half a bottle of cheap whiskey.

The woman didn't move. She stared in horror at Jackson's midsection and he realized her attention was focused on the Colt revolver still grasped in his right hand. He glanced down reflexively and saw what had held her gaze so effectively. A clump of the dead sheriff's hair was stuck to the grip, crusted in place by his dried blood. It bristled in the breeze exactly as the field grass had done when he was exiting the forest.

He smiled at the thought, and that seemed to jolt the woman out of her shocked inaction. Her eyes widened and her gaze left the gun, running up his disheveled body to his face, and she opened her mouth to scream.

And Jackson hit her.

14

Sharon was halfway across the dusty Ridge Runner parking lot when her cell phone rang. With every other available member of the tiny Paskagankee police force busy at the scene of last night's double murder, Mike had asked her to examine the excavated pit closely in search of any evidence that might shed some light on exactly what had happened down there.

She glanced at the caller ID and smiled before pressing the *Send* button. "Hello, Chief, how can I help you?" She had gotten so used to calling him "Mike" during the months of his retirement that addressing him more formally now that he was back at work was going to take some getting used to.

"Sharon, have you gotten to the Ridge Runner yet?"

"Yes, I just drove in and am getting out my unit now. What's wrong?" She could sense the tension in his voice.

"You're going to have some company in a few minutes. Two FBI special agents are on their way over there. They left the station a few minutes ago."

Sharon held her cell phone away from her ear and glared at it accusingly, as if it might be trying to get away with telling a particularly bad joke. Then she returned it to her head and said, "Could you repeat that, Chief?"

"I think you heard me," Mike said. "There will be two FBI special agents visiting the Ridge Runner crime scene this morning. Names are Ferriss and Cooper."

"You called the FBI and their people are already here? That

doesn't even seem possible."

"No," Mike answered. "I didn't call anybody. There were at the station waiting for me when I arrived this morning. Claimed Pete Kendall notified them about the human remains uncovered behind the Ridge Runner and wanted to take a look at the scene. Something about a possible connection to a missing persons cold case they were working some time ago."

"Pete notified them? When would he have had time to do that? He was with me most of the afternoon and then was busy getting killed overnight. I suppose he could have called Portland in the short time between when we left the Ridge Runner and when he called us at home, but..."

"I agree; it seems unlikely. And why would he suddenly decide to call in the Feds? I can't imagine how he would have known about some FBI missing-persons connection. Plus, I think he would have mentioned it to me if he was planning on calling Portland, and he never said a word."

"Very strange." Sharon said.

"You don't know the half of it. These guys acted more like thugs than buttoned-down Feds. They claimed to have stopped by the station as a courtesy before visiting the scene, but I think the only reason they were there at all was to throw their weight around and to try to intimidate the small-town cops."

"Fat chance of that," Sharon laughed.

"You got that right. But listen; be careful when those guys show up. Stay out of their way and don't hassle them, but keep a close eye on them at the same time."

"No problem, boss."

"Do me a favor and check in with me when they leave."

"Will do."

"And Sharon? Watch your back, something's not right about those two."

She clicked off and eyed her phone thoughtfully. Mike McMahon was not one to worry over her like she was some helpless child who needed protecting. She knew he regarded her as a solid, reliable cop who could handle herself on the job and off. Plus, she had a 9 mm equalizer strapped to her hip.

But his concern was evident in both his words and his tone and that, in turn, made her a little uneasy.

She shook her head and dropped her phone into her breast pocket, then resumed walking around the deserted Ridge Runner toward the excavation site in back. She was a little surprised but grateful that Bo Pellerin wasn't already on the scene, hassling her about all the business he was losing being forced to stay closed, and pushing to learn when the crime scene tape would be removed so he could get his precious septic system installed and once again serve the needs of Paskagankee's drinking public.

As she approached the corner of the building, the crunching of tires on gravel told her that either Pellerin had decided to put in an appearance or the Feds had arrived. She tried to decide which option she preferred and realized there was no good answer. Reluctantly she turned and watched a dark blue G-car motor slowly across the lot and pull to a stop next to her own vehicle.

The FBI was here.

* * *

The two special agents followed Sharon to the gaping hole dug into the ground behind the Ridge Runner. Perfunctory introductions had been accomplished when the men climbed out of their vehicle, after which neither one seemed inclined to speak. She could feel them staring at her ass and was tempted to whirl around just to catch them so she could read them the riot act, but Mike had asked her to play nice, so she would try to do so.

For now.

The overcast layer had disappeared overnight, with the sun putting in an appearance for the first time in more than a week. The pleasantly warm temperatures had dried the ground out nicely. Most of the mud inside the excavated hole had hardened into flaky, powdery dirt, and Sharon was thankful for that. Maybe she would actually be able to find some useful evidence down there.

The small group arrived at the edge of the pit, the stationary earthmover looming above them like the skeletal remains of a gigantic yellow dinosaur. Sharon lifted an aluminum ladder off the ground where it had been deposited next to the construction vehicle and slid it into the massive hole, noting with distaste that neither one of the FBI agents made any move to help.

She briefly considered offering the ladder to her companions first, then discarded the thought and clambered down. It was her crime scene; the Feds could come or not, their choice. As she passed below ground level, the temperatures dropped dramatically. The trapped air still out of direct sunlight had not yet warmed.

The human remains were gone, transported to the morgue last night by Pete Kendall. He had also supervised a thorough photographing of the entire scene by patrol officer Harley Tanguay. It had been one of Pete's final duties before being called to the Bronson Choate murder scene, where he had later lost his life.

Sharon's job today was to examine the eerie room in search of anything the investigators might have missed yesterday, as well as to try to get a feel for exactly what had happened down here. She gazed for a moment at the tons of earth covering the portion of the room that had not been opened like a sardine can by Dan Melton's earthmoving bucket and said a quiet prayer that today wouldn't be the day the whole thing collapsed. Then she took a deep breath and walked to the far corner to start her search.

Behind her, the two FBI men descended the ladder and began a search of their own. Mindful of Mike's instructions, she tried to keep an eye on them while still concentrating on the task at hand. Her initial impression of Special Agents Ferriss and Cooper seemed to validate Mike's concerns. The two men's "search" consisted of a single walk around the circumference of the ancient room, where they glanced with apparent disinterest at the rotting wooden tables and chairs, and then confined their investigation mostly to the area that had been exposed by Melton's equipment.

Sharon did her best to ignore their shoddy work habits, dedicating herself to her search despite having no idea what she might be looking for. She briefly considered coming right out and asking them what their game was, since neither special agent was acting anything like a trained investigator, then abandoned the idea as pointless. If they hadn't told Mike what they were up to, they certainly weren't going to confide in her.

After less than an hour, the agents climbed back up the ladder and out of the hole, presumably for a smoke break. She heard the men talking in hushed voices but could not make out their words. A few minutes later they returned, still doing little apparent investigating. Sharon continued her methodical search.

An hour later, she had covered nearly half of the room but found nothing that would indicate what its purpose might have been or why two (or possibly three) people had died in it. Her two FBI companions had by now given up any pretense of investigating and spent most of their time staring at her with unnerving openness. She began to get a very bad feeling and was thankful for the service pistol strapped at her hip.

She was running her hands along the earthen wall and moving slowly to her left, when her boot struck an object buried just below the surface of the dirt floor with a heavy *clunk*. The sound resonated through the enclosed space and the feds looked at her with renewed interest.

Bending down, Sharon dug through the hard-packed earth with her fingers. Less than an inch below the surface she struck something hard and smooth. It felt metallic and cool to the touch. She began scraping away the dirt along the object's edge, and soon it became clear the item was perfectly round. It was also big.

After a few moments she thought she had removed enough earth that she might be able to pull the object free if she could slide her hands underneath it. With a grunt of effort, Sharon wriggled her fingers, pushing and prodding to get the leverage required to lift the item. By now Ferriss and Cooper had moved close. They loomed over her, watching quietly, neither man offering to help.

Finally she felt as though she had enough of a grip that she might be able to break the earth's hold. She pulled upward, straining, and after a moment with no result, it suddenly lifted free. It looked perfectly round, about a foot in diameter, and it was heavy.

And it appeared to be solid gold.

Sharon stood in the muted light of the bizarre death-chamber and stared in surprise at her discovery, absolutely baffled as to what it might be.

The two feds stood next to her, both gaping at the circular object. Cooper said quietly, "Hoooly shit, he was here. He was really here," and then Ferriss glared at him with a look that would have melted steel and he closed his mouth, cringing under his partner's angry gaze.

Sharon furrowed her brow. "Who was here? Do you know who this belongs to? What is it?"

Ferriss growled, "Can't say. But that's evidence in the case we're working, and it's coming with us."

Her reached to take the mysterious metallic object out of Sharon's hands and she tightened her grip, yanking it away and turning to block the agent with her body. "I don't think so," she said tightly. "Whatever it is, it's evidence in *our* case, and you're not touching it until the Paskagankee PD is done with it."

"Is that right?" said Ferriss. His tone was simultaneously mocking and dangerous, and once again Sharon was thankful she was armed. She had never before had that feeling in the presence of other law enforcement officers. The agent continued, "I'll just make a call or two and that evidence'll be out of your hands and clear of this hick town before you know what hit you, little lady."

"It's Officer Dupont to you, jackass, and you're not touching this until I hear otherwise, from someone whose opinion I respect." She leveled a hard stare at the man and he took an instinctive step backward. His partner didn't move, though, so Sharon stepped nimbly around him and moved to the ladder, careful to maintain a firm grip on the disputed evidence as she climbed.

She was in her cruiser and driving out of the Ridge Runner lot before the Feds had even exited the pit.

15

Rose Pellerin spit blood out of her mouth and glared up at the man who had hit her. She tried not to think about the clump of bloody hair she had seen stuck to the grip of his beat-up pistol and thanked the good Lord he had seen fit to strike her with an open palm rather than shoot her or hit her with the gun.

"Git up," the man hissed with the hint of a southwestern accent, "and keep your damn mouth shut or the next time I hit you you'll wake up with the angels."

Rose rolled to her hands and knees, ignoring the bath towel and the sprinkling of clothespins she had dropped when she fell. She stood slowly, keeping a wary eye on the stranger, who seemed to have materialized out of nowhere. He was dressed in a manner that would have seemed comical had he not just assaulted her. His clothes were ill-fitting; they hung off him like a scarecrow's outfit. They clearly didn't belong to him.

But the fit of the man's attire wasn't what bothered Rose. Something that looked suspiciously like dried blood was smeared all over the man, splashed liberally on his clothes as well as his exposed skin. It almost looked like he had run through a sprinkler, except it had been spraying blood instead of water.

And the man smelled. He smelled as though he hadn't showered in decades. The stench of body odor and something unidentifiable wafted off him in waves. Rose felt her eyes begin to water from the awful stench and tried not to gag. Her jaw throbbed where she had been hit, and as she struggled to her feet she worried what might happen next.

She didn't have to wait long to find out. "I said I want food," the stranger croaked, "and you're gonna git me some."

"Okay," she agreed, nodding slowly, doing her best to show compliance but not fear. It wasn't easy. She thought about that awful bloody hair on the man's weapon and shuddered. "Okay," she repeated. "Let's just go inside and see what I can whip up for you, how does that sound?"

"Move," he said, gesturing toward the open back door with his bloody gun.

Rose didn't want to turn her back on her attacker but she knew she was being silly. She would be sixty-three years old in two weeks and this disheveled mess of a man looked like he was barely half that. If he wanted to hurt her it wouldn't matter in the least whether he was standing in front of her, behind her or next to her.

She took one last, quick glance at the man's face. It was hard and unfeeling. She turned and walked slowly toward the house. Once inside, she pulled a wooden chair away from the small kitchen table and gestured at it with one hand. The man sat without speaking.

"How does an omelet sound?" she asked.

"And coffee."

"Of course, and coffee. What would you like in your omelet?"

"Everything."

"Excuse me?"

"Whatever you got, put it in there. I feel like I ain't eaten in years."

Rose nodded and turned toward the fridge, risking a sidelong glance at the telephone hanging not three feet away on the wall. The stranger was watching her with his hard gaze from the table and she knew he would be on her before she punched the "9" in 9-1-1. The phone might as well have been in the next county. She tried to control her rising fear and opened the refrigerator door.

*   *   *

The pan was sizzling when Rose asked, "Would you like to freshen up before you eat?"

The stranger stared back with his flat gaze and just said, "Where's the fire?"

Rose furrowed her brow in confusion. "Fire? What fire?"

"The fire. To cook the food. Where's the fire?"

"This isn't a gas stove, it's electric. There is no fire." She tried not to grimace as she glanced at the blood and dirt staining the stranger's clothing and body. "Now, how about washing up?"

The man narrowed his eyes suspiciously but dropped the subject of fires. "Food first," came the curt reply. "How much longer?"

"It's almost ready," Rose answered, wishing she had some rat poison handy. The man might be a lot younger than she was, but he looked terrible, like he might be suffering from some kind of terminal illness. She thought if she could just slow him down a little, she might be able to escape, to rush to her car and get the hell out of here. She would drive straight to the police station and come back with Sheriff Kendall and as many officers as he could muster.

But there was no rat poison.

She tried to think of another option and wondered if she might be able to attack the stranger when he wasn't expecting it. The skillet currently sautéing vegetables for the omelet was made of cast iron and was also, as a nice bonus, red hot from the stovetop's burner. If she could manage to crack the man in the skull, there was every reason to believe he would drop like a sack of Aroostook County potatoes.

But she would only get one chance, and he was seated all the way across the kitchen, a distance of over ten feet. The odds of her being able to lift the pan, cross the kitchen floor and then slug him before he could react were so slim as to be laughable. She was old, and as the years had passed she had packed on a few extra pounds – *okay, more than few*, she thought to herself grimly – and there was little doubt the younger man's reflexes would be quicker than hers, regardless of how sick he may or may not be.

It wasn't going to work. Braining her attacker with a frying pan was a satisfying fantasy, but that was all it would ever be. Rose sighed and stirred the ingredients simmering in the pan, then moved to the coffee maker. She dumped coffee into the filter and poured water into the reservoir, then pressed the "Start" button.

A few seconds later, the coffee began to burble through the system, hissing audibly as it dripped into the glass carafe seated on the hotplate. Rose turned back to the stove and then whirled at the sound of feet scrabbling on her vinyl floor tiles.

The stranger was sitting up perfectly straight, the back of his wooden chair pressed against the wall as if he might be trying to force himself through to the other side. His eyes were wide and he stared at the coffeemaker unblinkingly. "What kind of joke is this?" he growled menacingly.

Rose ran her fingers gingerly over the side of her face where the man had hit her. It throbbed incessantly. She didn't want to be struck again, and the man was making it perfectly clear he was losing patience with her.

But what in the world was so scary about a coffeemaker? The stranger's frightened gaze suggested he was looking into the face of the devil himself. "I–I'm sorry," Rose stammered. "I thought you said you wanted coffee. I can turn it off if you'd like…"

She reached for the electrical cord, strung out behind the coffeemaker like a serpent. She would yank it right out of the wall and stop the coffee-brewing process in its tracks. Anything to keep the lunatic calm.

"I do want coffee," he said, his eyes flicking from the offending appliance to Rose and then back again. He stood and took a tentative step toward her, a development she interpreted as a very bad sign. "Where's the coffeepot and what the hell is…*that* thing?" He flicked his head at the Mr. Coffee machine.

"There is no coffeepot. The coffee is brewed inside the coffeemaker and then drips into the glass carafe, where it's kept warm by the hot plate," she said gently, wondering what rock this strange man had grown up under. What grown adult in the year 2013 didn't understand how a coffeemaker worked?

Her response seemed to allay the man's fears, if only slightly, and he took a step backward. He didn't sit back down but he was no longer advancing threateningly, either. Rose took a shuddering breath. *How am I going to get out of this?*

And then the telephone rang.

Rose's phone was an old, hard plastic wall-mounted model straight out of the 1970's that had been in perfect working order when she bought the house. She had never had a problem with it over the intervening decades and so had never had occasion to replace it. It was canary-yellow and featured a loud, jangling bell for a ringtone that Rose thought could probably be heard by folks living along the Canadian border.

She froze, fearing the worst. If the dripping of coffee into a glass carafe had spooked the stranger, what would happen now?

She didn't have to wait long to find out. The man's entire body jerked as if an electric shock had blasted through his system, and then he stood stiffly, searching desperately for the source of the noise, his long, stringy hair flying in a dirty arc around his head as he tried to look in every direction at once.

The first jangling ring ended and the man stopped moving, and then of course the phone began ringing again. The man stumbled forward now, his eyes bright with panic. He spun Rose around so he was positioned behind her, then encircled her throat with his left arm and began to squeeze, choking off her airway.

"Make it stop," he growled, his voice shaking.

Rose tried to speak and couldn't. She tried to breathe and couldn't. In a matter of seconds, bright blue and black spots began blossoming in her vision.

The telephone rang again.

The man squeezed harder. "MAKE IT STOP!" he shouted, and Rose knew she was about to die.

16

Mike straightened a pile of paperwork and shuffled it into a wooden "Out" box placed at an angle on the corner of his desk. The bureaucratic bullshit generated by even a small-town police department was staggering, and dealing with it had been his least-favorite duty when he was chief the first time around. He considered the irony of being buried under a mountain of it now that he was back on the job, when there was so much real police work to be done, and shook his head glumly.

He pushed his chair out from behind the desk and stood, stretching and yawning, wishing he could sneak in a thirty-minute nap. Going well over twenty-four hours without sleep could catch up to you quickly.

The nap would have to wait, though. He needed to get to the scene of the double murder – was already late, in fact – to check on the progress of the investigation.

He should also be hearing from Sharon soon with the results of her search of the earthen pit out at the Ridge Runner. He was curious to get her take on the two FBI agents who had joined her. Mike had found Sharon Dupont to be, among many other things, a keen judge of human nature. She was likely to provide insights into the feds that he might have missed.

He stepped around his desk and moved toward the closed office door when it opened with a crash, nearly clipping him on the shoulder. Sharon marched in, holding a large, dirt-encrusted, golden-colored disk clutched to her chest. He hadn't seen her coming through his office windows because he had lowered the blinds in an effort to discourage visitors. There was simply too much work to be done; the welcome-back greetings from officers coming on duty would have to wait until later.

Sharon's clothes were caked with dust, and the nylon gloves she had worn to conduct her search out on Route 28 – gloves she had still not removed in an effort to avoid contaminating whatever she was holding – had seemingly morphed from their normal baby blue to a dark brown, almost black.

She kicked the office door closed behind her and said, "Those guys are going to…"

The door burst open again, and FBI Special Agents Ferriss and Cooper trooped in, their faces scowling and angry. A vein pulsed in the middle of Cooper's forehead and Mike hoped the man wouldn't stroke out right here in the middle of his office.

Sharon thrust the disk toward Mike and then everyone was talking excitedly, their voices indecipherable in the confusion. He stepped around them and eased his office door closed, then returned to his original position behind his desk, still without touching the disk.

He stared at all three without saying a word, his gaze moving from Sharon to Ferriss to Cooper and then back to Sharon. Slowly the chaotic stream of babble began to fade, and then it died out completely. "I'm tired," Mike said, "and it's already been a long day, so I'm not going to shout over everyone to be heard. Let's all have a seat and discuss whatever the problem is like the professionals we're supposed to be, shall we?"

Sharon nodded wordlessly and stepped out of the office, returning a moment later holding the heavy golden disk pressed against her body with one arm while using both hands to drag a pair of chairs across the floor. She plunked the chairs down in front of the desk with a thud and then slid a wheeled chair over from the corner and sat in it, her expression stony. She held the disk in her lap, Mike noticed, covered with both hands as if trying to shield it.

"I uncovered this," she said, speaking quietly and nodding at the strange-looking circular object, "as part of my investigation. I dug through that site for hours, while these two clowns did little else besides stare at my ass when they thought I wasn't looking. The minute I pulled this...*thing*...out of the ground, they suddenly turned into super-sleuths and pulled rank. They want to take possession of it, Mike, but if they do, you know and I know we'll never see the damned thing again. I spent the morning digging through that death-chamber, I found this evidence – whatever the hell it is - and until we learn its relevance to our investigation, they're not getting it. They can have it when we're done with it."

Mike glanced between Sharon and the two agents. He had no trouble believing her story. She was dirty and bedraggled and looked as though she had crawled a mile through a sewer tunnel, while the two feds seemed to have survived the search of the construction site mostly unscathed. A small clump or two of stubborn dirt was stuck to their dress shoes, and a thin film of dust covered their suits, but compared to Sharon's appearance, they looked ready for a night on the town.

He nodded slowly, turning his attention to the heavy metallic disk. "What is it?" he asked.

Sharon shrugged. "I have no idea. Why don't you ask these two geniuses? They seem to have all the answers."

Mike raised his eyebrows and looked at Ferriss. Based on their earlier meeting, he knew that man was the senior of the two agents. The FBI man gazed back with a sour look on his face. Then Ferriss glanced over at his partner, who shook his head obstinately. The thick purple vein continued to pulse in Cooper's forehead.

"Come on, guys, spill it," Mike prodded. "You can't expect us to release evidence into your custody when we don't even know what it is, or what application it might have to our own investigation."

"That's *exactly* what we expect," Cooper answered, surprising Mike. He had thought Ferriss would do all of the talking.

Ferriss raised a hand, silencing his partner. "I already told you," he said evenly, "that we're not able to divulge the details of our investigation. You're just going to have to trust us when we tell you we need that disk a hell of a lot more than you do."

"Just trust you."

"Yep."

"Well, here's the thing," Mike said pleasantly. "On the one hand, I've got a dead cop, and not *just* a dead cop, but a dead chief of police, along with a dead civilian, both killed at the same location just hours apart. I've got a bizarre underground death chamber, complete with what appears to be the skeletal remains of two human beings. I've got a witness who swears the room originally contained a third body, which has now disappeared seemingly of its own free will, and is unaccounted for."

"Oh yeah? Well—"

"—I'm not done yet," Mike interrupted, raising his voice and cutting off the Fed. After the easy camaraderie of his initial statement, the outburst had the exact effect he wanted: the FBI man stopped talking, momentarily shocked into silence.

"As I was saying," Mike continued, his tone amiable again. "I've got all these events, which I'm willing to bet a month's salary are related, although I couldn't begin to tell you how. In addition, I've got my best officer sitting in front of me telling a story of investigative ineptitude at best, and sexual harassment at worst."

"That's ridiculous," Ferriss spat. "We might have glanced at her butt a couple of times, but, hell, who could blame us for that? She's a damned fine-looking lady. Besides, it's not like we groped her or anything." While Ferriss talked, Cooper's face had grown steadily redder, until now it resembled an out-of-control bonfire, with the reliably pulsing vein stuck in the middle.

"Well, see, that's where you should consider yourself fortunate," Mike said. "I believe my officer showed remarkable restraint under the circumstances, but if you'd tried to lay a hand on her, I'm pretty sure you would have found yourself regaining consciousness in the hospital down in Portland sometime tomorrow."

"And facing a lawsuit the likes of which you couldn't imagine in your worst nightmare," Sharon added, fuming.

"None of my nightmares involve lawsuits, missy," Cooper said, his voice tight with fury.

"Hey!" Mike said, banging the desk with a fist. "Let me finish saying what I have to say. This is the last time I'm going to tell you."

He waited a heartbeat, then two, for his message to sink in, and then continued. "Everything I just mentioned is what I have on one hand. On the other hand I have two federal agents, neither of whom I've ever worked with or have even seen before. These agents show up in my office the morning after a brutal double murder, speaking cryptically about missing persons cases and claiming, without offering anything to back up their statement, that the evidence *my* officer uncovered through her own diligence is so critical to their mysterious case – the case they're unable or unwilling to discuss – they must take possession of it immediately."

Mike lifted his hands chest-high, palms up, like a set of scales. "This is what I have on both hands. Now, put yourselves in my shoes, gentlemen. What would you do?"

"I've had it!" Cooper burst out, his throbbing vein working overtime. "Just grab the damned disk and let's get the hell out of here!"

Ferriss ignored him, as did Mike. Sharon shot him a scornful look, which he either ignored or didn't notice. The senior FBI agent waited a moment and then said, "Okay, I put myself in your shoes. It doesn't change a thing. That disk is our evidence, and we're taking it back to Portland."

Mike shook his head. "Wrong answer, guys."

He turned to Sharon and said, "Go process that thing, whatever it is, and then place it in the evidence room. Double-check to be sure the room is locked when you leave."

Sharon stood without speaking. She stared down each agent, in turn, and then walked out of the office, pulling the door closed behind her.

"You're making a mistake, *Chief,*" Ferriss hissed, his voice low and threatening.

"Maybe so," Mike said, unruffled. "It certainly wouldn't be the first time. When you're willing to spell out why that evidence is so critical to your case, we can revisit the subject of releasing it into your custody. Alternatively, if you'd like to have the Special Agent in Charge down in the Portland field office give me a call, I'd be happy to discuss the subject with him.

"Until then," he said, "it looks like we're done here. Now, if you'll excuse me, I have a lot of work to do. As I believe I mentioned before, it's already been a long day, and it's going to get a lot longer. As pleasant as it's been chatting with you fellas, unless there's anything else, I'll have to ask you to get the hell out of my office."

The men sat for a moment, unmoving, staring across the desk at each other, Mike doing his best to ignore the throbbing vein in Agent Cooper's forehead. Finally, Ferriss said, "This isn't over," and the two agents stood as one and marched out of the office.

Mike moved to his office window and watched as the pair plodded through the bullpen, looking neither right nor left, and disappeared through the lobby door. He hoped they would climb into their G-car and head south to Portland, but somehow he doubted he had seen – or heard – the last of them.

17

The telephone abruptly stopped ringing. Rose noted this development from somewhere that seemed very far away. She had fallen limp in the stranger's arms as the blue spots in her vision were replaced by rapidly growing roiling black clouds. A buzzing sound began inside her head, increasing in volume, becoming more insistent, and she knew instinctively that she was seconds away from losing consciousness. A few seconds after that happened she would be dead.

But then the phone stopped ringing and the stranger's iron grip on her airway relaxed, just a little, just enough for Rose to choke a wheezing breath into her lungs. The black cloud receded. She managed another shuddering breath and the cloud disappeared entirely.

The stranger seemed to remember her then, and he removed his arm from around her neck, but thankfully continued supporting her, as she was afraid she might still fall to the floor if he let go. He stared at her wide-eyed, face white, body shaking.

And then the answering machine clicked on. "I'm not here right now," Rose heard her recorded voice say. "Please leave a message and I'll get back to you as soon as I'm able."

The unrestrained panic returned to the stranger's eyes and he spun a full three hundred sixty degrees, releasing his hold on Rose to do so. She stumbled forward a couple of steps, wondering whether she would break her hip when she collapsed to the floor, but surprised herself by somehow managing to stay on her feet.

Through the answering machine's speaker, a sweet-sounding female voice was saying, "Hello, Rose, this is Annette. I know you haven't been feeling well, and when you didn't show up for work I just wanted to check in on you, make sure everything's okay..."

The stranger stopped looking around the kitchen and was now homing in on the origination of the voice. He took a step toward the kitchen counter, hesitated, then took another, finally reaching the counter and extending an arm toward the answering machine, a small plastic box Rose had placed on the countertop directly under the wall-mounted phone.

The man's actions were so bizarre she momentarily forgot about being attacked, forgot about nearly being choked to death, even forgot about her intense fear. As Annette Middleton, the young assistant at *Needful Things*, voiced her concern about Rose not showing up for work, the stranger hovered over the machine, a look of intense concentration etched on his face. Then, without warning, he swiveled his arm up like he was preparing to hammer a nail and smashed the butt end of his pistol down on the machine's case.

The plastic cracked with a loud POP and Annette's voice erupted in a high-pitched electronic squeal and then abruptly died away. The stranger leaped backward like he had been kicked in the chest by a horse, almost knocking Rose down in the process. He spun on his heels and his narrow, angry eyes locked on to hers and he said, "You've got some explaining to do, old lady. What in the hell is going on here?"

Rose's fear rushed back and she said, "I'm sorry, but I don't know what you want me to say. What don't you understand?" She felt her panic rising and choked off a sob, trying to keep herself under control.

"WHERE'S THE OTHER LADY?" he shouted, his face just inches from hers, splattering her with spittle. "WHAT WAS THAT GODDAMNED RINGING NOISE BEFORE? WHAT'S HAPPENING HERE?"

And just like that, it clicked in Rose Pellerin's head. This man's unreasoning terror stemmed from the fact he had either never heard the ringing of a telephone before, or, more likely, had suffered some kind of traumatic brain injury and didn't *remember* ever having heard a phone.

The same was also true with the answering machine. Annette Middleton's disembodied voice had had thrown him for a loop. He looked like he had just seen a ghost because he *had* just seen a ghost, practically speaking: a third person was talking but was invisible to him.

The man stood panting, his chest heaving, pistol held loosely in his right hand. The disgusting clump of matted hair was still stuck to the gun's handgrip. Even the violent blow to the answering machine had failed to loosen it.

Rose steadied herself with a deep breath. Her attacker was dangerous, but he was also clearly confused and terrified. He might not be quite as afraid as she was, but Rose guessed he was probably close. Speaking gently, she said, "That was Annette, my assistant. I own a small curio shop in downtown Paskagankee. I've been rather ill lately, and when I was late showing up for work today, she obviously became concerned. She wanted to make sure I was alright, that's all."

"Where is she?" He seemed to have relaxed slightly, but the fear still radiated off him.

"She's at the shop. The ringing noise you heard was her calling on the telephone, and when I didn't answer, she left a message on the answering machine."

The man backed up a step. "Telephone? Answering machine?"

"It's all right," Rose said soothingly. "Neither of those things will hurt you. They're just machines, designed to make life easier, although, to tell you the truth," she said with a smile, "many times they seem to have the opposite effect." She was trying to keep things light, to ingratiate herself with the plainly unstable man and keep him calm, until she could figure out what to do next.

He continued to gaze at her in obvious confusion, the concept of a telephone foreign to him. "May I sit down?" she ventured. "As I said, I've not been feeling well, and the day's events have worn me down just a bit." She didn't mention the part about being struck in the jaw and nearly choked to death. The volatile stranger had finally begun relaxing, just a little, and Rose didn't want to do or say anything that might counteract the minimal progress she'd made.

"I could still use that food and coffee," he mumbled. "I guess after that you could sit."

The omelet had by now practically burned to the base of the pan, and when Rose scraped it onto the plate, the bottom was charred a nearly uniform black. She grimaced at it and told him she'd make a new one, but he waved her off. "Looks fine," he said gruffly.

He was obviously ravenous, and by the time Rose poured a cup of coffee and brought it to the kitchen table, the man had already worked through more than half the omelet, burned and all. He nodded wordlessly at the chair on the opposite side of the table, and she sat, grateful to be off her feet.

Rose tried to imagine where on earth this strange man might have come from that he would be so unfamiliar with a telephone its ringing would send him into a frenzy. She couldn't come up with a single guess, so she decided to ask. As gently as possible, she said, "So, where are you from, Mr...?"

The stranger looked up from his food blankly. For a moment she thought he would refuse to answer. She began to wonder if he had even heard the question. Then, between large bites of burned egg, he took a deep breath and said, "I was born in Kansas City and moved to Texas as a young boy, but I left there a long time ago. I've lived all over. Wherever my horse'll take me, basically."

Rose furrowed her brow. Despite her fear and pain she was intrigued, though she took note of his refusal to give his name. "Your horse? What do you mean? You raise horses?"

The stranger chuckled. "Raise 'em? Nope, just ride 'em. How else would I get around?"

"Well, by car, like everyone else. Do you own a car?"

"A car? I don't know what you mean."

"You know, a car. An automobile."

The stranger shook his head in utter confusion, and Rose Pellerin began to feel an odd sense of...clarity...begin to sink in. As hard as it was to swallow – Rose Pellerin had always been a pragmatic Yankee, a believer in things she could see, feel and touch – this confused man's lack of familiarity with seemingly every modern convenience might not be due to *where* he grew up, she began to suspect it was due to *when*.

She sat quietly, watching the man eat and thinking about time travel, and about the science fiction novels she had read and loved as a young girl, and about all the secrets of the human brain that mankind has yet to unlock. She considered how to proceed, and even *whether* to proceed. For all his confusion and vulnerability, this uninvited and unwanted houseguest was still extremely dangerous, as evidenced by the gruesome clump of hair hanging off his gun and his frenzied attack on Rose, an attack that had been precipitated by nothing more dangerous than a ringing telephone.

After a silent but vigorous internal debate, she decided to ask her questions. She realized with some surprise there had never been any real doubt whether she would. The man would be finished eating soon, and then he would either move on, or...not. What would happen to her if he chose the second option was something Rose very much did not want to think about, but she doubted a few harmless questions would affect his decision one way or the other. Her fate had probably already been determined in his mind, anyway.

She cleared her throat and said, as casually as she could manage, "Do you happen to know today's date, Mr...?"

"My name's Jackson," he said, surprising Rose.

"It's nice to meet you, Jackson," she said, knowing how ridiculous the statement sounded, given the circumstances. "So, about the date..."

He thought about it for a moment. "I dunno the exact date," he finally said. "I was...out of circulation for a time. Not sure about how long a time, but it may have been several days. I assume it was more than a day or two, anyway, 'cause I've been so damned hungry since waking up. Anyway, I know it's June, but that's about the best I can do."

Rose sat for a moment, wondering about his phrasing. *Waking up?* Then she decided to go for broke. What did she have to lose? "Yes, it's June, and what's the year again?"

The stranger had finished his omelet, cleaning the plate of every last crumb. If Rose didn't know better, she would have thought the dish had been washed and dried and placed in front of the man empty.

"The year?" He took a sip of coffee and eyed her over the top of the mug, plainly convinced he had entered the home of a lunatic. "The year's 1858, of course."

18

Ward Cooper leveled a hard stare out the windshield of the Bureau-provided Chevy Suburban, currently parked along a desolate stretch of Paskagankee, Maine roadway. He chewed on a stick of gum relentlessly, attacking it as if competing in a professional sport. "What the hell do we do now?" he said sourly.

"Christ, would you just relax already?" Alton Ferriss looked his partner up and down with equal parts concern and amusement. "This is the biggest break we've gotten in…well…ever, and you can't even seem to enjoy it!"

"Enjoy it? What's to enjoy? We were this close," he held up a hand with his thumb and forefinger positioned an inch apart, "to getting that goddamned disk and now it's locked up tight." He took a deep breath, his jaws working like pistons to punish the offending stick of gum. "You think we can convince the boss-man to pressure that hick cop to release the disk into our custody?"

"I doubt it," Ferriss replied. "The chief might be a hick, but he's right about one thing: the disk is evidence in a double-murder investigation. We don't have anything to trump him with. Hell, we don't even have a real case; at least not a law-enforcement case. That disk isn't going anywhere."

Cooper chewed with renewed fervor. "What about breaking into evidence storage and just taking it?"

Ferriss shook his head disgustedly and stared down his partner. "Will you please pull your head out of your ass? There's always somebody at the station. How do you propose to break into their evidence room without being seen?"

"Who gives a shit about an eighty year old dispatcher? I think we could handle him without too much trouble, don't you?"

"Jesus, get a grip! We're not going to 'handle' an old man. That would bring us grief we don't need, not when we're this close to getting what we want after all these years. Just relax and use your head for once."

Cooper said nothing, but continued grinding his gum into submission. He didn't seem to have gotten the message about relaxing. He started impatiently out the windshield at the expanse of Great North Woods looming just across the empty pavement, looking like he wanted to climb out of the car and beat the crap out of someone. Knowing Cooper, he probably did.

Ferriss let his partner stew for a while. He knew his message would eventually sink in. At last, Cooper turned and said, "Okay, smart guy. You want me to use my head? Tell me how."

Ferriss smiled. He had known Cooper for so long he thought of him as a little brother. "We don't need the disk," he said softly. "Healy's scared and confused and has no idea what the hell's going on. Eventually, he going to come to the conclusion his best option is to leave town and figure things out as he goes."

"He's probably already reached that conclusion."

"Maybe," Ferriss agreed. "But he's not about to skip town without his precious disk. And he doesn't know it's locked up safe and sound in the Paskagankee Police station. He thinks it's still in that big, muddy hole in the ground. All we have to do is go there and wait. He'll be along eventually."

Cooper thought about it for a while. Ferriss let him. For a long time, the only sound was the popping and snapping of Ward Cooper's overmatched gum. Eventually Cooper turned and offered Ferriss a crooked smile.

Ferriss started up the Suburban and executed a perfect three-point turn. Then he accelerated slowly away, toward Route 28 and the Ridge Runner.

19

Mike McMahon stood motionless in the living room of Bronson Choate's small cabin, absorbing the sensations of violence and death. The bustling activity of the active homicide crime scene had ended, at least for the moment, with the departure of the crime scene technicians and medical personnel and investigators, and he had the home to himself.

As a cop on the Revere, Massachusetts police force for a decade and a half, and then as chief of the tiny Paskagankee force for nearly two years, Mike had been present at dozens of scenes where violent crimes had taken place – rapes, assaults, murders – and to his mind they always retained a subtle air of tragedy once the victims, perpetrators and investigators had moved on.

This one was no different. A butcher-block end table stood at a crazy angle next to a small, worn couch. The smashed remains of a glass lamp littered the floor next to it. A hard-backed chair stood empty in the middle of the room, a length of electrical wire coiled messily on the floor behind it.

The chair was where Choate presumably had been held captive by his attacker. He had somehow managed to free himself from his bindings – the home invader had used electrical wire to immobilize Choate, not the smartest move he could have made – and tried to fight back just as his girlfriend arrived. The lamp must have been knocked off the table and smashed during that struggle.

Choate had made it as far as the front door, warning Jodie Miller off before being struck in the head from behind with a blunt object, killing him in the open doorway of his own home. Bronson Choate had quite literally saved his girlfriend at the expense of his own life.

But what was his attacker doing here? Why had he picked this house? Choate was employed as a merchant marine engineer, spending weeks at a time at sea, and had returned home from one of those stints only yesterday. Had his attacker been squatting in the cabin and gotten surprised by Choate's sudden return?

The theory made sense but for one problem: Mike couldn't get past the nagging certainty that Bronson Choate's murder – not to mention the subsequent similar attack and murder of Pete Kendall – was somehow related to Dan Melton's uncovering of human remains next to the Ridge Runner and his insistence that there had been *three* bodies lying on the floor of the underground room, rather than the two that were presently being examined by County Medical Examiner Jan Affeldt.

The Runner was located no more than a half-mile north of this cabin, if you walked a straight-line path through the woods, and Mike suspected that fact was critical to understanding what had happened here. Someone had managed to steal the remains of a human victim right out from under the nose of Melton – for what reason Mike could not imagine – and then had hidden the remains somewhere in the thick forest. That person had then started walking, stumbling onto Choate's cabin and holing up here.

The question was, why? Why take the remains of one person from the pit and leave the other two? And if that *had* happened, how did the mysterious thief/murderer even know Melton would uncover the long-buried underground room in the first place? Could Melton have been involved? And what about Bo Pellerin, longtime owner of the Ridge Runner?

Mike considered all of these possibilities, walking aimlessly around Choate's empty cabin, and eventually eliminated both Melton and Pellerin as suspects. He had had more than one run-in with Bo, the most serious one back when he was investigating the disappearance of Earl Manning last year, but while he felt Pellerin could be rude and dismissive and wouldn't hesitate to skirt the law where his bar was concerned, he also felt reasonably confident the man was nothing more than a small-town bully who had been genuinely surprised at the discovery of the bizarre underground room next to his business.

And the idea that Melton would somehow construct a secret room next to the Ridge Runner and bury bodies in it, only to then dig it up himself and invent a story about disappearing victims, was frankly ludicrous.

His mind wandered back to the contentious meeting this morning with FBI Special Agents Ferriss and Cooper. Something didn't smell right about their interest in the case, and while their story of a hush-hush missing-persons case was technically feasible, it didn't hold water. If the federal agents were really working a case, why could they not share even the most basic details of it with local law enforcement?

And their demeanor was particularly perplexing. Their FBI ID's were legitimate. Mike had scrutinized them closely and had made a quick call down to the Portland field office after this morning's confrontation. But the behavior of Ferriss and Cooper was unlike that of any federal agents he had ever encountered in nearly eighteen years of law enforcement. FBI field agents tended to be buttoned-down, terse and overbearingly polite.

The exact opposite of Ferriss and Cooper, in other words.

Mike wished now he had had more time to question the Portland SAC, but he knew he would likely not have coaxed any significant information out of the man. They were Feds and he was not, and that was a line of demarcation that was rarely breached, especially where small-town police officers were concerned.

He sighed and took one last look around Bronson Choate's living room, then walked outside to re-examine the exterior of the property, where his friend and fellow cop Pete Kendall had been murdered.

Glancing at his watch, Mike did a double-take. He had been inside the little cabin much longer than he had planned to be. There was still a little time to do a walk-through of the spot where he had stumbled over Pete's body in the predawn darkness roughly twelve hours ago, but then he would have to hurry back to the station.

Choate's girlfriend, Jodie Miller, was due at three p.m. for a second, more in-depth interview, one that Mike intended to conduct himself. She was the only person he knew of who had come face-to-face with the killer and lived. She was lucky to have escaped, and he was determined to go over every second of the encounter in the hopes of uncovering some piece of evidence, some hidden memory, that would help bring the murderer to justice.

Pete Kendall had been his friend. His memory demanded it.

20

Rose wasn't surprised when the telephone began ringing again. She had been expecting it to. Annette Middleton, her young assistant at *Needful Things*, was a natural caregiver, the type of person who, upon encountering a baby bird with an injured wing, would nurse the thing back to health and then release it back into the wild weeks later.

There was zero possibility that Annette would let the issue drop when Rose didn't answer the phone the first time. Annette would allow a reasonable amount of time for Rose to get her message and return the call, and if that didn't happen, she would try again. If a second call was unsuccessful, she would probably close the shop and drive out to Rose's home herself.

And that was something Rose was determined to avoid.

Her attacker had calmed somewhat, but the shrill jangle of the telephone's ringer caused him to stiffen in his chair and again look around the kitchen in a near panic. After a moment, he seemed to recognize the ringer as the noise he had heard before, and he turned his attention to Rose, eyes narrowed, waiting for her to make a move.

"All I have to do," she said gently, "is answer the phone and get rid of the caller," knowing full well who would be on the line. "But if I don't pick up, whoever is calling might get concerned that I'm not answering. That person might then come over to check on me. I assume you wouldn't want that."

"No visitors," he said tersely.

By now the phone had rung four times. Rose's answering machine was set to pick up after three rings, but the machine had been smashed into several plastic pieces by the stranger's gun. Rose assumed her young assistant would be well aware of the setting for her answering machine – she had called Rose at home many times – and when it didn't activate, she knew Annette would become even more concerned than she already was.

"Alright," the stranger finally said with obvious reluctance. "Do what you have to do. But don't be stupid."

Rose, who had moved next to the phone, picked up the handset immediately. "Hello," she said, doing her best to sound unafraid, certain she wouldn't be able to manage it.

"Oh, Rose, hello," came the reply, in Annette's sweetly innocent voice. "You had me worried! I called a little while ago and your machine seemed to malfunction in the middle of my message."

"Yes," Rose said, eying the stranger, who had gotten up from the table and now stood next to Rose watching her closely. He glanced nervously at the telephone handset every few seconds. The man was jumpy and scared and Rose knew she had to allay Annette's fears and get her off the line as quickly as possible.

"I'm sorry about that," she said into the phone, wishing she were a better liar. Her brother Bo could make up whoppers with the best of them, and then deliver the lies with the sincerity of an altar boy, but that skill was one she had never mastered.

"Uhh…my machine died, I just noticed it. I'm not feeling well, so I decided not to come into the shop today. I apologize for not calling," she continued, knowing she was beginning to ramble. She was rattled worse than she wanted to admit by the dangerous man standing next to her and she hoped that fear wasn't apparent to Annette. "Just go ahead and close up the shop whenever you're ready to go home, and don't worry about it. We'll pick up our regular hours again tomorrow."

There was a long pause, and the stranger moved closer to her. He was now standing right next to her, towering over her, his presence intimidating. She concentrated on not retching from the awful stench rolling off him. After what felt like forever, Annette said, "Ooookay. Are you sure you're alright, Rose? I can be over there in fifteen minutes if you need me."

"NO," Rose replied without thinking. It came out much louder and sharper than she intended, and even the stranger flinched in surprise. "I mean, thank you, Annette, but I'm just a little tired today, that's all. I'm perfectly fine. It's not necessary to drive all the way over here. In fact, I'd rather not entertain visitors today."

Annette sighed and the stranger glowered. It was clear he had exhausted his patience with this one-way conversation that he obviously did not understand. Rose guessed he was seconds away from striking out with his pistol, with the horrible dried blood and clump of hair, and either hitting her with it or smashing the telephone. "I've really got to go now," she said hurriedly. "Goodbye, Annette."

She turned and replaced the handset on its cradle without waiting for an answer. She hoped she had been able to deflect the young woman's concern sufficiently that Annette didn't come running over here. Given her skyrocketing level of fear, she thought she had done a pretty darned good job of sounding calm and collected.

She took a moment to compose herself, then turned and faced the stranger, who had blessedly moved a few steps away. She wondered what would happen now. She didn't have to wait long. The man eyed her warily and, after a moment's hesitation, said, "Why'd you ask me about the date earlier?"

Rose's fear spiked and she froze in her tracks. "Uh, I couldn't remember, that's all. You'll find as you start to age that keeping track of things like the day of the week becomes much more difficult, and even what month it is becomes hazy, and…" Rose knew she was babbling and gradually her voice faded away to silence.

The stranger's eyes narrowed. "I ain't talkin' about the day of the week, I'm talking about the year. Even folks who're a little slow know what year it is. Why'd you ask about the year?"

The man had taken two shuffling steps toward her as he talked and now stood inches away again, glaring down at her like an angry teacher at a truculent student. "Why the year?" he repeated. "Answer me!"

"I…uh…" Rose tried to think, to come up with some way to deflect the man's suspicions. Why hadn't she let the issue drop? The stranger's face began to redden and she felt he was moments away from snapping.

So she told him the truth.

"You're unfamiliar with telephones, and answering machines, and electric coffeemakers. Your whole manner of speech strikes me as that of someone from...I don't know...a bygone era or something. I was just curious, I guess. I'm sorry, I wasn't trying to pry or to upset you."

"Upset me?" The man seemed genuinely taken aback by her statement, but the redness had faded from his face and his eyes didn't look quite so tight. He appeared to be breathing a little easier. "*You* didn't want to upset me? Everything I've encountered in this damned town has upset me since the minute I rode in here last night, or last week, or whenever the hell it was."

Rode in here? That's an odd way to put it, Rose thought, *and exactly what I'm talking about.* She debated whether to bring it up to the stranger, but before she could open her mouth, he surprised her. He said, "Okay, ma'am, I'm going to ask you the same question you put to me. What year is this?" He said it slowly and in a tone that indicated he would accept no waffling.

Rose's first thought was to pacify him, to lie and tell him it really was 1858, of course it was, what other year would it be? But she abandoned the idea immediately because she doubted she could pull it off. If her face, the tone of her voice, or anything in her demeanor gave away the fact that she wasn't being truthful, she was afraid of how he might react.

She reached up and ran her fingers over her bruised and swollen jawline and then answered, her voice quiet but direct. "It's 2013."

The redness returned to the stranger's face, and his eyes, instead of narrowing as they had done before, grew wide with terror. She tried not to react to the massive explosion she feared was to come, but couldn't help herself. She cringed.

But the stranger didn't hit her.

For a moment he didn't do anything.

He stood before Rose, his expression haunted. Then he backpedaled, keeping his frightened eyes locked onto Rose's. He shuffled backward until striking the kitchen wall hard enough to jar his entire body.

He gave Rose one last confused glare, then turned and sprinted out of the house. The back door creaked open and then slammed shut and Rose could hear the heavy pounding of running feet. After a moment the pounding faded away, and silence rushed in to take its place.

21

Gordie Rheaume had been the Paskagankee Police Department's day shift dispatcher for decades. He often worked the night and weekend shifts as well. Gordie had been on the job longer than any other member of the department, and at the age of seventy-two, with a wife lost to cancer more than a decade before and two grown children who had long since moved away, he had let it be known he was more than happy to work as many hours at the station as permitted.

Gordie liked to think of himself as inquisitive. He knew most everyone else would probably substitute the term "nosy," but he didn't allow that knowledge to bother him much. In a tiny, out-of-the-way village hard by the Canadian border where residents relied on one another to an extent unheard of in most other places, it was only natural for folks to take a healthy interest in the goings-on of their neighbors.

That was Gordie's theory, anyway, and in his case, without much else to do, it seemed only natural to expand on that "healthy interest" a little. He knew which residents were having marital problems and who had just purchased a new car. He could recite the averages of every member of the Paskagankee PD bowling league, updated weekly. He knew who had been laid off at the struggling paper mill down in Millinocket and who had begun drinking too much of late.

So when the caller ID at the switchboard indicated a call was incoming from *Needful Things,* Gordie knew immediately the voice at the other end of the line would either belong to Rose Pellerin or Annette Middleton. He knew further that Rose had been suffering from respiratory problems recently, and that she feared the onset of lung cancer, which had taken the life of her father many years ago.

He made a mental bet with himself that the caller would be Annette, then he punched the flashing button to activate the circuit. "Paskagankee Police," he said, and congratulated himself when a voice much too young to be Rose Pellerin's answered.

"Yes, hello," the voice said hesitantly. "This is Annette Middleton over at *Needful Things.*"

"Hello, Annette," Gordie said. "How can we help you?" Gordie had dropped candy bars into a young Annette's goodie bag at Halloween for many years and saw no reason to provide cold, impersonal service simply because he represented the police department.

"I...I'm not exactly sure," she said. "I just talked to Rose at home, and I got the definite impression that something was wrong."

"Wrong, how? Did she sound sick?"

"That's the thing, I don't know. She may have been sick, but it sounded more like..."

"Yes?"

"Gordie, I might be crazy, but she sounded terrified, like she was trying to hide how frightened she was, but couldn't quite do it."

"She sounded afraid? Did you ask her what was the matter?"

"She couldn't wait to get me off the phone. Gordie, I hate to ask, but could you..."

"We'll send an officer out there right away," he interrupted. "It's no problem."

"Thank you so much," she said, the relief evident in her voice. "I'm sure I'm just being silly, but something just seemed...wrong."

***

Standard operating procedure in Paskagankee was to have two units patrolling during the day and one at night from Sunday through Thursday. On weekend nights, a second unit would be added. Sharon was working the day shift today with Harley Tanguay, and she had told the other officer when they were coming on duty that she expected to spend the majority of her day in the Route 28 area, specifically in the vicinity of the Ridge Runner. Harley had agreed to cover the remainder of Paskagankee, an area massive in size despite being lightly populated.

Common sense would seem to indicate the killer of Bronson Choate and Pete Kendall was long gone by now, probably halfway to the West Coast, but Sharon wasn't so sure. If he were going to flee, he would have done so after killing Choate, but had apparently chosen to stick around. He had to have been hiding in the thick forest to get the jump on a good cop like Pete Kendall. Who was to say he wasn't doing exactly that now?

The prospect was creepy and frightening, and Sharon wondered if maybe the double murderer was somehow drawn to the area for reasons as yet unknown. Hell, maybe he was a Paskagankee resident, although why anyone would want to kill Bronson Choate and Pete Kendall, two men seemingly with nothing in common, she couldn't imagine.

In any event, the theory was worth pursuing, and she had spent most of her shift cruising Route 28 within a two to three mile radius of the Ridge Runner and criss-crossing the many back roads and fire trails interconnecting the remote area.

So when Gordie's call came in, Sharon responded to it immediately. She had never visited Rose Pellerin's home, but was well familiar with its location. Rose lived only about a mile-and-a-half east of the Ridge Runner, not far from her brother Bo's house.

On Route 28.

The only information Gordie had passed along was that Rose hadn't shown up for work today, and when her young assistant called to check on her, she said Rose had seemed preoccupied and frightened.

Another disturbing incident in roughly the same geographical area as the disappearing body and the two murders.

Sharon goosed the powerful Police Interceptor engine and the cruiser barreled along the mostly deserted road. She would arrive at Rose's home within minutes, and although the nature of the call couldn't have been more routine, she felt a nervous tension begin to fill her gut and unfocused dread begin to worm through her.

She wasn't a friend of Rose, but having grown up in Paskagankee, she had known the woman – at least to smile and wave hello to – for as long as she could remember. Rose was the polar opposite of her brother Bo: where he was suspicious and taciturn, she was open and friendly. With all that had happened recently along this lonely stretch of Route 28, Sharon felt her concern was justified.

She spun the wheel in her hands with practiced ease, whipping around hairpin turns and cresting hills with barely any reduction in speed. After nearly a lifetime spent in the little town, Sharon felt she could probably drive even its most remote roads with her eyes closed.

Another sharp turn and a rare quarter-mile straightaway and Rose Pellerin's saltbox-style home rose in the distance. It was surrounded by a neatly maintained yard, with acres of gently waving field grass beyond, and Paskagankee's ubiquitous massive, hulking forest looming in the distance.

Sharon slowed just enough to make the turn, then accelerated up the long dirt driveway. A rooster tail of dust rose from behind the vehicle, eliminating any possibility of a quiet entrance, but there was no way to avoid alerting potential lawbreakers to her arrival. The only alternative would be to park the cruiser at the end of the driveway and hike the several hundred feet to Rose's front door, but the sick feeling in Sharon's gut was telling her she couldn't afford to waste that much time.

She jerked the cruiser to a stop and leapt out while the car was still rocking on its springs. Jogging up the walkway, she scanned the front of the house, particularly the downstairs windows, looking for any signs of life, but there was nothing. The house stood silent.

She took the steps two at a time, lifting her hand to rap on the door, and was surprised when it swung open before she could knock. In the foyer stood Rose Pellerin, white-faced and shaken but very much alive. "He left maybe ten minutes ago," she said before Sharon could speak.

"Is anyone else here?" she said, placing a hand on the gun holstered at her hip.

"No," Rose answered. "It was just the one man and he's gone. I watched him disappear into the woods the same way he came."

Sharon looked closely at the older woman. A mottled purple bruise had formed on the right side of her face along the jawline. "Are you alright? What happened here, Rose?"

"I'm okay," she said quietly. "I don't know who he was. A man, maybe mid to late thirties, with long stringy hair. And filthy. It was like he hadn't bathed in weeks. He walked out of the woods while I was hanging up my laundry, appeared out of nowhere. He was on me before I even noticed him."

"What did he want?"

"Food," Rose said, surprising Sharon. "He wanted food, said he was ravenously hungry."

"All he wanted was a meal?"

"Apparently," Rose said. "He ate the omelet I made him even though it was burned almost beyond recognition. He had a cup of coffee with it and then just walked out the door."

"Did you recognize him? Maybe seen him around town, or in your shop?"

Rose shook her head firmly. "No. I'm certain I've never seen him before."

"Would you recognize him if you saw him again?"

"Oh, yes. I spent over an hour staring at his face in my kitchen."

Sharon pulled a neatly folded piece of paper out of her breast pocket. Jodie Miller, the girlfriend of the murdered Bronson Choate and the woman who had somehow survived her face-to-face encounter with the killer, had spent the previous evening with a police sketch artist developing an image of the murderer. A copy of the sketch had been handed out to each patrol officer as well as faxed to law enforcement agencies around the state. Sharon smoothed her copy on a nearby table and watched as Rose glanced at it.

She nodded immediately. "That's him."

"Take a good look. Are you sure?" Sharon asked.

"Oh yes, dear, I'm sure. That's the man who was eating at my table not twenty minutes ago."

Sharon pursed her lips and blew out forcefully. "Then you're extremely lucky. We have a witness who watched as this man murdered a Paskagankee resident in his home last night, and he's also the only suspect in last night's murder of Chief Kendall."

Rose gasped and clapped a hand to her mouth. "Pete Kendall is dead?"

"Yes, ma'am, I assumed you would have heard. It's been all over the news, both locally and nationally."

"I haven't turned on the television or the radio today."

"I'm sorry you had to find out like this, Rose. Now, if you'll excuse me for just a moment I'll call an ambulance to transport you to the hospital in Portland."

Rose waved her hand impatiently. "I don't need to go to the hospital," she said. "I'm feeling much stronger already, despite the horrible news about Chief Kendall. A good night's sleep is all I need, and then I'll be right as rain."

Sharon narrowed her eyes and gazed at the older woman closely. Her preference was for Rose Pellerin to get checked out, but she couldn't force the issue if the woman refused. Finally she nodded. "Okay. But listen, it's very important you keep all your doors and windows locked until we catch this guy. And we will get him. He should have run like a rabbit last night, but he's staying right in this area for some reason. And while we don't know what that reason is – yet – it gives us a leg up on locating him."

She refolded the sketch and slid it back into her pocket. "If you see or hear anything suspicious – and I mean anything – call the station and we'll have someone here in minutes." She jotted her number down on a slip of paper and handed it to the woman. "This is my home number. Call it any time you think you need to."

Rose folded the paper and slipped it into a pocket. "In the meantime," Sharon said, "I'm going to call this in. You can expect to see an increased law enforcement presence in the area, as well as searchers canvassing the forest behind your house. Don't be surprised if you see or hear them working later on today, okay?"

"I understand," Rose said. "And I know you're in a hurry. But there's something you need to know about this man."

Sharon waited impatiently. The more time she spent here, the harder it would be to pick up the killer's trail.

"There's something...off...about him, even above and beyond the fact that he's a murderer. When my telephone rang, it was like he had never heard the sound before. He was like a spooked animal. Same thing with my coffeemaker. He was scared to death of the damned thing. My *coffeemaker*," she repeated for emphasis.

Sharon chewed on her lower lip, thinking. "Sounds like maybe he was high on something."

"I don't think so," Rose said. "He was jumpy and nervous and almost as scared as I was, but he wasn't slurring his words and his eyes weren't bloodshot or anything. He stunk to high heaven, but he didn't strike me as being impaired by drugs or alcohol."

"Okay," Sharon said, shrugging. "I admit, that sounds a little odd, but the guy killed two people last night. He's probably not thinking too clearly right now."

Rose said, "You don't know the half of it."

"What do you mean?"

"He thinks it's June, 1858."

"Excuse me?"

"The man thinks we're living more than one hundred-fifty years ago."

Sharon stared at Rose without speaking. She had absolutely no idea what to say.

22

Mike looked at Sharon quizzically. "1858? What are you talking about?"

She smiled at his obvious confusion and the sight dazzled him just as much now, nearly two years into their relationship, as it had the very first time he had experienced it. "That was my reaction, too," she said. "But Rose swears the man who killed Bronson Choate and Pete Kendall thinks we're in the middle of the year 1858."

The couple was finally home. In what had become a nightly ritual, Mike lay on the bed watching Sharon brush her hair before bed. Mike tried to remember the last time he had been this tired and couldn't.

The remainder of the afternoon had been an exercise in frustration. After getting word from Sharon that Rose had positively identified the man who had accosted her in her home as the killer, he had organized a massive search of the woods behind the Pellerin house. Dozens of Paskagankee residents, fearful and angry about the murder of their police chief, had taken part.

As Mike had suspected, the FBI agents, Ferriss and Cooper, must have been hanging around town monitoring their police-band scanner, because they had shown up a few minutes into the search and been pressed into service as well.

Mike had done his best to stay out of the pair's way, not wanting to take the focus off the search for the fugitive by getting into another confrontation. But the feds had – surprisingly – been reasonably cooperative, at least compared to earlier in the day, and Mike was surprised how at-home they seemed in the vast wilderness north of Paskagankee, Maine.

Despite their best efforts, however, the search had turned up nothing, and when the sun disappeared below the horizon and darkness fell shortly thereafter, the search was suspended.

With all that had happened between the attack on Rose and the intense forest search, Sharon had neglected to mention the fugitive's bizarre conviction that he was living more than a century and a half ago to Mike until now. He gazed at her, trying to absorb the information, distracted by the sight of his beautiful fiancé in her short silk nightgown. "1858," he muttered.

"I know what you're thinking," she said, the smile returning.

Mike chuckled. "I imagine you do," he said. "It's the same thing I'm thinking every time I see you in that nightie."

She playfully swatted him on the arm. "I mean I know what you're thinking about the whole 1858 thing."

"Is that so?" he challenged. "Let's find out. Give it your best shot, sweetheart."

She locked eyes with him, smiling playfully but speaking confidently. "You're thinking about the condition of the rotted wooden furniture in that underground room next to the Ridge Runner. You're trying to figure out if there's a connection somehow, if it's possible that furniture has been down there – along with those human remains – for the last one hundred and fifty-five years. That's what you're thinking."

Mike laughed out loud despite his exhaustion and the disappointments of the day. "Why do I ever doubt you?" he asked. "I wish I knew how the hell you do that."

She blew him a raspberry. "You're not that hard to figure out, dude."

"Really?" he countered, reaching out and encircling her waist with his arm. He pulled her down to the bed next to him and she snuggled close. "And what am I thinking now?'

"The same thing I'm thinking."

And then the phone rang.

*   *   *

"I'm so sorry to bother you," the voice on the other end of the line said. "But you said I should call at any time if I remembered something."

"Of course, Rose," Sharon said. "It's not a problem. You're not bothering me at all, I was just...getting ready for bed."

"Oh Lord," the older woman exclaimed. "Just forget I called, and we can talk about this tomorrow."

"No, I insist. It's really no bother. What can I do for you?"

"Well," Rose Pellerin said. "You remember I told you my attacker was convinced the year was 1858?"

"Yes," Sharon said with a chuckle. "That's not something I'm likely to forget."

"Well, as you might imagine, after you left it was all I could think about. Something about his mention of that particular year bothered me. I couldn't quite put my finger on what it was, but it was niggling around in my brain. So I did a little research and I finally figured it out."

"Okay..." Sharon said, waiting for her to continue.

"Well, this isn't the sort of thing we can really do over the phone," Rose said. "I think you might want to come out here and see for yourself."

Sharon thought about Mike's exhaustion, and how she was nearly as tired as he, but when she glanced over at him, he returned her look with an alert stare. "Alright," she said. "We'll be right over."

"Thank you so much," Rose replied. "But I'm not at home. Come see me at *Needful Things.*"

23

The roads of Paskagankee were even quieter than usual at this time of night, and Mike and Sharon made good time getting from Sharon's house on the outskirts of town into the small strip mall housing *Needful Things*. Rose Pellerin's curio shop was located on the south end of the concrete block structure next to a pizza/sub shop that had closed its doors for the evening by the time their car rolled into the lot.

In fact, all of the storefronts were dark with the exception of Rose's. The interior of *Needful Things* was brightly lit, although the proprietor was nowhere to be seen through the plate-glass window.

As they stepped out of the vehicle Sharon murmured, "I hope to hell she didn't leave the place unlocked for us. I told her to be extra careful this afternoon."

They crossed the lot and Mike tried the door, Sharon nodding with satisfaction when it refused to budge. There was no bell, so he rapped his knuckles sharply on the glass, and a moment later Rose came bustling around a corner at the rear of the store. She moved carefully around rows of greeting cards, knickknacks, stuffed animals and scented candles before unlocking the door and throwing it open.

"Thank you so much for coming," she said with a bright smile. "Again, I'm very sorry for calling you at such a late hour."

Mike shook Rose's hand and said, "Put any worries out of your mind. If you've got *any* information that can help us get to the bottom of whatever is going on here, this will be time very well spent, believe me."

Rose's smile flickered uncertainly and she said, "Well, I'm not sure that what I have to show you will be of any use whatsoever. In fact, it might serve to muddy the waters further. But I thought you should see it, anyway, and make up your own minds about what it may or may not mean."

"Fair enough," Mike said. "So, what do you have for us?"

"It's in the back storage room," Rose said, turning toward the rear of the shop and the small doorway she had walked through upon their arrival.

They followed her as she retraced her steps around all of the display merchandise. Sharon said, "Rose, you look so much livelier than when I saw you this afternoon. Are you feeling better?"

"Oh, yes dear, much better. I took a short nap and although I doubted I would be able to fall asleep with the thought of that young man lurking outside my house somewhere, I slept like a baby and when I awoke, I felt like a new woman. Also, the idea that I'm helping in some small way to get to the bottom of this mystery gives me a tremendous boost. I hate feeling helpless, do you know what I mean?"

Sharon smiled and nodded. "I know exactly what you mean. Doing something to fight back is enough to make most crime victims feel immensely better."

By now they had reached the back wall of the shop, where Rose stepped through a small opening leading to a short hallway. At the end of the hallway was another door, which she opened and walked through. Sharon entered behind her, with Mike bringing up the rear.

The storage room was much bigger than Mike would have expected, and more chaotic as well. Sturdy cardboard boxes, some sealed and some opened, were stacked haphazardly in one corner. Mike assumed they were filled with merchandise that had yet to be inventoried and stocked. Shelves lined the walls, mostly covered with delicate-looking collectible figurines. He tried to recall whether he had seen any of the collectibles on the sales floor and could not.

Along the far wall a long table had been set up and was apparently being used as a makeshift workspace. A computer and laser printer held down one end of the table, with boxes of supplies – computer paper, printer ink, toner, etc. – placed on the floor directly beneath. To the left of the office equipment, stacked neatly, lay a small pile of yellowed newspapers.

Rose walked to the newspapers and gestured at them like a television game-show model introducing the prize behind Door Number One.

The papers looked dried-out and brittle, and Mike imagined them breaking apart and turning to dust if they were opened. They were clearly very old, and he glanced between Rose and the newspapers and said, "Okay, I'll bite. What am I looking at?"

"A few years ago," Rose said, "the Portland Public Library was forced to dispose of many older items they had been storing in the basement. The library underwent extensive renovations, and the city fathers determined it would be too expensive to put those items in rented storage for an extended period of time, only to return them to the basement upon the building's reopening."

"So you attended an auction, or something similar, and pur-chased these newspapers," Sharon said, gesturing at the pile on the table.

"Among other things, yes," Rose said, nodding. "I bought decades worth of old *Portland Journal* newspapers, not having any idea what in the world I was going to do with them. I just knew I couldn't sit by and see them thrown into a furnace like common trash."

Mike stroked his chin. "You mean the city was just going to dump all of this? What about the historical value?"

"All of these newspapers have been scanned into the library's computer network," Rose said, "so the information contained in them is readily available to anyone who visits the Portland Public Library. But, still, the thought of these beautiful old relics being disposed of without so much as a second thought was more than I could bear. So I bought them."

Sharon said, "I don't come into *Needful Things* very often, but I'm pretty sure I've never seen any of these items on display in the store. Have you ever tried to sell them?"

The elderly woman shook her head. "These aren't the sorts of things my customers would be interested in. I didn't buy them to resell; it was really more of a sentimental purchase. I had the cartons stacked in here when I bought them, and this is where they've stayed ever since."

"Until now," Mike said.

"Yes, until now," Rose agreed. "I mentioned to Officer Dupont on the phone that the man who attacked me is quite convinced he is living in the year 1858."

Mike nodded. "So she said."

"Well, I've been fascinated with local history for as long as I can remember, which is one reason why I was so reluctant to let those old copies of the *Portland Journal* be destroyed. When my attacker mentioned that particular year, it rang a bell in my head. I seemed to recall that something quite significant had happened in our little town in 1858; I just couldn't put my finger on what it might have been."

"So you came down to your shop and looked it up," Sharon said with a smile.

"Yes," Rose said. "It seemed like the thing to do, wouldn't you agree?"

"Absolutely," Mike said. "And the fact that you called us down here means you found something. What was it?"

Rose picked up the top newspaper and turned it over for their inspection. It didn't break apart and turn to dust as Mike had feared would happen, it simply flattened out on the surface of the table.

A bold banner headline ran in faded black newsprint under the *Portland Journal* logo, proclaiming, PASKAGANKEE TAVERN BURNS TO GROUND. Underneath the headline, in slightly smaller print, a second headline proclaimed, ONE DEAD, TWO MISSING AS AUTHORITIES SEEK ANSWERS.

Mike leaned closer and checked the newspaper's publication date. The print was even more faded than the headline copy, but remained legible: *June 20, 1858.* He shared a glance with Sharon and then turned to Rose. "The Paskagankee Tavern. I don't suppose that would be…"

She began nodding and answered before he could even finish the question. "Yes," she said. "The Paskagankee Tavern was the precursor to the modern-day Ridge Runner, which as you know

186

is now owned by my brother, Bo. The structure that burned to the ground in 1858 was eventually rebuilt using the existing granite-block foundation, which survived the fire with virtually no damage.

"Now," she continued, "I'm going to go make you folks a cup of tea. You read the story and I'll be back in a few minutes." She turned and retraced her steps out of the storage room.

Mike and Sharon leaned over the table, moving in almost perfect synchronization, straining to read the story:

In an intense blaze, thus far of unknown origin, the Paskagankee Tavern burned to the ground sometime in the overnight hours of June 18-19. Nothing but smoking embers remain of the popular drinking establishment, the only one located in this isolated village just south of the Canadian border.

A search of the ruined tavern – delayed for nearly a full day as investigators were forced to wait for the embers to cool enough to enter – revealed the remains of a single victim, whose body was found in the basement and is believed to be the building's owner, Lucas Crosby, age 33.

Still missing are Crosby's wife, Sarah, age 28, and liquor distributor Matthew Fulton, age 39. Authorities have thus far refused to speculate on the cause of the blaze, and have as well refused to rule out the possibility of foul play in the death of Mr. Crosby.

Anyone with information regarding the Paskagankee Tavern fire, or the whereabouts of Mr. Fulton and Mrs. Crosby, is strongly encouraged to contact the Sheriff's Department at the earliest possible convenience. More details as they become available.

Mike picked up the paper gingerly and turned the page, looking for any related stories, but found none. He stood up straight, stretching his back, and ran a hand through his hair absently. He could feel Sharon staring at him with those laser-beam eyes, and she said, "Well? What are you thinking?"

"I'm thinking about coincidences," he said, "and how little stock I put in them. We have a bizarre underground room uncovered next to the Ridge Runner, where two sets of human remains are uncovered. We have the guy who dug up the room swearing there was a third body present, a body that up and disappeared into thin air when no one was looking.

"Then we have a stranger who shows up out of nowhere and brutally murders two people, one of them an experienced law enforcement professional. We have the same stranger assaulting an elderly woman the following day and then disappearing again, but not before making wild statements about the year being 1858.

"Now we have newspaper evidence of a horrific tragedy – and possibly a criminal event – *that took place in exactly that year*.

"What am I thinking? I'm thinking that every one of these events revolves around the Ridge Runner. I just can't put together how."

The clanking of ceramic cups signaled Rose Pellerin's return. She stepped expertly around the boxes of paraphernalia, handing Mike and Sharon each a steaming mug, then said, "Quite a story, isn't it?"

"It certainly is," Mike agreed. "Timely, too, given the discovery Dan Melton made next to the Ridge Runner yesterday morning. Any idea how it ended?"

"There are follow-up stories in a few issues of the *Journal* over the next several weeks. I've placed them all in the pile next to my computer," Rose said, nodding at the small stack of equally yellowed newspapers. "Feel free to peruse them at your leisure. But according to the paper there was never any solid evidence uncovered that would explain what really happened in the Paskagankee Tavern that night. The liquor distributor's delivery wagon was discovered hidden in the forest the next day, horse and all.

"No trace of the distributor, Matt Fulton, was ever found, nor of the tavern-owner's wife, Sarah Crosby. The prevailing theory at the time seemed to be that Fulton and Sarah Crosby had been having an affair, and that the pair murdered Lucas Crosby, then set fire to the tavern to cover their tracks. After that they rode off into the sunset together."

Mike thought about it for a moment, then shrugged. "Makes sense," he said.

"There was only one problem with that theory," Rose said. "Sarah Crosby's sister Emma said she would swear on the bible that Sarah had never met Matt Fulton and certainly hadn't been having any affair. She claimed, in a *Journal* interview conducted a few months later, that she was as close to her sister as was humanly possible, and there was no way Sarah could have carried on an illicit affair without her knowledge. She claimed Sarah was utterly devoted to her husband, Lucas, and that she would not rest until the story of what really happened to her sister and brother-in-law was brought to light."

Mike glanced at Sharon, one eyebrow raised, and then turned back to Rose. "And?"

"And as far as I know, nothing ever came of it. As I said, no trace of Fulton or of Sarah Crosby was ever found. But Crosby's sister did mention one other thing during her interview that you might be interested in."

Mike nodded and sipped his tea, waiting for the elderly woman to continue.

"Emma claimed Lucas Crosby had been heavily involved in the Underground Railroad movement, the loose affiliation of people sympathetic to the plight of escaping black American slaves that worked to provide shelter for the fleeing escapees as they made their way to Canada and freedom. She said Crosby had modified the tavern somehow, in order to hide escaping slaves, and that she feared some harm had come to her sister and brother-in-law as retaliation for their participation in the Underground Railroad movement."

Mike stopped drinking, his tea lifted hallway to his lips, as he digested Rose Pellerin's statement. He thought about the potential implications of that information from a law enforcement stand-point. Finally he said, "I assume nothing ever came of this claim?"

"Not that I could find," Rose said. "The way the claim was reported leads me to believe even the reporter wasn't taking it seriously. No reference to it was ever made again, at least not in any of the *Portland Journal* articles I found on the subject."

"Hmm," Mike said, finishing his tea and glancing at his watch. It was nearly one a.m., and while he knew he should have been exhausted, he felt wide-awake and invigorated. He smiled at Rose. "I must say you've been extremely busy. Great work digging all of this information up."

"Was it worth getting out of bed and coming over here for?" she asked timidly. Mike couldn't help thinking what a differ-ence there was between this lovely old lady and her unfriendly, obstinate brother.

"Oh, absolutely," he answered. "This is extremely helpful, but I think at this point we should all get home and get some sleep. Daybreak will be here before you know it."

The small group began strolling through *Needful Things*, retracing their steps toward the front entrance and the parking lot. Mike and Sharon saw Rose to her car, the two women chatting comfortably about mutual friends and acquaintances in the tight-knit community.

Mike studied Sharon's face as she interacted with the older woman. She looked engaged and happy, and he thought about how she had lost her own mother at a young age, and how she hadn't had a mother figure since she was twelve years old.

Rose started her car and drove slowly toward the road. They watched as her taillights turned right and disappeared. "She'll be okay at this time of night going home alone, won't she?" Sharon asked anxiously.

"I asked Phil Shankman to spend most of his overnight patrol time on Route 28, concentrating on the area between the Ridge Runner and Rose's home. She's as safe driving home as she would be inside her house with the doors and windows locked," he said confidently.

They slipped into Mike's car and he turned the key, pretending not to notice Sharon eyeing him intensely. When it became clear she had no intention of turning away, he gave in. "Yes?"

"Well?"

"Well, what?"

She spread her hands impatiently. "What do you think about everything that just happened back there?"

"There's one thing I know with complete certainty."

Sharon now rotated her hands in a circular motion, telling him to get on with it, and he grinned. "I can say for sure that Rose Pellerin makes the best cup of tea I've ever had. Man, that was good!"

He ducked, laughing, as Sharon tossed a backhand his way and said, "You know what I mean."

Mike eased down on the gas and watched the pavement roll beneath the car. There was no moon and the night was as black as coal. "I think that underground room dug up by Dan Melton now makes perfect sense, given the story Sarah Crosby's sister told."

"You think Crosby *was* running slaves out of the country?"

"It makes perfect sense, doesn't it? If you're a northern Maine tavern owner and you're smuggling slaves out of the country in the 1850's, you had better have a rock-solid place to hide them, because black faces would stick out like a sore thumb around here. A secret underground bunker would have been fit the bill perfectly."

"But what about the liquor distributor who disappeared along with Sarah Crosby?"

"Think about it," Mike said, working it through in his head. "The distributor was probably involved. What better way to sneak the slaves into Paskagankee than in a beer wagon? Nobody would have paid any attention to the thing, and a regular delivery schedule would have given them plenty of opportunities to smuggle freedom seekers into and then through the town."

"So you think it's possible someone discovered the whole thing and killed Crosby in retaliation?"

"Again, it makes sense, don't you think? Especially given the fact that two sets of human remains were discovered inside the room. The murderer locks Fulton and Crosby's wife in the underground room, then kills Crosby. The room's a well-guarded secret, so Sarah Crosby and Matt Fulton slowly starve to death, dying in agony right under the noses of a whole town full of people searching for them."

"But why not just lock Crosby in the secret room as well?"

"Who knows? Maybe he put up a fight and was killed before he could be herded inside the room. The theory's not perfect, I'll admit, but it fits the evidence pretty well."

Sharon was quiet as she considered the possibility. "What a horrible way to go," she said, her voice a whisper.

Mike nodded. "There's one thing I don't understand, though."

"What's that?"

"What the hell does any of this have to do with a double murder that took place one hundred fifty-five years later?"

24

Jackson rose slowly and brushed the twigs and dirt of the forest floor off his already filthy clothing. He had barely slept overnight. Between his concern about the town organizing a posse to come after the man who had murdered their sheriff, and the fact that even in the summer the temperatures got damned cold at night up here in the North Woods, Jackson had tossed and turned until the first hint of light insinuated itself into the sky. Then he just admitted defeat and got up.

But lack of sleep and deep-forest solitude had given Jackson plenty of time to think, which was something he sorely needed to do. It was also something he had not had much time to do since waking up two days ago at the bottom of that muddy hole.

Something was very wrong; he knew that without a doubt. Jackson Healy was many things, including cold, calculating, disloyal and greedy, but he was not stupid. And the world he had observed since climbing to freedom through the ceiling of that underground room barely resembled the world he knew based upon a lifetime of experience.

He had sprinted out of the old lady's house yesterday afternoon with no plan and no destination in mind. He just ran, leaving the house in a panic after the lady's two simple words – "It's 2013" – simultaneously confirmed his worst fears and sent a chill of terror shooting through his body like a lightning bolt striking the Texas plains.

Nothing he had seen of this cursed town since awakening the

day before yesterday resembled the tiny village he had ridden into in a desperate attempt to flee to Canada ahead of the pursuing Krupp brothers. The bizarre self-propelled buggies everyone seemed to ride around in, the strange-looking clothing everyone seemed to wear, all of the impossible, futuristic gadgets inside the old lady's home yesterday, all of it indicated to Jackson a shift in reality that he could not explain.

Was it possible the old spinster was telling the truth? Could the year really be 2013? Could Jackson have somehow survived more than one hundred fifty years trapped in that underground hellhole, his unconscious body hanging in some unexplained state of suspended animation, not alive but not dead either, while the two corpses trapped down there with him slowly rotted away to nothing more than bare bones?

Was any of that really possible?

He thought about the things he had witnessed in Peru, in the Valley of the Spirits, spying on the shaman priests during their otherworldly middle-of-the-night ceremony. He thought about Puerto de Hayu Marka, the Gate of the Gods, and about the alien-looking figure dressed in flowing robes that had materialized through the door carved out of solid stone, and about the gel-like liquid Jackson had brought back from South America that was supposed to make a man live forever but that he was too fearful to drink.

Then he thought back to the moment he had, in sheer desperation, unable to come up with a single alternative, poured the bitter-tasting liquid down his throat, convinced he was facing a long, slow death of starvation and dehydration.

He tried to recall what had happened after swallowing the liquid and realized he could not; at least not with any degree of accuracy. He had a hazy recollection of stumbling around the chamber, a single flickering candle throwing terrifying shadows on the wall, capering monsters and misshapen alien beings.

He remembered being tired, so tired.

And then he had gone to sleep, only to be aroused from his unnatural slumber by the cold slanting rain pelting his naked body. He had been clothed when he went to sleep, he was certain of that much. Would clothing rot away in a damp underground room over the course of a century and a half? Jackson didn't know for sure but he guessed that, yes, it probably would.

That was what clinched it for him: waking up without a stitch of clothing on his body to find himself in an almost totally unrecognizable world.

As hard as it seemed to be to believe, Jackson Healy decided the most likely explanation for the confusing events that had befallen him was that the years was, in fact, 2013.

And as utterly horrifying as that conclusion seemed, as impossible as it was to believe, Jackson knew that if it was true, he could adjust. He was nothing if not flexible. It wouldn't be easy; he would need time, and probably help, and *definitely* money, and while he had no idea how he would manage the first two items on that list, he knew exactly where he would find the money: the solid-gold disk that no one else in the world knew about was still sitting somewhere down in that hellish underground prison.

He simply had to work up the courage to descend into the death chamber one last time and search until he uncovered the disk. Then he would have all the money he would ever need. He knew he could do it, too. When cash was involved, Jackson Healy was capable of just about anything. He had proven that many times over.

Now that he had developed the beginnings of a plan, Jackson found himself getting excited. His exhaustion melted away, and even his fear began to recede. He continued strategizing. Once he had the disk in his possession, he would turn his attention to leaving Paskagankee behind forever and finally – a century and a half later – slipping across the border into Canada. He would sell the disk and then settle down in some tiny, isolated village not unlike this one.

Now that he really stopped and thought about it, there was one very distinct advantage to waking up in the year 2013 as opposed to 1858: he would finally be free of the damned Krupp brothers, who must have died off and been shoveled into their graves at least a hundred years ago. No Krupps meant his days of endless running were finally over.

Jackson leaned against a tree and allowed himself the luxury of a momentary smile. His plan to escape the dogged pair of brothers, who chased him for years and across two continents, had worked! Not in the way he had expected it to, of course – it had taken far too long and involved untold misery – but still, he was finally free of his pursuers.

Now he just needed to locate that disk and slip out of town.

25

FBI Special Agent Ward Cooper munched methodically on potato chips, one after the other, working his way through the bag. Alton Ferriss knew his partner wouldn't stop until he had pulverized every last chip, and it was driving him crazy. Crunch, crunch, crunch, swallow. Wipe hands on seat. Reach into bag and begin again.

Cooper was bored and impatient, and Ferriss knew it was impossible to try to have a conversation with the man when he was in such a black mood. So he sat across the front seat quietly, idly picking his teeth with a well-worn toothpick and keeping a close eye on the construction site behind the Ridge Runner, glancing over every few seconds to see if there was any activity, then looking away.

Cooper's gaze, however, was focused on the site like a laser beam. An ant wouldn't be able to climb out of the hole without Ward Cooper spotting it. He stared through the windshield with the single-minded intensity of a peeping tom with his face pressed against a pretty girl's bedroom window.

The pair had parked diagonally across from the Ridge Runner, and as far down the road as was possible without losing sight of the stakeout area. The agents had left the black bureau Suburban in the lot at their Portland hotel, reasoning it was a little too conspicuous, and instead had rented the most invisible car they could find under short notice: a white, late-model Honda Civic.

Cooper, predictably, had disagreed with the decision, arguing that they had no idea how long the stakeout would last and that the Suburban would be a hell of a lot more comfortable than a tiny econobox car.

Ferriss didn't care. He didn't think Jackson Healy would notice the black Suburban with the smoked windows – a vehicle that practically screamed "U.S. Government" to most people – any more than any other vehicle, given how terrified and confused he must be by now, but there was no reason to take chances when they were this close to achieving their goal. So on the off chance Healy *would* get spooked by the big SUV, he had overruled his partner and insisted on the rental.

Cooper had pissed and moaned and grumbled – had been himself, in other words – and finally dropped the subject after being steadfastly ignored by Ferriss.

Funny thing is, Ferriss thought, *he's right. This damned clown car is about as comfortable as an amusement park roller coaster.* His back was stiff, his ass hurt, and every so often his right leg would cramp up, sending shooting pains through his calf and halfway up the back of his thigh. He refused to give Cooper the satisfaction of hearing him complain, though, or even of opening the door and stepping out to stretch his legs unless he had to take a leak.

Ferriss glanced around the interior of the car as if he hadn't already done so a hundred times before looking over at Cooper. He expected to see the same thing he had been forced to look at all day: the constant chewing of chips and the repetitive motion of hand into bag and then up to mouth.

But this time, when Ferriss gazed dully across the front seat, Special Agent Cooper was sitting bolt upright with his nose pressed almost into the windshield. The nearly empty bag of chips sat forgotten in his lap. He said, "Hooooly shit, there he is," his voice tinged with a note of awe and perhaps even a little trepidation as well.

Ferriss' gaze lingered for another split-second on his partner. To say he was surprised would be a gross understatement. Ward Cooper was a hard man, stoic, not given to displays of fear.

After a moment he followed Cooper's sightline and immediately spotted a man with long, scraggly hair dressed in filthy clothing slipping hesitantly out of the thick underbrush behind the Ridge Runner. The man walked five feet into the open field and then stopped, as if only now realizing how exposed he was. He looked around wildly, his head on a swivel, and then continued, ducking under the yellow crime scene tape ringing the construction and walking swiftly toward the big hole in the ground.

The figure was too far away to tell with the naked eye whether it was actually Healy, but Ferriss had no real doubts as to the man's identity. Just to be sure, he reached into the back seat for a pair of binoculars and raised them to his eyes, spinning the wheel between the two eyepieces to bring the image into focus.

His breath caught in his throat. It was Jackson Healy.

Cooper had already exited the car, closing the door gently to avoid alerting their quarry to their presence, although Ferriss doubted Healy would have heard the sound from this distance. Even if he did, it seemed unlikely he would understand its significance.

Nevertheless, as he climbed out of the Honda, Alton Ferriss took the extra second to ease his own door closed quietly. Then he hurried across the empty road and trotted after his partner, who was already advancing stealthily toward the filthy man, gun drawn.

26

Sharon Dupont was operating on autopilot mode as she drove her cruiser toward the Ridge Runner, lost in thought, navigating mostly by reflex on the quiet roads.

Her assignment was to remove the police crime scene tape from around the construction pit and the underground room. She had already notified Bo Pellerin that he would be free to resume construction of his new septic system by this afternoon, and the news had been greeted by the taciturn businessman with what Sharon thought was probably as chipper a response as he had ever uttered. "'Bout time," he growled. "Gotta go," he continued before she could say another word. "I need to get that lazy bastard Melton on the line and tell him to get over here and finish the goddamn job." He had hung up without another word.

Sharon couldn't contain her uneasiness, or her sense that something was wrong. She was certain it was too soon to allow the room to be filled in as part of the construction job.

The human remains had long since been removed for analysis, the scene had been thoroughly photographed, and she had dug through the small room with her own hands. It was empty. The only item of value seemed to have been the strange golden disk, now tagged and sitting in the police station's evidence room.

Everything else at the bottom of that hellhole while Sharon conducted her search yesterday had been pulled out and carted away earlier by Harley Tanguay. There was a table, a couple of chairs, and something that looked as though it may have been a rudimentary bed frame. All of the wooden artifacts were rotted almost entirely away and would provide little evidentiary value.

So Sharon understood Mike's decision. Bo Pellerin was dependent upon the income derived from the Ridge Runner for his livelihood – not to mention the fact that the bar represented Paskagankee's only claim to night life – and it could be financially devastating to delay the resumption of business without good reason.

But, still, the nagging sense of unease she had been feeling since before calling Bo refused to diminish. She tried to convince herself she was just being silly, that she was imagining problems where none existed, but the effort went nowhere. Alone in the cruiser, she shrugged and muttered, "Something's not right."

The Ridge Runner came into view in the distance, the bar set off to the right and about two-thirds of the way along the Route 28 straightaway. The parking lot was empty. Not even Bo had arrived yet. She pictured him haranguing poor Dan Melton about getting his "lazy ass" out here to finish the job that had been interrupted and couldn't help smiling.

Then her attention was drawn by a sense of movement, more felt than seen, in the open field behind the bar. She took her foot off the accelerator and the cruiser began to slow as she squinted to get a closer look.

Next to the open pit containing the underground room stood a man. Approaching from behind, as-yet unseen, were two other men. Even from this distance, highlighted against the bright yellow bulk of the still-parked Caterpillar earthmover, Sharon could tell right away that two of them were the FBI agents who had spent most of yesterday morning leering at her while she dug through the remains of the pit.

The first person, she had no doubt, was the double-murder suspect.

The suspect was peering intently into the pit as the two Feds stalked him quietly, guns drawn, making no move to alert him – yet – to their presence.

Sharon's uneasiness intensified and she punched the gas. The cruiser responded immediately, leaping forward toward the parking lot. She wheeled in without braking and moved to the front of the bar before pulling to a stop and killing the engine. The Ridge Runner stood between Sharon's car and the three men behind it and she hoped the building's bulk had served to shield the suspect from the sound of her car's approach.

She leapt out of the vehicle and hurried to the corner of the building, drawing her weapon.

She eased her head around the corner and was surprised to see the agents had yet to place the suspect under arrest. They had by now positioned themselves directly behind the man, who looked as though he hadn't bathed in weeks. *What the hell are they waiting for?*

She watched in astonishment as Special Agent Cooper drew his weapon to eye level and held it in a two-handed grip aimed at the back of the suspect's head. Then Cooper said, "Turn around, Healy," his voice gruff and filled with malice.

The suspect froze, his attention still directed at the bottom of the hole. He hesitated for a moment as if considering his options, then seemed to realize he didn't have any. He turned slowly to face the agents.

For a moment nothing happened and Sharon waited, wondering why the agents weren't placing the man under arrest. Abruptly the suspect's eyes widened, staring incredulously at the two law enforcement officials. His jaw dropped and he gasped and took one quick step backward, nearly tumbling into the pit, before stammering, "It...it...it's you. But it can't be, you're..."

"Dead?" Cooper said helpfully. Sharon could see his eyes glittering dangerously even from her position more than ten feet away.

"It's impossible," the suspect muttered. He was now breathing heavily and appeared to be on the verge of collapse. "You should be long dead."

Sharon furrowed her brow, unable to understand what that was supposed to mean, but aware things were going south quickly. "Well, guess again," Cooper spat. "You're not the only one to benefit from that funky Peruvian life-juice."

The suspect shook his head in disbelief.

"Now," Cooper continued, taking one step forward and placing his gun to the side of the man's head. "Get on your knees."

The suspect hesitated. Then, with obvious reluctance, he did as he was told, dropping to a kneeling position in the weedy grass. His entire body was shaking with barely controlled terror.

For maybe two seconds Sharon froze, unable to comprehend the scene playing out in front of her. These FBI agents weren't going to arrest the man at all; they intended to execute him in cold blood.

Ferriss took up a position next to Cooper, his gun trained on the kneeling suspect. Cooper had removed his weapon while the suspect dropped to the ground, and now he replaced it against the side of the man's head. In a low voice, he said to his partner, "You don't mind if I do the honors, do ya?"

Ferriss said nothing. He simply stared at the suspect with cold, dead shark eyes. More than anything else, the look on Ferriss's face was what forced Sharon out of her shocked inaction. She took a deep breath and stepped out from behind the Ridge Runner, lifting her service pistol to eye level and training it directly on Special Agent Ward Cooper.

"Stop right there," she said sharply. "Pull that trigger and you'll die less than a second later." Her nerves were thrumming and adrenaline was pumping madly through her body, yet her voice stayed strong and calm and her aim never wavered.

Time stopped and for what felt like an eternity nothing happened. Ferriss's shoulders slumped and he lowered his weapon, and then a moment later Cooper followed suit. He turned to face Sharon. His eyes were blank and cold. "Have it your way," he said quietly. "You're just delaying the inevitable."

"What the hell is wrong with you two?" she said in bewilderment. "You were about to murder a man in cold blood!"

Agent Ferriss glanced from Sharon to his partner and then back again. An oily smile slid across his face, but his eyes looked no less dead. "You've got it all wrong," he drawled, the unmistakable hint of a Southern upbringing coming out from the stress. "We wasn't gonna murder nobody, we was just subduing the suspect, weren't we, Agent Cooper?"

Cooper never took his eyes off Sharon's, the hatred undisguised on his face. "That's right," he finally agreed. "Subduing the suspect."

"Good thing you came along when you did," Ferriss continued. "You can help us take this man into custody."

Sharon hesitated, her gun still trained on Ward Cooper. She

knew what she had witnessed, and it wasn't a pending arrest, it was a pending execution. At Cooper's feet, the suspect started babbling, "Get them away from me, get 'em away, they're gonna kill me!"

"Shut your mouth right now," Cooper muttered angrily, prodding the suspect with his shoe, and to Sharon's surprise, the man stopped talking.

The small group eyed each other silently and suspiciously. Sharon had a moment of disbelief at the utter unreality of the situation. She was holding a loaded gun on two federal agents, who she was certain had been about to murder the only suspect in the killings of two Paskagankee residents. What the hell was going on here?

Ferriss took a slow step in Sharon's direction and she immediately turned her weapon toward him. Ferriss had holstered his gun and he raised his hands, palms out, in a gesture of conciliation. He said, "I think there's been a serious misunderstanding here. You seem to have misinterpreted our disarming of the suspect," he pointed to the Colt revolver in the grass next to the still-kneeling man, "as something...sinister."

He smiled. The gesture contained absolutely no warmth and the sight chilled Sharon. "You need to holster that weapon now, officer," he continued, "before something bad happens to you."

"Excuse me?" she said sharply. "Is that a threat?"

"Put your gun away now," Ferriss continued as if she had never spoken, "and you *may* still be able to keep your job. Continue acting in the reckless manner you've displayed here this morning, and not only will you find yourself unemployed, you'll spend the next twenty years in federal prison." His voice was silky-smooth and layered with menace. "I'm sure you're aware it's illegal to interfere with a federal investigation."

"You were going to kill that man," she replied stubbornly. "I know exactly what I saw."

"No one's killing anyone," Ferriss said. "Yet. Everything's under control. In fact, you're the only one I see pointing a loaded gun at someone else." He gestured to Cooper, who holstered his weapon reluctantly, with the look of a man who would rather be eating razor blades.

"I'm taking the suspect to the station," Sharon said after a long pause. She reached down with her left hand and yanked the man to his feet, keeping her weapon trained roughly midway between Agents Ferriss and Cooper with her right. The stench rolling off the suspect's body would normally have made her gag, but right now she barely noticed and didn't care.

She began walking backward, a big wad of her prisoner's shirt clutched tightly in her fist, refusing to turn her back on the two FBI agents. When she felt as though she had put a sufficient distance between herself and the feds, she eased her weapon into its holster and pulled a pair of handcuffs off the utility belt at her waist. She spun the prisoner around, hands behind his back, and deftly snapped the cuffs around his wrists. Then she marched him to her cruiser, keeping a wary eye on Ferriss and Cooper.

Neither agent moved. They stood quietly next to the big hole dug out of the ground, the Caterpillar earthmover looming behind them, staring back at her with undisguised contempt.

27

Mike looked up from his desk as Gordie Rheaume rapped his knuckles once on the open door and then entered. "Sorry to bother you, Chief," he said, "but Officer Dupont just radioed in and…"

Mike shrugged. "Yes?"

"She's got a suspect in custody."

"A suspect for what?"

"The murders, Chief!"

Gordie's face was flushed with excitement, and for a moment Mike had trouble making sense of his statement. "The murders? The Choate and Kendall murders? How is that possible? I sent her out to the Ridge Runner less than an hour ago to pull down the crime scene tape around the construction site. How did she go from that boring chore to arresting a double-murder suspect?"

Gordie shrugged. "I dunno. I asked her the same question, but she said she'd explain it all when she gets here." He looked at his watch. "And that should happen any minute."

"That's fantastic news," Mike said, standing and moving out from behind his desk with a smile.

"Uh, there's something else," Gordie added.

"What is it?"

"She said the FBI guys were there, too, and that there was some kind of trouble."

"What trouble?"

"She wouldn't say, but she wanted me to stress that you shouldn't let them anywhere near the suspect until you talk to her."

Mike ran a hand through his thick black hair. "Don't let them near the suspect? Why not?"

"She wouldn't tell me, Chief, but she was adamant. She made me promise I would come right to your office and tell you. She seems to think the Feebs will be right behind her, and she didn't want them getting to the prisoner before she could pass the message to you."

"Okay," Mike said, nodding. He had no idea what kind of dispute Sharon might have gotten into with Ferriss and Cooper, but her sense of intuition was almost always spot-on. If she thought the agents should be kept away from the prisoner, Mike would do everything in his power to make it happen until he had a chance to talk to her.

He looked up at the ceiling, lost in thought, and said, "Do we have anyone else in holding right now?"

The dispatcher shook his head. "Nope. Lee Evans was locked up overnight on a drunk and disorderly, but we released him this morning after he sobered up and made bail."

"Good. I'm assuming Sharon will bring the suspect in through the back so she can deposit him right into the holding cell, so I'm going to go down there and wait. I want to talk to her the minute she arrives."

* * *

It didn't take long.

Less than two minutes after Mike stepped through the reinforced metal basement door at the rear of the station, Sharon wheeled her cruiser into the small secondary lot. Right behind her, a nondescript two-door Honda sedan sped into the lot, driving much too fast, and slid into a spot next to the police vehicle. Special Agents Ferriss and Cooper were out of the Honda and walking briskly toward Mike before Sharon had even finished removing the prisoner from the cruiser's back seat.

Ferriss looked more or less unruffled, although there was a tightness to his posture that Mike didn't remember seeing before.

Ward Cooper, on the other hand, was plainly furious, his face flushed bright red with percolating anger. Mike felt a momentary pang of sympathy for Sharon having to face down the two federal agents by herself, regardless of the specifics of the confrontation.

"We need to talk," Ferriss said without preamble.

"You're damn right we do," Sharon said, approaching from behind as quickly as she could while still escorting the handcuffed prisoner with one hand on his elbow.

Cooper whirled on her. "You listen here, little Missy, we'll do the talking. You just shut your mouth and stand back." He made as if to pat her on the head.

Anger flashed in Sharon's eyes and she moved quickly at the much bigger man, standing on her tiptoes and getting in his face. For a second Mike thought she was going to take a swing at the agent, and he moved to step in between them. But she merely narrowed her eyes and growled, "Don't you ever talk to me like that again, little man. It would be the biggest mistake of your misogynistic life, and from what I've seen, that's saying something."

To Mike's surprise, Cooper said nothing. Instead, he turned away from her dismissively. Mike took advantage of the momentary lull in the hostilities and said, "Okay, here's what's going to happen. Officer Dupont will process the suspect and get him into a holding cell, and then we'll all meet in my office and hash out the problem."

He turned to Sharon without waiting for an answer from the FBI men. "I assume you read the prisoner his rights?"

She nodded. "I did it on the ride over here. He hasn't said a word since these two geniuses tried to kill him. In fact—"

"—Tried to *what?*" Mike interrupted.

"You heard me, they–"

Chaos erupted again, with both FBI agents talking over the beleaguered officer, who shrugged and spread her hands in a *what can I say?* gesture.

"ENOUGH!" Mike said, his voice not quite a shout but sharp and authoritative. Abruptly, the competing voices stilled and Mike said, "Nobody say another word. We'll talk it all out in my office."

He nodded at the prisoner, who appeared not to be paying the slightest attention to the squabbling taking place around him.

The man's eyes were open wide in fear, and glued to Alton Ferriss and Ward Cooper. It was exactly the sort of reaction Mike would have expected if the two agents actually *had* tried to kill him, although he knew that could not possibly have been the case. He told Sharon, "Take him in and process him. When you're finished, come to my office."

She nodded curtly and pulled the prisoner away without another word. She opened the heavy door and disappeared into the building. For his part, the suspect seemed only too happy to be putting distance between himself and the feds, and once again, Mike felt a sense of disquiet overtake him.

The moment the door slammed behind Sharon and her prisoner, Alton Ferriss said, "While we're waiting for her, Chief, we'll fill you in on what happened out there."

"No you won't," Mike said.

The hostility written all over Cooper's face now showed up in Ferriss's. "What did you say?"

"I said, 'No.' You're not filling me in on anything until Officer Dupont has finished with the suspect and is present in my office as well. She deserves to hear everything you have to say."

Ferriss blew out forcefully in frustration. "I've had about enough of this Podunk little town and this Podunk little police department. We've tried our best to include you in our investigation, and—"

"—Stop right there," Mike interrupted. "I don't want to hear it. You two have done nothing to include my department in your 'investigation.' In fact, you haven't even explained what, exactly, it is you're investigating. So save your self-serving load of bullshit for somebody who's buying. Give me your cell number, and go on down to the Katahdin Diner for a cup of coffee and some blueberry pie. I guarantee both are better than any you've ever tasted. When Officer Dupont's finished booking our suspect, I'll call you boys and you can come on back and we'll clear everything up then."

"Or we can call our SAC," Ferriss answered, "and he can be all over your ass in about three minutes."

"Do what you have to do," Mike shot back, "but do it from the diner, because you can get the goddamned *president* 'all over my ass,' and we're still not talking about a goddamned thing until Dupont's finished with the goddamned suspect!"

Mike knew he had gone overboard with the profanity but he didn't care. In fact, it felt kind of good. Ferriss said, "Lemme guess, while we're having coffee and pie, you'll be getting Officer Cupcake's side of the story, is that about right?"

"That's not even close to being 'about right,'" Mike said. "That's not how I operate. You deserve to hear what Officer Dupont has to say just as much as she deserves to hear your story. I'll say this one last time, since you don't seem to be getting it: I'm not talking to anyone about anything until every interested party is present in my office. You have my word on that."

Ferriss and Cooper stared at him for a moment, then Ferriss reached into an interior suit coat pocket and fished out a pen and a slip of paper. He jotted down a number and handed it to Mike, then turned and stalked back to the Honda. Cooper waited a moment and Mike thought he was going to say something, but then he followed his partner without another word.

As the car backed out of the parking space, Mike called through the open driver's side window, "The cell reception's spotty around here, so if I can't get ahold of you, I'll call the diner's landline and have a message passed to you." The two agents stared back stonily and drove away.

The car pulled around the building and then turned toward Main Street. Mike watched until it had disappeared in the direction of the Katahdin Diner. Once again, he was struck by how little resemblance the pair had to any federal agents he had ever dealt with.

28

Sharon knocked lightly and then slipped into the office, dragging two chairs for the FBI agents behind her as she had done during their first meeting. She rolled the third chair over from the corner and then took a seat in the one closest to the office door.

Mike said with a smile, "Planning a quick getaway?"

Her return smile was tight-lipped and angry. "I don't trust those guys as far as I can throw them. I want to make sure they can't get up and bolt out the door to get at the prisoner."

He gazed at her, recalling her earlier charge that the agents had tried to murder the suspect. She stared back defiantly. "You're serious," he said finally.

"You weren't out there," she said. "You didn't see what I saw. These guys—"

Mike held up a hand. "I told them I'd wait until they get here to discuss what happened out at the Ridge Runner."

Sharon sighed deeply and said, "Fair enough."

"But while we wait, did you get a name on the suspect?"

She shook her head. "He still hasn't said a word, and he had no identification on him. No driver's license, no Social Security card, nothing. In fact, he didn't even have a wallet. And the guy smells like he's been marinating in a pig pen."

"Hmm," Mike said, thinking. "Did he use his phone call to lawyer up?"

Sharon shook her head. "Nope. Like I said, he hasn't said a word to *anyone,* not just me. I offered him his one phone call and he just looked at me like I was crazy. Mike, I think we need to consider the possibility that this guy's mental capacity is diminished. He doesn't strike me as mentally deficient, and when I talked to Rose Pellerin – she spent enough time with him to get a read on him – she didn't give any indication that the guy was anything but sharp. Still, there's something definitely off about him."

"Maybe he's setting up an insanity defense now that he's been apprehended."

She shrugged. "Maybe, but that's not the sense I'm getting. He just seems…I don't know…overwhelmed."

Mike thought it over and finally shook his head. "Maybe we'll learn more when I question him. For now, we need to get this FBI fiasco over with. Did Gordie call Special Agents Tweedle Dee and Tweedle Dum back from the diner?"

"Yep. He made the call a couple of minutes ago, so they should be here any time now."

As if on cue, the two feds stalked through the bullpen toward the office. Mike could see both men eyeing them warily through the glass partition. They entered without knocking, and Ferriss said, "Well, aren't you two all nice and cozy? Who could've predicted this? Oh, that's right, me."

Mike shook his head wearily and said, "I told you we wouldn't discuss the confrontation without you and we haven't. But I'm about out of patience with you two. Why don't you keep your snide remarks to yourselves and sit your asses down so we can talk this thing out."

Ferriss and Cooper sat heavily, and Mike knew he had to take charge of the meeting immediately or it could get out of hand in a heartbeat. He looked at Sharon and said, "Who saw the suspect first?"

She nodded in the general direction of the agents, refusing to look directly at either of them. "They did," she said. "I spotted them moving up behind him as I drove toward the Ridge Runner. Then I lost sight of them behind the building as I parked my cruiser. By the time I got out and walked to the corner of the building, this guy" – another nod in Cooper's direction – "had forced the suspect to his knees and was about to put a bullet in his head."

Both Ferriss and Cooper immediately interrupted, their voices unintelligible as they attempted to talk over each other.

"AGENT FERRISS," Mike said loudly. The men stopped talking and he took advantage of the pause, ignoring Sharon's inflammatory charge for the time being and directing a question to the senior agent. "What in the world made you decide to stake out the Ridge Runner construction site?"

The two agents glanced at each other in unspoken communication. Neither answered.

"Another one of those investigatory issues you can't discuss?" he said drily.

"You guessed it," Ferriss answered, hostility evident in his voice.

Mike sat for a moment. "So, for reasons unknown to me and that you're unwilling to share, you knew the suspect in two murders would show up at the Ridge Runner, and yet you refused to share that information with me or my officers."

A smile flitted across Ferriss's face and disappeared. "I think it's an exaggeration to say we 'knew' the suspect would show up. Let's just say we were playing a hunch."

"A hunch," Mike repeated dubiously. "So, the suspect appeared out of the woods behind the Ridge Runner, I assume…"

"That's right."

"And then you moved to apprehend him."

"That's pretty much the size of it."

"Where was the stakeout location?"

"Down the road a ways, in our rented car."

"Down the road a ways," Mike repeated. "How were you able to get from 'down the road a ways' to the edge of the construction pit without the suspect seeing you?"

Ferriss grinned wolfishly. "We're just that good."

Mike ignored the comment and said thoughtfully, "His attention was directed at the bottom of that hole in the ground, wasn't it?"

"He did seem mighty distracted."

"What was he looking at down there, I wonder?"

"I…"

"I know, you can't say."

Ferriss looked at Mike innocently. "Sorry."

"I'll bet," Mike answered, thinking about the big, heavy circular gold disk currently under lock and key in the evidence room, and how the two agents' interest in it had seemed much more than casual. That disk had been retrieved from the bottom of the pit.

He made a mental note to examine the disk more closely as soon as he could, and then refocused his attention on Agent Ferriss. "You boys showed up in Paskagankee about five minutes after that underground room was dug up a few days ago. In nearly twenty years working law enforcement, I don't think I've ever seen the FBI move so fast on anything so seemingly innocuous as an unexpected hole in the ground."

"So? What's your point?" Ferriss asked.

"My point," Mike said, "is that I don't think you were interested in the secret underground room at all. I think you rushed all the way up here on a moment's notice because you knew the discovery of that room would bring our suspect sniffing around, didn't you?"

Ferriss returned Mike's thoughtful gaze with a wary look. Even Agent Cooper, who had been the epitome of impatience and anger during the entire conference, seemed taken aback. Instead of fury, his face reflected surprise and perhaps even a hint of concern. It was Cooper's that convinced Mike he was on the right track.

He continued, still connecting the dots. "And if that's the case, this unknown suspect we have sitting in a holding cell downstairs, the man without a single identifying document in his wallet – hell, without even a wallet at all – isn't unidentified after all. You know who he is, don't you?"

Ferriss and Cooper shared an alarmed glance. The look was involuntary and gone in an instant, replaced with the men's carefully cultivated hostility, but Mike had seen it as clearly as if they were wearing flashing neon signs on their foreheads. He immediately pressed the issue. "Come on, guys, who is he? This is information critical to a murder investigation. Give it up, or you won't have to call your SAC in Portland. I'll do it, and I'll let him know his agents are actively obstructing my investigation."

He reached for the phone on his desk and let his hand hover over it. "Your choice. What's it going to be?"

The two agents shared another glance and Ferriss spoke to his partner softly. "What difference does it make now? It can't hurt anything."

Cooper glared back before answering reluctantly, "Fine. Go ahead."

Ferriss turned back to Mike. "We know him as Jackson Healy," he said simply. "That's all I can divulge right now, without compromising our own investigation."

The statement was made with a tone of implacable finality, and Mike knew he had gotten all of the information he was going to out of the two very strange FBI agents.

For now.

It was time to get to the heart of the matter. "What do you have to say about Officer Dupont's statement that your partner was about to put a bullet into Mr. Jackson Healy's head when she arrived on the scene?"

Cooper's eyes flashed and he opened his mouth to speak, but before he could, Mike said, "My question's directed at Agent Ferriss. I'd like him to answer it, if you don't mind."

The purple vein in Cooper's forehead started throbbing again and he looked as though he very much *did* mind. In fact, he appeared ready to come across the desk at Mike, which was exactly what Mike wanted. His goal was to push the obviously unstable agent as far as he could with the intention of shaking more information loose. It was becoming crystal clear that the key to unraveling the mystery of the two murders would lie in uncovering exactly why these men were here in Paskagankee.

Agent Ferriss seemed to understand Mike's reasoning, though. Before Cooper could react, he put a hand out in front of his partner in a calming gesture, never taking his eyes off Mike's. To Mike's surprise, the volatile agent clamped his mouth shut in what seemed to take an act of extreme willpower.

After a moment of dead silence, Ferriss said simply, "That's not how it happened."

"My officer is lying, then?"

The used-car-salesman smile returned and then disappeared. "'Lying' is such a harsh word," he said. "Let's just say she didn't see what she thought she saw, and leave it at that."

Sharon snorted. "I didn't see the suspect forced to his knees at the edge of the pit, with Agent Sharpshooter, there, pressing his gun to the side of the man's head?"

Cooper's face flushed redder and the vein in his forehead throbbed away, once again giving Mike the impression the man was moments away from suffering a stroke. Ferriss, however, continued unperturbed. "This person is suspected in two brutal murders, one of a fellow peace officer. Surely you don't think we should have approached him with any less than the full measure of caution?"

"You weren't approaching him with caution," Sharon retorted. "Neither one of you was reaching for cuffs or reading the prisoner his rights. Another three seconds and he would have been executed."

"As I said," Ferriss continued, directing his attention and his comments at Mike. "Your officer is simply mistaken in what she saw. We were, in fact, just about to cuff the prisoner. Her mistake is understandable, though. As so often happens with women, she probably let her nerves get the best of her."

Now Sharon's face flushed red, and she balled her hands into fists in her lap. Before she could interrupt, Mike said, "So that's your story, then. You two, for reasons unknown, staked out the construction site, took advantage of the suspect's mysterious interest in the site to sneak up on him from behind, then disarmed him at gunpoint and were seconds away from placing him under arrest and putting him in handcuffs when Officer Dupont came around the corner and saw him on his knees, execution style."

"I can't think of a better one, can you?"

Mike shook his head. "How long have you two been in law enforcement?"

Ferriss smiled, and even Cooper seemed to lighten up a little. "Longer than you could possibly imagine" Ferriss said glibly.

"What's that supposed to mean?"

Ferriss shrugged. "Nothing. Forget it. Let's just say we've been involved long enough to know how things are done."

"Well," Mike said, stretching. "Apparently we're left with a jurisdictional conflict. The man we have in custody is the prime suspect in two local murders, as you've already noted. Since you won't reveal what crimes you're investigating him for, I'm still going to assume our interest in him trumps yours. Feel free to have your SAC contact me if any of my assumptions are off the mark, but until further notice, that suspect is staying right here under lock and key in Paskagankee. You're not taking him anywhere."

Mike sat back, prepared to weather a storm of protest, but none came. To his surprise, Special Agent Alton Ferriss said quietly, "That's not a problem, Chief. We're not going to bother the head of the Portland office with something we can handle perfectly well ourselves. And there's no need for us to remove the suspect from your custody at all, as long as you're willing to be a little flexible."

Mike rubbed his eyes and yawned. He was still exhausted from his whirlwind return to the Paskagankee Police Department and even though he had slept well last night, that short amount of rest hadn't been enough for him to completely shake the effects of the previous thirty-six hour workday. So he felt tired and slow, but was immediately suspicious of any offer of cooperation served up by these two, who had done nothing but obstruct since their arrival in town. "Flexible, how?"

"I assume you're intention is to interrogate the suspect as soon as possible?"

"Of course. I plan to do so as soon as we're finished here."

"Perfect. Then simply allow us to sit in on the interrogation and ask a few questions ourselves. We have no problem meshing our investigation with yours. Once we get the answers we're looking for, I promise you we'll go away and won't bother you again."

Mike looked between Ferriss and Cooper, suspicious of their motives but unable to think of any reason to deny their request. Finally he shrugged. "Okay, I don't think that will be a problem."

Sharon shot to her feet. "Did you not hear anything I said? You can't let these two anywhere near that man. You certainly can't allow them to take part in the interrogation!" Now her face was flushed in anger while the two FBI men sat quietly.

"That's enough," Mike said sharply. "Sit down!"

He waited until she had grudgingly slumped back into her seat and then told Ferriss and Cooper, "If you don't mind waiting outside for a moment, I'd like a word with my officer in private. As soon as we're done here, I'll have Mr. Healy taken to the interrogation room and you can join me there."

"Of course," Ferriss said, a look of smug satisfaction on his face. Cooper still looked pissed off. Mike was beginning to assume it was his default expression. The FBI agents stood and exited the office, pulling the door closed behind them.

"For the record," Mike said, keeping his voice level, "I didn't miss anything you said about those two, but we can't shut out another law enforcement agency – especially the FBI – just because you don't like the way they handled themselves during an arrest."

"I'm telling you, this isn't about how they 'handled themselves during an arrest.' They were about to execute him."

"Would you stake your career on that? Because that kind of explosive accusation, made without a shred of evidence, would be enough to end your career right where you are. You *might* be able to keep your job, but all you'll ever be is a patrol officer in Paskagankee, Maine. The FBI has the kind of political influence and pull – within state governments and even inside small town administrations, if they want to exercise it – to ensure you never move up or out of your current position. I've seen it happen before, and I don't want to see it happen to you. You're too good a cop for that."

"The charge isn't being made without a shred of evidence," Sharon said stubbornly, a grim set to her lips. *"I know what I saw."*

"I'm not questioning what you saw. All I'm saying is you can't *prove* what you saw, and if we can get rid of these two jokers simply by letting them sit in on one interrogation session, why not take advantage of that opportunity? They ask a few questions and then they leave. We've got nothing to lose, especially when you consider the trouble they could cause if we shut them out."

"Trouble? They already said they weren't going to involve their SAC down in Portland. And, besides, they can't just yank that guy away from us just to get even if we piss them off."

"Oh no? The federal government can do whatever they want. We have no clue what they're investigating this guy for, but the fact they've been staking out the Ridge Runner with a two-man team means they want him pretty badly. There's no reason to risk losing our prime suspect to the feds when keeping him here is so easy to do."

Sharon looked down at the floor, her lips set in a thin line. Mike could see she was struggling to control her emotions. She raised her head and looked into his eyes. "You're making a mistake.

I can feel it. Don't try to tell me you can't feel it, too."

"Maybe. But my mind's made up. I'm going to get downstairs and get this over with so we can send those two loose cannons back to Portland. You go back out on patrol, and I'll fill you in on the details of the interrogation tonight at home. Deal?"

Sharon shook her head silently, and Mike thought for a moment she was going to continue arguing. But she didn't. She stood and said, "Good luck," tightly, and walked out of the office.

He watched through the glass as she crossed the big open room, moving around desks and chairs, and exited the front door. She refused to acknowledge or even look at the two FBI agents, who were leaning against an unoccupied desk as they waited for Mike.

Mike looked at the clock on the wall and then buzzed Gordie, who was sitting at the dispatch desk glancing between the loitering FBI agents and the retreating form of Sharon Dupont, still visible as she crossed the parking lot to her cruiser. He looked like a man watching a ping-pong volley. When his console buzzed be pushed a button and said, "Dispatch."

"Hey, Gordie," Mike said. "Has Phil gone out on patrol yet?" It was the beginning of Phil Shankman's evening shift.

"I don't think so," Gordie said. "Last I knew he was still reviewing the day shift log."

"Good. Get ahold of him and ask him to escort the suspect in holding into the interrogation room and secure him in preparation for questioning." Then he replaced the phone and walked out of his office, thinking about Sharon Dupont's words: *You're making a mistake…don't try to tell me you can't feel it…*

He tried telling himself she didn't know what she was talking about, that he was doing the most sensible thing he could under the circumstances.

But he realized she was right, as usual. He couldn't shake the feeling things were spiraling out of control.

29

Mike led Special Agents Ferriss and Cooper down the back stairs and along a narrow corridor to the police station's single interrogation room, which had been constructed next to the large holding cell in the station's lower level. They met Officer Phil Shankman trudging along in the opposite direction. Shankman nodded once to Mike and then gazed with interest at the two FBI men before saying, "Prisoner's all ready for you."

"Is he still cuffed?" Mike asked.

"Yep. He's secured to the table. He won't be going anywhere." Shankman turned to the side to let the three men pass before continuing down the hallway and starting up the stairs to the station's main floor.

When they reached the interrogation room's heavy metal door, Mike took a quick glance through the small wire-reinforced window before entering. He observed the prisoner, whose name he now knew to be Jackson Healy, sitting at a dented and scuffed rectangular aluminum table. Healy's wrists were indeed still handcuffed, and the glittering chain links connecting the bracelets had been threaded through an iron tie-down ring bolted to the table's surface. Healy sat with his head down, apparently uninterested in his surroundings.

When Mike turned the knob and entered, the powerful stench of body odor and a heavy, damp smell that reminded him of rotting wood struck him like a sledgehammer. It was as though the prisoner had never been introduced to the concept of soap and water. He wondered idly how long the smell would remain inside Sharon's cruiser.

Mike tried to breathe through his mouth and stepped farther into the interrogation room. It was barely more than a large closet, constructed with cinderblock walls and painted a dingy off-white. There was no two-way mirrored observation window as there were in the interrogation rooms of many bigger departments. In fact, the room was mostly bare, containing only the table, bolted securely to the floor, four chairs, one of which was currently occupied by the prisoner, a small voice-activated digital recorder that Shankman had placed on the tabletop out of the prisoner's reach, and a console telephone hanging on the wall by the door.

At Mike's entrance, the prisoner lifted his head and stared dully at him. Healy took in the uniform and his eyes widened slightly at the sight of the holstered Glock on Mike's hip, but aside from that, offered almost no reaction at all.

That changed dramatically a second later, though, as first Special Agent Alton Ferriss and then Special Agent Ward Cooper entered the room behind Mike. The prisoner's eyes widened in unconcealed panic and he gasped and scrabbled backward, the legs of his chair squealing over the beat-up institutional vinyl floor tiles. He seemed to have forgotten he was chained to the table, because the cuffs clanked against the iron tie-down bar as the bracelets dug into his skin, jerking his progress to a painful stop.

Healy didn't seem to notice. Now stretched almost flat across the table, he stared at the two agents like he had seen a ghost and said, "No, no, you can't be here. Get away from me." He turned his panicked gaze to Mike and begged, "Keep them away from me!"

Mike stopped, surprised at the prisoner's reaction, and felt Ferriss bump into him from behind. He turned and looked questioningly at the two agents. Both were sporting identical looks of utter undisguised malice, their mouths open in hard smiles filled with dirty yellow teeth.

He flashed back to Sharon's comment that he was making a mistake – as well as to his own unfocused feelings of unease and the prisoner's extreme reaction to the arrival of the Feds – and made a snap decision about allowing the agents to participate in the interrogation. It was time to put a stop to this; he would deal with the fallout later. "You know what, guys," he said, lifting his hands, palms-out, in a *stop* gesture. "We need to rethink this whole interrogation—"

Before he had even finished the statement, Agent Cooper kicked the heavy door shut behind them and lifted his gun out of a shoulder harness under his unbuttoned suit coat. He stepped around Ferriss and from less than four feet away, leveled the weapon at Mike's face.

Mike reacted on instincts honed by nearly twenty years of law enforcement experience, reaching without hesitation for his holstered weapon. But before he could draw down on Cooper, the agent barked, "Stop right there and keep your hands where I can see them!"

Mike froze and from somewhere behind him, the sound thin and reedy like it was coming through a faulty landline connection, Jackson Healy rasped, "Wesley and Amos Krupp, you should be long-dead, I killed you myself, you should be rotting in your graves, it's impossible, you're ghosts, you're—"

"SHUT UP!" Agent Cooper screamed, whipping his gun in Healy's direction before retraining it on Mike.

Healy's voice trailed off after the warning, but he continued muttering what sounded like mostly gibberish, disjointed snippets about spirits and South America and rocks with doors in them.

Mike ignored the prisoner and said softly, "Guys, what the hell? You're committing assault with a deadly weapon on a law enforcement officer. Why don't we all take a step back and talk about this?" He directed his comments at Ferriss, who had demonstrated time and again he was marginally less unhinged than his partner.

Ferriss smiled, flashing his stumps of dirty yellow teeth. "Sorry, Chief, but we know exactly what we're doing. It's time to end things. In fact, it's well past time to end things." He glanced over at the prisoner, who was still stretched out as far as possible away from the two FBI agents, watching the proceedings with huge, frightened eyes. "Isn't that right, Jackson, old buddy?" he said to the man in a sibilant hiss.

Healy's voice was shaking when he responded. "How did you get here? How did you find me? How are you *still alive?*"

Ferriss smiled wider, his face cold, his eyes glittering with hatred. Mike thought it was the most frightening thing he had ever seen, which was saying something considering his history in Paskagankee. "We'll get to that," Ferriss said, "but first things first. Chief McMahon, would you please remove your weapon, very slowly, and hand it to me? And don't forget, my brother's gun is still trained on your forehead and he will not hesitate to splatter your cranium all over this room. Be smart, and you will leave here still breathing. Be stupid and you'll leave in a body bag."

Mike's gaze flicked from Ferriss to Cooper and then back again. "Don't worry," he answered evenly. "There's not much danger of me forgetting something like that. But I really can't give up my weapon. As a fellow peace officer, I'm sure you can appreciate the position you've put me in."

Ferriss laughed. Even Cooper snorted. "Fellow peace officer," Ferriss said. "That's a good one."

"Apparently I'm off the mark. How would you describe yourselves, then?"

The smile vanished off Ferriss's face and he said, "If you want to live to find out, hand over that weapon. I'm not going to ask again."

Cooper leaned forward and pressed the muzzle of his weapon against Mike's forehead. Mike thought if he moved fast enough, he might be able to snatch it out of the man's hand, but that left the problem of Ferriss. There was no way he could disarm both men before taking a bullet.

He sighed softly. Then eased his hand to his holster and unsnapped it. He lifted the Glock 9mm and in one slow, smooth motion handed it to Ferriss, feeling certain he had just signed two death warrants, his own as well as the prisoner's.

"Okay," he said, watching closely as Ferriss slid the weapon into his waistband at the small of his back. "I'm unarmed. What now?"

"Now you sit down in that chair," Ferriss pointed to the empty chair placed directly across the table, "and don't make a single goddamned move unless you're told to."

Mike moved around the table, thinking hard. "So, you two are brothers? I should have guessed."

Ferriss shrugged. "Yep. You might say we go way back." He grinned and turned to the prisoner. "Ain't that right, Jackson, old pal?"

Healy was no longer stretched out across the table in a pointless attempt to escape. While Mike was surrendering his weapon, he had sat back down and was once again hunched over the well-worn stainless steel tabletop. He refused to acknowledge the taunt.

Mike studied the interaction between the rogue FBI agents and the prisoner closely. It was obvious the key to defusing the situation and getting out alive would lie in understanding their relationship. The three men shared some kind of history beyond what was apparent here; that much was abundantly clear.

What was also clear was that Ferriss and Cooper, while maybe the worst, most corrupt FBI men in the history of the bureau, actually *were* legitimate Feds – Mike had checked them out personally after their arrival in town – and the fact that they were choosing now to abandon their careers meant this fiasco was unlikely to end well. They had nothing to lose.

"So," Mike said. He needed to regain control of the conversation and keep these men talking. "Mr. Healy here is obviously very important to you two on a personal level. How long have you been chasing him?"

Ferriss and Cooper shared a glance. Then Ferriss said, "What year is this again?"

"You know what year it is. It's 2013."

The mischievous grin returned. "Just funnin' ya," Ferriss said. "We been chasing this piece of human shit for...let's see..."

Cooper cut in, his voice harsh and deadly. "A hundred and fifty-seven years."

30

Sharon made it as far as Main Street and the Katahdin Diner before turning around. Her misgivings had been building steadily since leaving the station, as had the sense that something was amiss. Now, without any conscious thought, she knew she had to get back there.

She wheeled the cruiser into the diner's parking lot, barely slowing. Loose gravel scattered from under her tires as she spun the steering wheel sharply and accelerated back onto Main Street in the direction of the Paskagankee Police Station.

Mike was probably right. If she stepped between the FBI and the murder suspect now by accusing the two agents of conspiring to execute the man, she would effectively end any chance of promotion.

Ever.

Hell, it was entirely possible she would lose her job. She didn't doubt the federal government's ability to get people sacked at the local level if doing so was important enough to them.

But she was one hundred percent certain about what she had seen this morning. Something was off about those two agents, and she knew in her heart if she had been just two minutes later arriving at the Ridge Runner, the prime suspect in the murder of Chief Kendall and Bronson Choate would have been summarily executed, his body buried in a shallow grave somewhere in the vast expanse of wilderness surrounding Paskagankee.

There was no doubt in her mind.

She recalled something her mother used to tell her. It was one of her mom's favorite sayings, and when the twelve-year-old Sharon asked her what it meant, she smiled and said, "You'll understand when you need to understand." Then her mother had succumbed to cancer, and her father had started drinking, and the words had vanished from her mind, forced out by many other more pressing life events.

But now she remembered, and she understood with a clarity that brought tears to her eyes that her mother had been right all those years ago. The expression was, "It's more important to do the right thing than the prudent thing." She said a quick prayer of thanks, hoping more than knowing that her mother would be there to hear it.

For the second time today, she entered the police station lot at a rate of speed she would have ticketed a citizen for. She screeched to a stop directly in front of the entrance – another no-no – and leaped out of the car. Now that she had made up her mind, she felt driven, like every second mattered, like she might already be too late.

Leaving the cruiser's front door hanging open, Sharon rushed up the steps, banging through the front door and into the lobby. Gordie Rheaume looked up from the dispatcher's console with a smile and said, "Whoa, where's the fire, young lady?"

She ignored him, trotting as fast as she was able through the maze of chairs and desks to the rear stairway. She registered Gordie saying something else to her as she ran but ignored that as well.

She hit the stairway and took the steps three at a time. She knew it was a bad idea, that she was risking injury, but by now she was no more able to slow herself down than she would have been to lift the building off its foundation. She was being driven by an almost pathological need to stop whatever was happening in that interrogation room. And she *knew* something was happening in the interrogation room.

She leaped off the last four steps, landing in the hallway with a bone-jarring *thud*. Then she straightened out and sprinted the length of the hallway to the closed door.

31

Mike did his best to keep any hint of ridicule or skepticism out of his voice. "A hundred and fifty-seven years, huh? That would make you fellas close to two hundred years old. You're holding up amazingly well, under the circumstances."

Cooper glanced at him scornfully, but Ferriss looked almost introspective at his words. Then the FBI man seemed to come to a decision and he said, "What do you know about the Fountain of Youth?"

Mike tried to cover his surprise. This was an unexpected turn, but since his goal was to keep the two armed men talking until he could figure out his next move, he considered any subject they decided to explore to be a productive one. "What do I know about the Fountain of Youth? I know the legend says that if you drink from its water, you receive the gift of eternal youth. I know that people have been searching for this fountain for thousands of years. I know that it's nothing more than a myth."

Ferriss smiled. "Yeah? What if I told you you're wrong about that last part? What if I told you—"

A suddenly agitated Jackson Healy blurted out, "*I* took that liquid out of Peru after I shot you. *I* took it, and then drank it after you tried to burn me to death in the Paskagankee Tavern! *I* took it," he repeated, "so how could you be standing here?"

As if a switch had been flipped, the introspective look vanished from Ferriss's face. He turned to Healy with a snarl. "You shot us, but you never finished the job," he spat. "You never checked to see that we were dead. But you didn't care about that, anyway, did you? We were miles out in the wilderness, with nowhere to go for help and no one to save us, even if we *were* still alive."

Mike watched, open-mouthed, as Healy nodded a mute confirmation of Ferriss's impossible words.

"Well, here's what you didn't take into consideration," the FBI man continued, his words dripping with venom. "I'm sure you remember the sacred ceremony we crashed that night, right? When we killed everyone and stole the disk and the Fountain water? Remember? And then you gut-shot Amos and me? You remember all that, right?"

Healy nodded wordlessly, his eyes haunted.

"Well, here's the thing, Mr. Genius Outlaw: The ceremony wasn't over at that point. It was at some kind of halftime or something, like at a fucking football game."

Mike watched the exchange closely. Healy gaped at the FBI man as if not fully understanding his words. Then comprehension started to dawn as Ferriss continued speaking. "After you rode off into the sunset, leaving Amos and me to bleed to death and end up as a meal for some small animal, more of those goddamn shaman priests started to show up.

"They discovered all of their compadres slaughtered and then they found us, cursing and bleeding in the scrub brush. They carried us across the wilderness on the backs of goddamn donkeys to a village who the fuck knows how far away. It felt like forever, thanks to your lead injections in our bellies. And then they interrogated us. They asked us just how badly we wanted to live. Understanding them wasn't easy, either," Ferriss said, "and not just because Amos and I was just about delirious by then from pain and infection. None of them jungle-living bastards spoke a word of English, and of course our Spanish wasn't exactly up to snuff, neither.

"But eventually, them shaman guys managed to make their intentions clear. We agree to their terms, and they save our dying asses. We don't agree to their terms, and we can just crawl off into the jungle and finish dying all alone in the middle of nowhere, with not a single goddamn soul to ever know what happened to us or how we were double-crossed by one traitorous, cheating bastard!" The volume of Ferriss's words had gradually been increasing as he talked, until now he was just shy of a full-out scream.

He took a moment to regain control of himself before continuing. When he did, his tone was once again icy, his words hard as diamonds. "Well, as you might imagine, ol' Amos and I felt we had quite a bit to live for, what with the way things ended between you and us that night back in Bumfuck, South America. The thought of dying in the jungles of Peru was bad enough, but we had a score to settle." He gazed at Healy, flat-eyed and cold, and Mike saw that Agent Cooper was doing the same.

Jackson Healy looked from Ferriss to Cooper and back again. Nobody spoke. Finally Healy said, "A-an understanding?"

Ferriss grinned. "I thought you might focus on that part of our little story. Yep. We reached an understanding with them godless shaman guys. As I mentioned, it was an easy decision for us."

He stood across the table, keeping his flat-eyed stare trained on Healy, making the man squirm. "Wondering what the understanding was, ain't ya?"

Healy nodded, the rigid set to his body indicating to Mike he already had a pretty good idea what the answer might be.

Ferriss said, "The agreement was a simple one, really. In exchange for them shamans nursing us back to health, we would agree to spend the rest of our lives hunting down the murderous scum who slaughtered their fellow heathens at that cursed rock. It was a no-brainer, really. Shamans or no shamans, that would have been our intention, ain't that right, brother?"

"Goddamn right," Cooper agreed with a growl, his weapon still held rock-steady and trained on Mike. For his part, Mike had nearly forgotten all about the Glock, so intensely was he trying to follow Ferriss's bizarre narrative. He noticed the two FBI men slipping into more rural speech patterns. The transition was jarring, but somehow made perfect sense at the same time.

"But that ain't to say them Peruvian medicine men didn't sweeten the pot a little," Ferriss/Wesley Krupp continued. "Once they learned you had made off with the Youth Juice that unearthly demon gave them during the ceremony, they realized the hunt for you would likely be a long and difficult one. They had to assume you would eventually drink it – which you obviously did – and they knew it would take decades, maybe centuries, to even the score with you."

Ferriss paused, either for dramatic effect or to take a deep breath, Mike wasn't sure which. Maybe it was both. With his flat gaze still directed at Healy, Ferriss/Wesley said, "I'm thinking you might be able to guess how they sweetened the pot for us."

Healy's eyes widened and he said, with almost no hesitation, "They had more liquid, didn't they?"

"Give the man a cigar," Ferriss/Wesley Krupp crowed. "They had more Youth Juice. And they were so pissed off at the slaughter of their buddies back at the magical rock that they were more than happy to forgive us our little role in the confrontation, if only we were willing to follow you to the ends of the earth to extract revenge, on their behalf as well as ours."

He looked around, as if taking in the massive forest of Paskagankee, rather than the dingy off-white walls of the windowless interrogation room. "It looks like we've done exactly that."

Healy sat shaking his head. "I don't understand," he said not just with fear but also with genuine curiosity. "How did you know I was inside that damned tavern when you burned it down a century-and-a-half ago?"

"We didn't know," Ferriss/Wesley Krupp replied. "Not for sure. But we was only minutes behind you when we tracked you down that night. Where else would you have gone? Once the tavern burned and you never showed up, we thought maybe we had killed you after all."

"But how could you have killed me if I had drunk the 'Youth Juice,' as you call it?"

"Drinking that stuff don't make you invincible," Ferriss/Wesley said. "It simply stops the aging process. If you hadn't been nice and cozy in that goddamned secret underground room, you *would* have died. You could have drank a gallon of magic juice and it wouldn't have mad a damned bit of difference. But when the body of the tavern owner was the only one found in there after the fire burned itself out, we suspected you might somehow have escaped."

Healy shook his head in wonder. "So you've been waiting more than a century and a half for me to show up?"

"That's the curse," Ferriss/Wesley said, nodding. His eyes were still flat and hard but Mike thought his face looked rueful. "Until we *knew* you were gone, until we *knew* you had paid for what you did, we had to continue slogging along, watching and waiting for you to show your traitorous face."

"But…" Jackson Healy hesitated, working it out in his head. "The FBI? How did you manage that?"

Ferriss/Wesley shrugged. "Wasn't that hard," he said with a thin smile. "After we was back at full strength in Peru, we snuck across the border and started searching. I'm sure you recall we almost caught up to you a few times before we finally ran you down in Paskagankee."

"I remember," Healy nodded.

"Thought you might," Ferriss/Wesley said. "But after we burned down the tavern and you never showed up, we feared you might have somehow given us the slip again. So, within a year, we had transformed ourselves from Wesley and Amos Krupp into James and Hardy Frey. We hired on as law enforcement in the surrounding states, always keeping an eye on news and arrest reports, just waiting for you to poke your head out of your hidey-hole."

Healy looked stunned. "You've been working in law enforcement for the past one hundred and fifty years?"

"A hundred and fifty-three, to be exact," Ferriss/Wesley said drily. "I think it's fair to say we now have seniority over just about every cop and FBI agent who's ever worked in the country. Ironic, when you think about it."

Ferriss's sardonic remark went right over Healy's head. He was otherwise occupied, clearly thinking things through. "But if you never aged…"

"We would work in a town or federal agency for a while, then quit, or resign, or just disappear when everyone else started getting older and we became concerned they might take notice of the fact that we weren't. We would lay low, then turn up elsewhere with new identities and start the whole process over again. It wasn't all that hard, especially years ago."

"A hundred and fifty years of waiting," Healy said, as if he just couldn't believe it.

"Yeah," Cooper/Amos Krupp grunted. "It's been fucking forever. So let's get this over with."

Ferriss/Wesley turned his glare on his brother. "I've been

waiting just as long as you have," he said, pointing an accusing finger. "Now that the moment we've waited for is here, I ain't going to rush things. We'll do what we're here to do, don't worry about that, but there's no goddamned hurry. We have this nice, private room, no one's going to bother us, so we can just take as much time as we damn well please."

Cooper/Amos looked like he was going to argue, but he didn't. He clamped his jaw shut, his perpetually angry look still firmly in place. Mike could see his teeth grinding from all the way across the table.

He took note of the man's expression as his concern at being held at gunpoint began morphing into outright alarm. He didn't like the turn the conversation had taken, or what it seemed the two time-traveling FBI men were about to do. He needed to keep the men talking. He quickly said, "So when you saw the reports of a secret underground room being uncovered next to the Ridge Runner, complete with skeletal human remains, you came running."

"Yep. We're actually on emergency leave from our bureau jobs down in Portland," Ferriss/Wesley said with a sly wink. "Deaths in both of our families, don't ya know. It probably stretched the limits of believability, but it's soon to be a moot point. And besides," he grinned evilly and turned his own gun on Healy. "It'll soon be true, more or less."

Ferriss/Wesley then cut a look at Mike. "I know you called down to Portland to check up on us. I'm surprised Special Agent in Charge Griffin didn't tell you that."

Mike shook his head. "He never said a word about it. Just verified your employment and hung up. He probably felt it was none of my business where you guys were, and I don't really blame him. I wouldn't go giving out my employees' whereabouts to some random phone caller, either, even if he was in law enforcement."

"Whatever," Ferriss/Wesley said with a shrug. "Like I said, it's a moot point, or soon will be. And now that we've brought our friend and former partner in crime, here, Mr. Jackson Healy, up to date on what's been happening over the last couple hundred years, I guess it's about time to finish what he started so long ago."

Ferriss/Wesley's eyes narrowed. He had lowered his weapon

while speaking, but now he again brought the gun to bear on Healy, pointing it directly at the prisoner's head. Cooper/Amos perked up noticeably, clearly pleased the talking was about to end and the shooting would soon begin.

Mike desperately racked his brain for some way to forestall the inevitable, but before he could come up with a single idea, Jackson Healy – who obviously had a stake in delaying things as well – burst out, "But I don't understand something…"

Cooper/Amos blew out an exasperated breath. "Who gives a shit what you do or don't understand?" he growled, but Ferriss/Wesley, still very much in charge, snapped at his brother, "I told you before, we have all the time in the world."

Ferriss/Wesley turned back to Healy. "What don't you understand?" he asked, his voice as calm as if they were discussing the New England Patriots cheerleaders over drinks at the Ridge Runner.

"I didn't drink the magic juice until I was trapped inside that damned room and nearly dead on my feet. Drinking it was a last-ditch effort to save my life. Afterward, I must have passed out and have no memory of anything until waking up a couple of days ago at the bottom of a muddy hole with a steady rain falling on my face. How in the hell could I have survived for over a hundred and fifty years without eating or drinking anything?"

Ferriss/Wesley shrugged. "Good question. We ain't no experts on the stuff. It's been a century and a half, and in all that time, we've never once gone back to Peru. Had enough of that place to last a thousand lifetimes. But the Youth Juice comes from a goddamned alien wellspring; who knows what properties it contains? My best guess would be that the it has some kind of mystical ability to drop you into a state of suspended animation.

"Maybe," he continued, warming now to the subject, "since you can't die a natural death once you've drunk it, your body was simply going to hang, cursed, halfway between living and dead forever. God knows it's better than you deserve. But once the soil was peeled off the top of that room like a sardine can being opened, and your body was exposed to fresh air and rain, that Youth Juice somehow jump-started you, and brought you back from wherever the hell you were suspended."

"I was starving, hungrier than I've ever been, for the first day or so after I came back," Healy muttered, more to himself than to anyone else in the room. "That must have been some kind of reaction to being woken up such a long time."

"Beats me," Ferriss/Wesley said. "And to tell you the truth, I have to agree with my brother. I really don't give a damn. Now, where were we?" Once again, both he and Cooper/Amos raised their weapons. It was plain by the look on Ferriss's face that his patience for talking had come to an end. He and his nearly two hundred year old brother were going to execute Jackson Healy in cold blood, and undoubtedly turn their weapons on Mike immediately afterward. Then they would walk out of the nearly empty police station – likely eliminating Gordie Rheame on the way by – and disappear.

Ferriss/Wesley growled, "Got any last words, compadre?" to Healy, who said nothing but shrank backward as far as he was able. The handcuffs clanked tight against the tie down ring and Healy's progress was again jerked to a stop.

The two brothers were spread out in the small room, separated. Cooper/Amos was to Mike's right, standing next to the wall, Ferriss/Wesley off to the left in front of the table, standing roughly five feet from the interview room's closed door. They were too far apart for Mike to take them both down at the same time, so in a split-second decision, he decided to go after Cooper first. That brother seemed by far the more unstable of the two lunatics, so Mike's only hope was that if he launched himself over the table and brought Cooper down, Ferriss might be distracted enough to give Mike time to scramble to his feet and go after him as well.

It was foolhardy.

It was suicidal.

It was his only option.

Mike tensed his muscles and prepared to spring.

And then everyone froze at the sound of a quick knock on the interview room's door. A half-second later it swung open, revealing Officer Sharon Dupont.

32

Sharon sprinted along the basement corridor, driven by the same sense of impending doom she had been feeling since shortly after driving out of the police station parking lot. She had no idea what Ferriss and Cooper might be up to, but she knew allowing them to be alone in a tiny room with Jackson Healy – and with Mike – had been a very bad idea.

She chastised herself for not being stronger, for not making her case more clearly to Mike. He was in charge, but she knew how heavily he valued her sense of intuition and her instincts as a cop.

She should have been able to more clearly state her position.

She had failed.

Hopefully it wasn't too late.

She skidded to a stop in front of the heavy steel door, not bothering to peek through the tiny wire mesh-reinforced window, not wanting to waste the time. Every second counted now; she could feel it in her gut.

She took a deep breath and then knocked on the door, a perfunctory, *I'm knocking as a courtesy, but I'm damned well coming in no matter what you say* knock, and then turned the handle and threw the door open.

What she saw froze her in shock, standing motionless in the doorway for a critical half-second.

Agent Ferriss stood directly in front of her, his gun pointed at Jackson Healy's head. Agent Cooper was braced against the wall to her left, his weapon also trained on the prisoner. Healy was straining hard against his handcuffs, which had been locked into place on the table's tie-down ring; he looked as though he would gladly gnaw through his wrists and propel himself backward through the cinderblock wall. Mike was frozen in a half-standing position directly across the table from her. He looked like he had been preparing to launch himself at Cooper.

She took it all in in an instant and reached reflexively for her service weapon. Somewhere in a dark corner of her brain she registered that all of her fears and suspicions had been right on target, and then the thought vanished as the scene disintegrated into chaos.

Ferriss spun on his heel and squeezed off a shot, just as Cooper rotated to his right and did the same. Both slugs ricocheted off the metal door with a pair of rapid-fire pings. Mike was screaming "Get down, get down!" as he continued moving forward, scrambling over the table and plowing into Cooper shoulder-first, slamming him into the wall.

Sharon dropped straight to the floor, hitting it with a jarring crash and rolling backward into the hallway. She prepared to return fire but Ferriss beat her to the punch, squeezing off another shot that whistled over her head. Had she remained standing, Sharon guessed the slug would have pierced her heart.

Out of the corner of her eye, she observed Mike and Agent Cooper struggling for Cooper's gun. The FBI man had somehow kept his weapon in his right hand while absorbing the devastating hit by Mike, and Cooper appeared to be gaining the advantage now, as he peppered the side of Mike's face with a series of jabs with his left.

She rose to her knees and raised her gun. She knew Ferriss would not miss again. Before she could fire, the FBI man took one long stride and *kicked* the door closed. It swung noiselessly on its hinges and slammed shut inches in front of her face. Then she heard the manual lock click into place.

She scrambled to her feet and pressed her nose to the eye-level window, trying desperately to calculate the odds of getting off a successful shot through it. The glass was at least half an inch thick, reinforced with thick wiring in a criss-cross diamond pattern.

Even with a rushed glance she could see that hitting what she was aiming at with any degree of accuracy would be impossible. She would have to raise her weapon to eye level and aim it awkwardly down. Once she pulled the trigger, the slug would ricochet wildly off the thick glass and there would be no way to predict whom it would strike, if anyone.

She would be just as likely to shoot Mike or the prisoner as either FBI agent.

She cursed bitterly and slammed a fist against the door in frustration. Pain blossomed in her hand and she turned and raced along the empty corridor, feeling like she had just abandoned Mike, knowing there was every possibility she would never see him again alive. But her cop instincts took over, and she knew there was nothing she could do for him with just a Glock 9 mm sidearm.

It was time to get the heavy artillery.

33

Mike slammed Cooper/Amos against the cement wall, driving his shoulder into the agent's gut and churning with his legs. He heard air rush out of the man's lungs with an elongated *"Uhhhhh"* and felt a savage sense of satisfaction. The agent's gun rattled against the wall with a metallic *clack* but to Mike's utter disbelief, somehow Cooper managed to hold on to it.

Another shot rang out, the concussive blast as loud as a cannon in the enclosed room. As he fought for his life, Mike listened for the cry that would tell him Sharon had been hit but could hear nothing over the ringing in his ears.

And now he was in big trouble. He had counted on his jarring blow knocking the gun from Cooper's hand, allowing him to dive at Ferriss, but now that plan was moot. The minute Mike turned toward away from the still-armed Cooper, the agent would put a slug in his back.

A loud *bang* told him the interrogation room door had been slammed shut. Mike tried to push Ferriss from his mind and turned his attention back to Cooper/Amos. He had succeeded in knocking the wind out of the agent, but now he was at a serious disadvantage; bent over, his shoulder planted in Cooper's midsection. The agent began pummeling Mike's face, raining closed-fist blows down on him while Mike tried desperately to yank the gun from Cooper's grasp.

He slammed Cooper's hand into the wall.

Nothing.

Two more punches opened a gash in his face.

He doggedly slammed Cooper's hand into the wall again, willing himself to ignore the beating he was taking.

This time he felt the man's fingers splay open. The gun clattered to the floor, seemingly forgotten by Cooper as he continued his vicious assault on Mike's face.

Mike had had enough. He loosened the muscles in his legs and dropped immediately, disregarding the pain radiating through the left side of his head. His left eye was nearly swollen shut but that was irrelevant because so much blood had flowed into it he couldn't see anything, anyway.

But his right eye was just fine – so far – and through it Mike could see the Cooper's gun where it landed and then taken one big bounce toward the door. He crashed down onto his hands and knees and scrabbled after the weapon just as Cooper/Amos kicked out viciously, catching Mike in the side of the head and sending him sprawling onto his side on the dirty tile floor.

He managed to grasp the gun as he was being kicked, and in one smooth motion, Mike rolled onto his back, squinting through his now rapidly swelling right eye, aiming carefully down Alton Ferriss/Wesley Krupp.

But no one was there.

Ferriss had anticipated Mike's move the moment Cooper's gun fell, and he had dropped to the floor as well. Now, with his gun aimed at empty air, Mike felt the cold deadly muzzle of Ferriss's Glock as the FBI agent shoved it into the side of his head.

"Not one fucking move," Ferriss/Wesley said, his voice low and hard and furious. "Drop it right now, or the last thing you ever see will be my smiling face."

"Can't even see that," Mike said as he released his hold on the weapon. For the second time in a matter of seconds, it clattered to the floor. "Too much blood and swelling, if you hadn't noticed. I might as well be blind."

The statement was close to being true, with his left eye useless and the right one swelling as well. But that eye wasn't completely closed. He could still see – sort of – through a tiny slit, like a suspicious homeowner lifting one slat and peering through a drawn set of window blinds.

It wasn't much, but it was all he had left. Maybe he could convince the brothers he couldn't see at all and then take some kind of action if an opportunity presented itself. The crazy bastards hadn't shot him yet, surprisingly, and until they did, he wasn't about to give up.

Cooper/Amos bent down and grabbed his gun off the floor, glaring at Mike as he did so. He was breathing heavily, the air whooshing audibly in and out of his lungs as he tried to recover from Mike's shoulder to the gut, and Mike almost smiled.

Any sense of satisfaction disappeared, though, as Cooper/Amos shoved the barrel of his gun between Mike's eyes. "Think you can find anyone else to put a gun to my head?" Mike said drily. "I'm sure there's room for one more. Barely."

"Shut up," Cooper snapped. "Man, am I gonna enjoy this."

Mike had the crazy thought that maybe the two lunatics would shoot one another as they were blowing his brains out. Their weapons weren't quite pointed at each other, but he could always hope for a ricochet.

Then Ferriss/Wesley said, "Amos, we don't have time for this."

Cooper/Amos hesitated and Ferriss continued. "That chick officer got away, which means any minute now we're going to have more company than we can handle. If we're still fussing around with one lawman who's only trying to do his job when the cavalry comes, we may not be able to finish what dipshit over there started so long ago."

Cooper turned a black gaze in the direction of Healy, who was still cowering behind the interrogation table. Ferriss continued, "Mr. Small Town Police Chief's helpless now, he can't hurt us. Let's stay focused and get this over with."

For a long moment nothing happened, and Mike feared Cooper/Amos was going to pick this moment to finally disobey his brother. Then the pressure of the cold steel barrel against his forehead vanished as Cooper pulled his gun away, and he muttered bitterly, "You are one lucky son of a bitch, you know that, lawman?"

Don't answer, Mike thought, but before he could stop himself, he said, "Somehow I don't feel all that lucky right now."

To his surprise, Cooper/Amos barked out a laugh, and then Mike felt himself being jerked to his feet. "Get back in your chair,"

Ferriss/Wesley ordered, shoving him hard.

Mike stumbled backward and bounced off the table before falling heavily into the chair. He could feel his right eye continuing to swell, and knew he would soon be as blind as a bat. He was lucky to be alive, but any chance of disarming the two men and preventing the execution of Jackson Healy – and probably himself, once the outlaws had completed the job they came here to do – was slipping away.

And he was out of ideas.

34

Sharon raced up the steps and burst through the doorway leading to the police station's main floor. "Gordie!" she screamed, to get the attention of the older man she assumed would still be sitting at the dispatcher's station across the big room.

But Gordie Rheaume had already started across the floor. He had made it nearly to the door, and now he grabbed Sharon's arm to slow her down and said, "What the hell's going on down there? Did I hear gunshots? Is anyone hurt?"

She ignored the question and snapped, "Call the State Police right now! Tell them we have a hostage situation inside the station and we need a negotiator and tactical response unit immediately. Then get every Paskagankee cop in here, even the ones on their day off. We need people and we need them now!"

Gordie stared at her for a moment, his grey eyes watery and uncertain. "Hostage situation," he repeated. "How could the prisoner have gotten the jump on Chief McMahon AND the two FBI agents?"

"It's not the prisoner," Sharon said. "It's the FBI guys. They're holding Mike and the prisoner at gunpoint and I'm afraid they're about to kill them both. That's enough questions, make the calls now!"

She waited long enough to see Gordie hurry back to the dispatchers' station and punch the line connecting the Paskagankee station to the Maine State Police unit in Orono. Then she ran to the weapons locker against the far wall, unlocked it, and removed a

247

Mossberg 590 riot gun and shells. She loaded the weapon quickly, hefted it, and retraced her steps toward the back of the room. Just before reaching the stairway she ducked into the chief's office and grabbed a master key off a small pegboard hanging behind Mike's desk. Then she darted out of the office.

Gordie looked up in alarm and removed the phone from his shoulder. "Sharon!" he shouted. "You can't go down there alone. Wait for backup! The Staties are on their way and I'm talking to Shankman right now. He was relatively close on patrol and will be here inside of two minutes!"

Sharon ignored him. She had by now reached the stairway leading to the basement and the interrogation room. She paused just long enough to look back at Gordie Rheaume, who had accumulated more service time with the Paskagankee Police Department than all of the current patrol officers combined. Worry was etched on his craggy face.

"I can't wait, Gordie," Sharon said, locking eyes with the kindly dispatcher. "Two minutes will be too late. In fact, I might already be too late." She pictured Mike lying in a pool of blood and pounded down the steps.

At the bottom of the stairs she sprinted the length of the hallway. Reaching the door, she threaded the master key into the lock with shaking hands. Without time to develop a workable plan and with no backup, she was counting on the element of surprise and the superior firepower of the Mossberg shotgun to force the two rogue FBI men to stand down.

Assuming they hadn't already killed Mike and Jackson Healy.

She slid the key home and it rattled in the metal lock, sounding to Sharon like the chatter of machine-gun fire.

She cringed and sank to her knees, hoping that her previous strategy would work one last time and the slugs would whistle over her head when the men started shooting at her. She turned the knob as quietly as she could and eased the door open slightly, then took a deep breath, steadied the shotgun in both hands, and drew back her foot to kick the door open fully.

But before she could, two nearly simultaneous gunshots blasted from inside the room, the sound heavy and piercing even through the mostly-closed metal door.

She spit out a curse and kicked at the door, her heart refusing to acknowledge what her brain was telling her: that she was too late.

35

"It's been a long road," FBI Special Agent Alton Ferriss/Wesley Krupp said to Jackson Healy, who was yanking and jerking on the handcuffs in a desperate but futile attempt to escape. Healy's skin was raw and bleeding from his efforts, but he didn't seem to notice. His eyes rolled wildly in his head and his ever-present body odor had seemed to intensify in direct proportion to his panic.

"But all things come to an end, even for someone who's been alive for nearly two hundred years." Ferriss stepped around the table as he talked, moving next to Healy. He rested his pistol lightly against the side of the prisoner's head.

Agent Cooper/Amos Krupp now flanked Healy on the other side. He had sidled carefully past Mike's chair, training his gun directly on Mike's chest as he did so, being careful to keep the weapon out of his reach. Mike thought briefly about going for it anyway, despite the fact he could by now barely see.

The endgame had clearly begun. Time had run out. Mike thought he might be able to take Cooper down by standing suddenly and bringing the crown of his head directly up under Cooper's chin. With luck, he might stun the agent enough to make a play for his gun.

But the problem with this hastily devised plan was obvious. Ferriss would need only a half-second to pull the trigger on Healy, and there would be no way Mike could demobilize Cooper that quickly, even operating at one hundred percent, which he was not.

So he reluctantly allowed the man to pass, and now Cooper

held his weapon against the other side of Healy's skull. The prisoner had stopped struggling and sat completely still, breathing heavily but unwilling to move a muscle, as if the act of doing so might cause one of the men to squeeze off a shot.

Mike tried one last time to reason with the men. "Guys, don't do this. You don't have to kill him. You don't have to kill anybody. With me as a hostage, you can get out of here safely and get away clean. I'm law enforcement, there's no way SWAT or anybody else is going to risk shooting me. As long as you have me, you'll be as safe as a baby in its mother's arms."

"Shut up," Cooper growled, swinging his weapon Mike's way and then immediately returning it to bear on Healy.

Ferriss shook his head. He seemed almost sympathetic. "Haven't you been listening? It's not about getting away. It's about finishing what this traitor started a hundred and fifty years ago. We're not interested in getting away clean, dirty, or otherwise. We sickened of this endless life long before you were born, and we want nothing more than to end this goddamn curse."

Ferriss/Wesley Krupp looked at his brother. "Are you ready?"

Cooper/Amos Krupp nodded. "I'm way past ready."

Mike could see what was coming, and he started to rise from his chair. He would have to make a play for Cooper's gun, it was the only option left, and—

--And he heard what sounded like a key rattling in the door's lock just as the two FBI men fired their weapons in near-unison, the criss-cross effect of the two 9mm slugs ripping into Jackson Healy's skull in a spray of blood, bone and tissue. The nearly headless corpse slumped back in the seat, an obscene splattering of crimson gore striking the dingy wall behind the table as if tossed from a bucket.

Mike froze in open-mouthed horror halfway between his seat and the now-dead prisoner as Agent Cooper/Amos Krupp swiveled smoothly and trained his gun on Mike.

The door burst open and he heard Sharon's voice, loud and amped on adrenaline. She shouted, "Everybody freeze!" and he watched as Agent Ferriss/Wesley Krupp lifted his gun and pointed it at the door.

36

It was a perfect standoff.

Sharon leveled the shotgun at Ferriss, who pointed his Glock back at her with steady hands. Cooper held his weapon in a two-handed shooter's grip aimed directly at Mike, less than five feet away.

For what felt to Sharon like a long time nothing happened.

The two echoing gunshots seemed to reverberate much longer than they should have, the sound trapped by the concrete walls of the small interrogation room. In her peripheral vision, she could see the devastation: the corpse of Jackson Healy, his head hideously misshapen and bloody. The gore littering the area around the body. The unidentifiable gristle dripping off the clothing of the two assassins.

"Drop the guns now," Sharon barked, not because she thought there was any chance in hell the men would, but more because she couldn't think of a single thing else to do.

Ferriss/Wesley ignored her and spoke to his brother, never taking his eyes off Sharon. "Never mind the lawmen," he said. "Let's do this," and Sharon stared in utter disbelieving horror as Cooper nodded once and then the two men swiveled their arms smoothly, bringing their weapons to bear on each other's foreheads.

Before she could say another word, the brothers squeezed their triggers, again firing in near-perfect unison, and the centuries-old assassins blew each others' brains all over Mike McMahon and the ruined body of Jackson Healy.

And Sharon screamed.

37

It was after midnight by the time they left the station. Mike carried a canvas equipment bag slung over one shoulder while Sharon maintained a firm grip on his arm. They moved as quickly as they could to navigate the gauntlet of television cameras, flashbulbs and shouted questions. Mike felt off-balance, with one eye swollen shut and the other nearly so.

He stopped roughly in the middle of the chaos, Sharon sticking closely by his side. Even nearly blind, Mike could see that the skin of the assembled journalists had been bleached a glaring white by floodlights erected haphazardly around the lot like fast-growing weeds. He scanned the throng with his half-open good eye as he waited for the buzz of excited voices to recede, picking the expectant face of the Portland *Journal*'s Melissa Mannheim out of the crowd, as well as those of representatives from Fox News, CNN all of the other major networks' news divisions. He wondered how they had gotten to the flyspeck of a town in extreme northern Maine so quickly, then realized they wouldn't have had to – he and Sharon had been answering questions by investigators from the FBI and the Maine State Police for more than eight straight hours.

He waited patiently, and when it became clear to the reporters no one would get any information until everyone stopped shouting, they reluctantly closed their mouths and waited for Mike to speak.

Finally he did. Sort of. "We have nothing to say at this time. A joint press conference will be held here tomorrow at 9:00 a.m., and will include myself, as well as representatives from the FBI's Portland office and the Maine State Police. At that time, we'll give a short statement regarding today's events and then answer any questions you might have to the best of our ability, given that the investigation is ongoing. Thank you all for your patience, and we'll see you tomorrow."

A frustrated groan spread through the crowd and the shouted questions resumed as Mike and Sharon turned away from the cameras and walked determinedly toward Mike's car, which he'd left at the far end of the lot. The voices rose in volume and intensity, blurring together into an indistinguishable roar as the journalists battled each other to be heard, but then Mike froze as Melissa Mannheim's unmistakable screech ripped through the crowd: "Chief McMahon, is it true two FBI agents executed a suspect in cold blood inside your station this afternoon while you stood by and did nothing?"

He whirled to confront Mannheim, almost losing his balance thanks to exhaustion and near-blindness. Sharon steadied him and then tightened her grip on his elbow, practically dragging him to the waiting car. "Don't let her bait you," she whispered fiercely. "You'll be giving her exactly what she wants."

Mike allowed himself to be pulled to the car. Sharon opened the door and he dropped heavily into the front passenger seat. He knew she was right, knew that confronting the pushy reporter to answer her infuriating charge would be playing right into her hands, not to mention would also cause pandemonium and do nothing to convince the media jackals that what she said *wasn't* true.

The worst part was that he wasn't even entirely convinced that her statement *was* untrue. He *had* given up his gun to the killers, and then he *had* stood by while Wesley and Amos Krupp – there was no point referring to them by their current FBI names; he knew without a shred of doubt that they really were the notorious Krupp brothers, wanted in the mid-1800's for bank robbery and murder – executed a man inside the Paskagankee Police station before turning their guns on each other.

Sharon started the car and eased out of the lot, weaving around reporters and network film crews trudging to their vehicles. Mike leaned against the headrest, squinting hard, and watched as a small knot of journalistic die-hards, apparently refusing to accept the notion that there would be no more news to report until morning, continued milling around the police station's granite front steps.

When they reached the road, Sharon picked up speed and turned toward their home. Mike considered telling her to keep an eye on the rear view mirror in order to ensure they weren't being tailed by an enterprising reporter, then thought better of it. For one thing, Sharon was smart enough to do exactly that without being told, and for another, the Portland *Journal*'s Mannheim the Maneater already knew where they lived. If she wanted to hassle them, all she would have to do would be to let slip the address of Sharon's little house and then stand back and watch the action.

He sighed quietly. As bored as he had been sitting around waiting for another job while Pete Kendall had been running the department, as much as he had missed police work, he would never have wanted to return to the job under these circumstances.

Sharon cleared her throat. Mike smiled – as much as he could, with sutures covering half his face like some horrible road map and his skin bruised and swollen – and said, "What's on your mind, babe?"

She stared out the windshield as the headlights cut twin beams of light through the coal-black northern Maine night. "You're not really buying Mannheim's idiotic implication, are you?"

Mike sat in silence, watching the thick cover of the ever-present forest slide past, crowding in, as always, from all sides. A pervading sense of claustrophobia was never far off in Paskagankee, Maine.

After a while he spoke, but not to answer Sharon's question. How can you give an answer you don't have? "You should never have kicked in that door, you know, not all by yourself. Protocol would have been to call for backup, get everyone out of the station, and then wait for help. And if you *were* going to come charging in there like some modern-day Dirty Harry, you should have at least taken the time to put on a vest."

"I know the protocol," Sharon said tightly. "But I wasn't going to wait while those two...*freaks*...blew your brains out. And putting on Kevlar takes time I didn't feel could be spared. Sue me."

"As a cop," Mike continued, ignoring her angry aside, "I can't condone what you did. But as your fiancé, I don't know how to thank you. I owe you my life, literally."

She turned and smiled, her face radiant, her teeth glowing white in the weak moonlight struggling through the side window. "As I recall, you saved me a couple of years ago from a fate worse than being shot in the head, so the way I see it, we're even. Maybe now we can get to the point where one of our lives doesn't constantly *need* saving."

They fell silent for a while, and when Mike spoke again it was to address a different subject. "I owe you an apology," he said simply and without preamble.

"Apology accepted."

"Don't you want to know what it's for?"

"I already know what it's for. You're not that hard to read, remember?'

"Try me," Mike said, although he had no doubt she knew exactly what she was talking about.

He wanted to hear her say it. *Needed* to hear her say it.

"You're sorry you didn't listen to me about Ferriss and Cooper being determined to execute Jackson Healy. You feel like if you had given more weight to my warnings, this whole fiasco might have been avoided."

Mike chuckled despite the pain it caused his injured face and head. "You're right on, as usual," he said. "About most of it."

"Really," she countered. He could see she was now genuinely curious. "What did I miss?"

"There was no way anyone was going to stop the Krupps from killing Healy. If they hadn't been able to do it today, they would have killed him tomorrow in his holding cell, or ambushed him outside the station as he was being taken to jail in Portland, or they would have taken him down some other time. But they were on a mission, and they weren't going to stop until they completed it. Hell, they had been single-mindedly pursuing their objective for over a hundred and fifty years, what would a few more days or even weeks have mattered to them?"

"You really believe all that stuff Ferriss was saying about Peru, and the Fountain of Youth, and being betrayed back in 1858, don't you?"

Mike hesitated and then nodded forcefully. "I sure do." He turned in his seat and stared until she looked over, then he held her eyes and said, "And so do you."

"Is that so?"

"Yep. As I recall, wasn't it you who quoted the fictional Sherlock Holmes in saying, 'if all other possibilities have been exhausted, then what's left, however unlikely, must be the truth'?"

She grinned. "That would be me."

"Well, then, think about it. The FBI has already begun examining the personal histories of Special Agents Ferriss and Cooper, and once you dig more than a year or two prior to their hiring, guess what you find?"

Sharon answered instantly. "Nothing."

"Bingo. The trail is completely cold. You know how hard it is to live completely off the grid, to live so anonymously you leave no footprint for investigators to find and follow? It's damned near impossible, and it *never* happens with federal agents."

He paused and took a deep breath. "You're damn right I believe it," he repeated.

Sharon turned into her driveway and Mike blinked in surprise. He had been so caught up in their conversation he hadn't even been aware of the miles rolling by. Sharon switched off the engine and they sat in the darkness, comfortable in each other's presence, enjoying the nocturnal stillness.

"What are you going to do about the press conference tomorrow?"

Mike started in surprise. He didn't realize he had dozed off before Sharon's question. He shrugged. "I'm going to explain what happened to the best of my ability."

"Are you concerned about more questions like Mannheim's?"

"Not really," he said, realizing he meant it. "I took what I felt was the best course of action at the time. There will always be those who second-guess you. The more significant the decision, the more vociferous will be the criticism. The important thing is to be able to look yourself in the mirror afterward. It's the only thing you can control, when all is said and done."

Sharon nodded and he said, "Besides, I'm only a minor story in this goat-rope. The feds are the ones who have to try to explain two of their agents shooting an unarmed, handcuffed man after beating the crap out of one officer and shooting at another. I almost feel sorry for Fred Griffin."

"Who?"

"Fred Griffin. He's Special Agent in Charge of the FBI's Portland Field Office, and he'll be here in the morning for the press conference. He's going to be roasted alive by the media."

"And you *almost* feel sorry for him."

"Yeah, almost, but not quite. The guy's an officious prick, and living proof that the bureau needs to refine their hiring and promotional procedures."

Sharon laughed. It sounded like a softly pealing bell. "Well, if this doesn't get them to do something, nothing will."

She opened her door and Mike squinted against the sudden brightness of the interior dome light. "Come on, old man," she said teasingly, "let's see if we can't get at least a few hours of sleep before that stupid press conference."

He shook his head. "Sleep is going to have to wait a little longer, at least for me."

"Why's that?"

"Because my work tonight isn't done yet."

38

Sharon extinguished the headlights as the car turned into the empty Ridge Runner parking lot. The crunching of gravel under the tires in the three a.m. stillness sounded to her as loud as a Fourth of July fireworks display. Mike had insisted on coming here alone, but she steadfastly refused to listen, telling him, "We're in this together, and I'm sticking it out to the end."

And she meant it, as far as that went, but the truth was Mike McMahon looked like hell. Lack of sleep, stress and the beating he had taken at the hands of Ward Cooper/Amos Krupp had taken its toll on him, and she feared he might fall asleep at the wheel on the way over here and drive into a tree.

The moment the vehicle rolled to a stop, Mike was out the door and reaching into the back seat for the equipment bag he had carried out of the station a couple of hours earlier. He moved with more energy that Sharon would have expected under the circumstances, slinging the heavy bag over one shoulder and marching toward the excavation in the field behind the bar.

She grabbed her flashlight and shovel they had thrown across the back seat and hurried to catch up. Ahead, Mike murmured, "Did Bo happen to mention when the septic system project was going to be finished, now that the pit's no longer a crime scene?"

"He said the system is being installed in the morning, and Dan Melton's coming back tomorrow afternoon to fill the hole back in."

"Perfect," Mike said as he rounded the corner of the building.

The stationary earthmover loomed in the distance, looking in the diffuse moonlight like a grazing dinosaur. Sharon fell into step next to Mike. "Are you absolutely certain you're comfortable with this? I'm sure you're aware we're tampering with evidence."

"I know what we're doing," he said. "And it's exactly why I wanted to do this alone. I don't want to put your career at risk."

"That's not what I'm worried about. I know you. You're as straight an arrow as they come. Will you be able to live with yourself afterward?"

Mike stopped next to the pit and turned, lasering his hypnotic eyes on her. Even now, more than two years after meeting him, the intensity of his stare sometimes took her breath away. "Everyone connected with this thing is dead. All three of them died in a violent manner. And those are only the ones we're aware of; who knows how many other people tied to this thing died horrible deaths over the last hundred and fifty years? This case is going to end in a whitewash by the FBI – there's no other conceivable way it *can* end, given the circumstances – and any story they come up with to explain the actions of their agents won't include *this* thing." He nodded at the heavy bag still hanging off his shoulder.

"But still, it doesn't belong to us. What about returning it to its rightful owners?"

"Why? So someone else can misuse it and cause another two centuries of violence and terror? The 'rightful owners' died at least a hundred years ago, and to their heirs, what's inside this bag is nothing more than a myth, a fanciful story passed down from generation to generation. Returning it to its 'rightful owners' now will accomplish nothing positive, and could potentially cause untold misery."

He turned back toward the hole, and Sharon realized she had been holding her breath. "So," he said. "To answer your question, yes, I'm completely at ease with this."

He walked to the earthmover and picked up the aluminum ladder lying next to it in the damp grass. Then he walked back to the hole and slid the ladder down the side until it rattled to a stop. He tossed the bag to the bottom, where it landed with a muffled *whump*. Then he climbed down the ladder and waited for Sharon to follow.

Stepping onto the pit's dirt floor, Sharon felt trapped, claustrophobic, like the dirt walls were closing in. She hadn't noticed the sensation while searching the underground room in the daylight. Tonight, in the darkness, it reminded her of a casket. A vague whiff of corruption hung in the unmoving air, as if the secret death-chamber was hanging doggedly on to the remains of the two still-unidentified human beings who had perished inside it so long ago.

"Let's get this over with," Mike muttered uneasily, and she knew he felt the disturbing sensation, too. He knelt down and unzipped the bag. Reached in. Lifted the heavy golden disk clear of the bag with both hands and set it down on the hard-packed dirt. Stood and moved next to Sharon.

She had begun digging a hole roughly eighteen inches in diameter in the middle of the pit, but now she stopped and gazed at the circular object. It glittered dully in the reflected beam of the flashlight. Now knowing the part the strange disk had played in the tragic story spanning two centuries and two continents, she had fully expected to feel some kind of power emanating from it, some evil vibe, but it was even worse than she had imagined. A suffocating dread began to fill her, a sense of pervading evil unlike any she had ever known.

"Do you feel that?" she said, looking up at Mike, trying to control the shaking in her voice and mostly succeeding.

"What?"

"It feels…I don't know…like we're not alone, like there's a presence down here with us or something."

"A presence," he said, an edge to his voice, and Sharon knew by his tone and lack of direct denial that he felt it, too. She looked back down at the disk. It lay on the dirt, unmoving and apparently benign.

Mike took the shovel from her hands. He bent over his work and within minutes had excavated a hole deep enough to accept the disk. Then he dropped the shovel and for the final time, picked up the golden disk, setting it carefully it into the bottom of the hole.

Without speaking, he stood and began filling the dirt back in. He worked quickly, and soon the hole was gone. He stamped down on the newly replaced earth until it was packed hard, once again resembling the rest of the secret room.

"Shine your light on it," he said. Sharon directed the beam at the ground, and in the weak, uneven light there was no detectable difference between what had been dug up five minutes ago and what had been in place for over a century and a half.

"Guess it'll have to do," he said, and zipped the now-empty equipment bag closed.

He picked up the shovel and said, "Let's get the hell out of here," but took one look at Sharon and stopped in his tracks. "What is it?" he said.

"Something's wrong about this," she whispered. "I can feel it. And don't try to tell me you don't feel it, too, because I know you do."

"Doesn't matter," he said. "It's done now, and there's no going back."

"Of course we can go back! We can dig the damned thing up and put it back in the evidence room."

"Nothing's changed," Mike hissed. "The fact that this thing gives off some kind of weird, dangerous vibe makes it even more critical we get it out of circulation. Maybe there's no right thing to do with it, but I'm certain this is the *least wrong* thing. Sometimes that's the best you can hope for." He grabbed the ladder with both hands and climbed quickly out of the pit.

Sharon stood a moment longer. The darkness at the bottom of the deadly hole, a darkness of both light and of spirit, was nearly overwhelming. She realized Mike was right. They were doing the only thing they could.

She realized also that she needed to get the hell out of there and back to the land of the living. She climbed out as quickly as she could and then removed the ladder, placing it once again next to the Caterpillar. Then she followed Mike to the car, anxious to take a shower and get a little sleep. The press conference would begin in just a few hours.

Mike reached back and took her hand as they walked. "Thanks again," he said. He didn't specify what he was thanking her for. He didn't have to.

"Always," she said, and squeezed his hand. In the distance, high above the evergreens, the first shafts of daylight began brightening the sky over Paskagankee, Maine.

About the author

Allan Leverone is the *New York Times* and *USA Today* bestselling author of nine novels and a 2012 Derringer Award winner for excellence in short mystery fiction. His dark thriller MR. MIDNIGHT was named one of the "Best Books of 2013" by Suspense Magazine. Allan lives in Londonderry, New Hampshire with his wife Sue, three grown children and one beautiful granddaughter. He loves to hear from readers and other authors; connect on Facebook, Twitter @AllanLeverone, and at AllanLeverone.com